THE DEATH TRIP

She could smell her fear in the closed atmosphere of the coffin. She knew she was hyperventilating, but it was no use, terror filled every cell of her body.

I'm suffocating! O dear God, help me, I'm suffocating!

Carin screamed in the airless darkness, pounding the wood above her head with both fists, the weight of the earth above her immovable.

I'm dying. Someone help me, please. I'm dying!

Deathscape

by the author of Soul Snatchers

Michael Cecilione

Diamond Books by Michael Cecilione

SOUL SNATCHERS
DEATHSCAPE

DEATHSCAPE

Michael Cecilione

DIAMOND BOOKS, NEW YORK

This book is a Diamond original edition, and has never been previously published.

DEATHSCAPE

A Diamond Book/published by arrangement with the author

PRINTING HISTORY
Diamond edition/December 1992

ISBN: 1-55773-826-2

Diamond Books are published by The Berkley Publishing Group,
200 Madison Avenue, New York, New York 10016.
The name "DIAMOND" and its logo are trademarks belonging to Charter Communications, Inc.

PRINTED IN THE UNITED STATES OF AMERICA

10 9 8 7 6 5 4 3 2 1

To Christy—
Wife, lover, friend, *everything* . . .

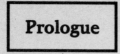

Prologue

ACCIDENTS HAPPEN

If man could see
The perils and diseases that he elbows
Each day he walks a mile, which catch at him,
Which fall behind and graze him as he passes,
Then would he know that life's a single pilgrim
Fighting unarmed among a thousand soldiers.
—Beddoes, *Death's Jest Book*

Wet footsteps on asphalt.

Following the streak of crimson gore to its source.

Bending down over the soft, bleeding sack of leather, flesh, and broken bone.

The girl almost dead.

Barefoot.

A red high-heeled sandal lying on its side by the storm drain.

As if she'd stripped at 125 mph in her rush to make it to this rendezvous.

The left side of her once-pretty face smeared over a quarter mile of the street. Her right leg bent outward at a forty-five-degree angle, the bone protruding almost comically through her inner thigh; the soft white flesh of her belly peppered with bits of grit and stone, as if she'd taken a blast from a shotgun.

She was wearing a fashionable leather jacket, a bare-midriff blouse, a cotton miniskirt. Suicide clothes. On a Harley.

Her boyfriend was half a block back, twisted inside the mangled machine, the hot pipes and burning chrome part of his own entrails, as if he were some kind of bionic centaur. His black helmet was still strapped securely to the back fender. Macho man. His head had rolled to a stop near the storm drain. It had split open like an overripe melon, spilling its secret gray meat in the gutter.

Stuck a finger in the pulp.

No taste. No images.

Too late.

Dead.

Leaning closer over the girl. Could still hear her sucking breath through the shattered bones of her nose. Blood burbling around her nostrils, as if she were drowning. Lungs punctured by the jagged ends of broken ribs.

Leaning closer.

Smelling the harsh, acrid incense of urine, blood, and pain.

Hearing her heart beat. Remarkably steady for someone in such hellish agony. For someone so close to dying. Most likely the effect of the Quaaludes she and her boyfriend had consumed only an hour before. Her one remaining eye opened wide. Shocked. Amazed. The eyelid fluttering. The blue iris swimming in blood.

Hearing the sirens in the distance.

Too far away. They would never get there in time.

Reaching forward.

Holding her nose closed, delicately pinching the bloodied nostrils together.

No struggle left in her. No protest. Feeling her surrender. The one eye opening wider, widest. Impossibly wide.

Seeing happy times, childhood, birthdays, friends, old relatives, a long tunnel, a soft, white, welcoming light.

And behind it. Croaker.

I WATER SPORTS

Do not go gentle into that good night,
Rage, rage against the dying of the light.
—Dylan Thomas

Go on pull the trigger,
It's easy that way;
Take a sip of poison,
Lovers do it every day.
Drag a rusty razor across your wrists,
He will take you away.
—Grimm, "Deliver Us From Life"

A living dog is better than a dead lion.
—Ecclesiastes 9:4

1

LAURA KANE broke the surface with a gasp.

She had come up a little short on her dive and was already about half a body-length behind the girl in lane two. Ordinarily that would be no big deal except for the fact that the girl in lane two was Terry Myers, and the big, rawboned blonde from Texas would relish the opportunity to beat her. She had already taken advantage of her quick jump, opening up a full body-length between them.

Along the side of the pool, stopwatch in hand, Coach Morgan was following their progress, shouting, trying to make himself heard over the splashing water.

"Come on, Laura, dammit, move it, move it, move it!"

The coach always rode her harder than the other girls. She was the team's best swimmer, unbeaten in twenty-one straight races, and, if you listened to Coach Morgan, had an outside shot at the '92 Summer Olympics; at least that was the kind of talk he kept drumming into her head to make her try harder.

Laura had gotten used to the pressure. But sometimes she really hated all the extra attention Coach Morgan focussed on her. It made her feel self-conscious. Besides, she knew it made the other girls jealous, particularly Terry Myers.

They had already made the turn at the end of the first lap and Myers had opened up her lead even further. Laura could see the bottoms of the other girl's big feet churning up white water ahead of her.

The coach seemed to be yelling right in her ear, his face level with the water. Laura wondered if he had dropped to all fours and was crawling along the side of the pool.

"Kick, goddammit, kick!" he was yelling like a maniac.

She knew there would be no point in telling him that she hadn't felt much like swimming today. If she had explained to him about the classmate who had died he would have just looked at her, his face blank, waiting for her to explain the connection, unable to comprehend how the fact that a woman who had been killed in a motorcycle accident the night before yesterday could have any possible bearing on her desire to practice today.

To Coach Morgan, swimming was life itself; he breathed chlorinated water. Laura just didn't share his obsessive dedication to the sport.

She hated to disappoint him. But in her heart she suspected she would never be an Olympian.

They had pushed off the wall marking the second lap and were midway through the third with no change in their relative position. If anything, the other girl had opened up her lead another half body-length.

Water, Laura had learned in physics class, was an excellent conductor; Laura could sense the other girl's excitement at the prospect of winning.

Laura saw Myers somersault at the wall and speed past her in the opposite direction like a torpedo. A split second later, Laura ducked under the water, planted her feet against the wall, pushed off, and started the final lap.

If this had been breaststroke, Laura wouldn't have stood a chance: Terry had shoulders like a lumberjack. But freestyle was Laura's strongest stroke, and now that the prospect of losing to her main rival was growing more and more likely by the second, she could feel the adrenaline rush through her system.

It was true that Terry was both bigger and stronger, but in freestyle strength could easily work against you as it was working against Terry now, causing her to beat at the water rather than glide through it. Over the shouting of the coach and the noise of the other swimmers, Laura could hear Terry slapping excitedly at the water, greedy for the victory that she sensed was just within reach.

Meanwhile, Laura deftly cut the water with long, clean strokes, her legs kicking powerfully and efficiently behind her, propelling her forward.

She was clearly gaining on Terry, there was no doubt of that, now if only there was enough water left before the finish line . . .

Terry felt her coming and redoubled her efforts, but it was in vain. Like someone drowning, the more she struggled the less she achieved.

Water, Laura often reflected, held many lessons like that.

Laura shot forward, inexorable as a shark, cleanly passing Terry and touching the wall almost a full body-length in front of her opponent. She leaned back against the wall, treading water, gasping for air. She could feel her heart pounding against her rib cage. Her body, weightless in the water, seemed to dissolve, leaving her with nothing but the awareness of that wildly beating heart.

Maybe she had what it took to be an Olympian, after all.

She was still basking in the afterglow of her last-second victory when Coach Morgan's angry voice exploded in her ear.

"What the hell were you doing out there, Kane!" he yelled. "The dead man's float? For Chrissakes, you looked like you were asleep!"

Laura whirled around in the water.

"I won, didn't I?" she yelled back angrily. She could feel Terry's murderous gaze like twin red lasers between her shoulder blades, but she was too mad to care about that now.

"How many times do I have to tell you?" Coach Morgan growled. "You're racing the clock, not the other girls. You have to beat the clock!"

He held his stopwatch in front of her face and Laura had to force back the almost irrepressible urge to knock it out of his hand. Instead she kicked off the side of the pool and did a loose backstroke to the other side.

"All right, ladies," the coach yelled, his voice echoing off the tiled walls, off the water. "That's enough for today. Everybody out of the pool. Hit the showers. Kane, I want to talk to you."

The other girls quickly gathered up their gear and headed for the locker room, talking in hushed voices, leaving Laura alone in the pool.

She pulled herself up over the side and walked back to her things, grabbing a towel out of her gym bag and drying herself off.

Coach Morgan sauntered over, hands in the pockets of his shorts, staring at the ground as if planning what to say.

Seth Morgan was a tall man, about six foot three, trim and fit, with the kind of long rubbery muscle that was peculiar to swimmers. His close-cropped blond hair prematurely tipped with silver, his blue eyes alert and crisp, and his strong clean-shaven face all bore testament to a lifetime dedicated to physical fitness; Seth Morgan was the perpetual athlete.

He had been a member of the USC swim team back in the early 1980's, one of the stars, actually, though apparently not the brightest, for two of his own teammates beat him out for the '84 Olympics. If he was bitter about the disappointment, he never showed it, except maybe in the almost sadistic attention he paid to Laura's progress as a competitor. Sometimes Laura felt as if Coach Morgan had more stake in her success than she did, as if he were somehow trying to reclaim his own lost opportunity through her.

He looked up from the concrete between his flip-flops as if he'd finally found the answer he were looking for and fixed Laura with his clear blue eyes.

She would have felt embarrassed standing in front of any of her other teachers in a wet bathing suit, even rumpled, kindly old Mr. Lasky, whom she'd once caught eyeballing her from over his Shakespeare one hot summer day when she'd decided to wear a tank top, but she didn't feel the least bit embarrassed in front of Coach Morgan. Although there were always rumors—all of them, it seemed, unfounded—that he had once gotten into trouble with the administration for sleeping with one of the girls on the team, there had never been even a suggestion of anything sexual between her and Coach Morgan.

At first, Laura wondered if there wasn't something wrong with her. She was somewhat disappointed and then even a little hurt that he didn't even seem remotely attracted to her. Like most of her teammates, she had developed something of a crush on the handsome young coach, but besides that she would have considered it a validation of her abilities as an athlete if she could have been "chosen" in that way. Even in this age of enlightened sexual equality, Laura instinctively understood that more often than not a man expressed his admiration for a woman's talents with an erotic interest.

Of course she didn't want anything to happen—that was just the point. Going out with a teacher would have been scandalous and would have made her the target of an unending source of ribbing, even if it did happen more often than the school administration wanted to believe. Still it would have been nice to know that a man like Seth Morgan thought of her as a real woman, and more than once it had been his lean hard body, still wet and cool from the pool, that she imaged covering hers as she lay in bed at night stroking herself to orgasm.

But as time went on Laura realized that his "coldness" toward her was actually the greatest compliment he could pay her. The fact that he didn't even see her as a woman was proof that he saw her as something even more important to him: a championship athlete. And he would do nothing to jeopardize her success—or his part in it.

"Laura," he began reasonably enough, trying to keep his temper under control, "I don't know where your head is at but it's not on the water."

Laura didn't say anything; she was determined not to rise to his bait.

"You don't understand, do you?" he went on, despite her silence. "You've got a chance of a lifetime in front of you, the

chance to become an Olympic champion. That's a gift most athletes would kill for, and you're just throwing it away."

Laura felt herself flush with anger, but she tried to ignore
him. Instead she finished drying herself and pulled off her rubber bathing cap. She shook out her blond hair. Many of the girls
had cut their hair short in imitation of the style adopted by
swimmers on television, to increase their speed—even though
the effect was mostly psychological—and as a sign of their dedication to the sport. But Laura couldn't bring herself to cut off
her own golden locks.

Coach Morgan just stared at her for a moment, the unexpected sight of all that yellow hair after the neutering effect of
the bald rubber skull cap throwing him off as if he were suddenly looking at a whole different person. Laura didn't notice
his momentary discomfort. In any event, he recovered soon
enough.

"Dammit, girl, what the hell is the matter with you, anyway?
Talk to me!"

Laura looked up, her eyes blazing. "All right, you asked for
it. If you really want to know what's wrong, a woman in my bi-
ology class was killed in a motorcycle accident."

To her surprise, Coach Morgan looked genuinely shocked.

"I'm sorry," he said quietly. "Did you know her well?"

"Well, no," Laura said. "I mean I saw her in class, in the hall
once in a while . . ."

She could see the expression on his face changing and knew
what he was going to say even before he said it.

"Look," he started. "You've got to put these kinds of distractions behind you. If you want—"

"Distractions!" Laura exploded, her voice bouncing off the
walls. "A woman is killed and you call that a distraction?"

"It's a matter of priorities, Laura. You said yourself you
didn't know the woman. You've got to start putting things in
their proper perspective. You need to concentrate, to focus on
your goal and forget everything else. That's what it takes to be a
champion!"

"Well then maybe I don't want to be a champion!" Laura said viciously. "Maybe I'd rather be a human being!"

Coach Morgan shook his head sadly. "I thought you had the drive, the talent to be somebody. I guess I was wrong."

"I guess you were," Laura said, turning away to the locker room.

"Laura, wait!" the coach called out to her.

"I quit!" she yelled over her shoulder.

"Laura, come back here!"

Laura didn't look back. She went right on walking to the locker room, her rubber flip-flops slapping the wet concrete like the sound of someone slowly and patiently slapping a face.

2

THINGS WERE EVEN WORSE in the locker room.

When she stormed through the door Laura was almost stopped cold by the wall of silence that met her on the other side. It was obvious that they had all been listening to what had transpired at the pool. Now they looked down, or talked in whispers to each other, though a few couldn't resist sneaking a peek at her.

Laura tried to ignore them as she made her way to her own locker at the end of the row. She only hoped they couldn't see the blood coloring her face or the tears stinging her eyes.

When she passed Terry, she heard the Texan snicker.

"Whatsa matter? Lover's spat?"

Laura spun around.

The big girl was standing by her open locker, her hands on her hips, her legs slightly spread. She was stark naked.

Whereas most of the girls had developed an easy familiarity with each other's nakedness that came from spending so much time together in various stages of undress, Terry pushed such intimacy a step further. She always seemed to take twice as long as necessary to get dressed. She seemed to enjoy strutting naked up and down the row of lockers, spouting off jokes and obscenities. She took obvious pleasure in showing off her body and intimidating the other girls.

Laura hated the routine and always made it a point to get

dressed and out of the locker room as quickly as possible. Though she hardly admitted it to herself, her reason for doing so was to stay out of Terry's way.

Now she had no choice.

Laura looked the other girl up and down. Terry was tall, nearly as tall as Coach Morgan, and her large-boned frame was covered with lumpy muscle, bulging at the thighs and biceps in a way disturbingly unnatural to a woman. One look at her flat ass and flatter chest provided all the back-up anyone needed to confirm the locker-room gossip: Teresa Myers took steroids.

There was also the matter of her temper.

She had nearly been thrown out of school the semester before for beating up her girlfriend, a thin, mousey looking little bookworm named Marie. Only some fast talking by the athletic director and an empty promise that Terry would schedule regular appointments with the school psychologist saved her scholarship.

Though she would have loved to plant her fist in the Texan's flat smug face, Laura knew she didn't stand a chance against the bigger girl. If anything, she would be playing right into her hands. Terry would have jumped at any excuse to beat her up.

Laura swallowed the bitter lump of anger in her throat and continued on to her locker. She yanked open the door and started peeling off her Speedo one-piece.

"You know what I think," Terry's taunting voice jabbed at her back, "I think you need to give ole Seth a blow job. Maybe that'll put the old spark back in your romance. Get him off your ass."

Laura was naked now, reaching for her panties.

"Unless, of course, he's already getting off in your ass."

Everyone froze; the locker room was suddenly as quiet as a morgue. All eyes were on Laura, waiting to see what she would do next.

Laura felt her face burn, the anger trapped inside her like a pacing cat, its tail twitching. She wished Terry would just give it up and go away. But the big girl wasn't backing off; she was itching for a fight.

"Hey, I'm talking to you, bitch!"

"Come on, Terry," a quiet girl named Dell said. She was also a lesbian, and she and Teresa often went cruising the gay bars together looking for femme types. She was the only girl on the team who could stand up to Terry without getting knocked on her ass for her trouble.

But this time Terry was really mad and not even Dell could calm her down. The beating Laura had given her in the pool had really burned the big Texan, and now she wanted to even the score.

Terry turned to her friend. "What the fuck," she snarled. "Are you telling me what to do now?"

"No," Dell said with a shrug, trying to sound reasonable. "Just trying to keep the peace, is all."

"Well, keep the fuck out of it. This little bitch wants trouble and she's found it!"

Laura felt her heart pounding faster. She wanted nothing more than to get dressed and out of there in a hurry. She found her panties where they had fallen to the bottom of the locker and bent over to pick them up.

She heard the towel snap before she felt the ice-cold patch just above her right hip, and then a hot stinging sensation as if someone had burned her with an iron.

The blow ignited an anger that Laura suddenly realized had been steadily building for months. There was no backing down now. Her hands balled into fists and her eyes narrowed as she started forward.

"Let's go!" Terry bellowed, and stepped forward to meet her. Suddenly, from out of nowhere, Coach Morgan came running down the row of lockers.

He somehow managed to get between the two girls before they could reach each other. He grabbed Terry by the arm and yanked her to one side, using his other arm to hold Laura away. The big girl still had that wild look in her eyes, as if she would go for Laura's throat at the first opportunity.

"What the hell is going on here?" Coach Morgan demanded.

Terry shot her arm forward, stabbing a finger at Laura.

"Her!" she spat, rage making it impossible for her to speak clearly. "She fuckin' started it!"

The coach turned to Laura for an explanation.

"Laura?"

Laura met the coach's glittering blue eyes. His chest was heaving under his blue polo shirt, the muscles of his arm tensed as he held Terry back. She saw his gaze drop for just an instant and once again she felt the warmth flood her face, only this time it wasn't anger, it was embarrassment.

For she suddenly became aware of the panties balled up in her right fist and the fact that she was standing in front of Coach Morgan stark naked.

3

IF IT WEREN'T for the monitor above the bed, Detective Neil Stone wouldn't have known if his father was alive or dead.

The old man lay motionless on the thin hospital bed, the starched sheet above his narrow chest barely rising and falling. His face was stiff and white, almost statuesque. His mouth hung open, slack and wet, dribbling spittle onto his yellowed beard. Above it, the large hooked nose was more pronounced, beaklike, in the wasted features. What was left of his hair, dry and sere, was no longer combed carefully over his bald pate, but hung down from the left side of his head like a patch of dead sod.

It was a shock to see his father like this. Even though Stone had known it was coming for weeks now, had steeled himself against this very moment, there was no way to prepare for it.

As a cop, it was his job to protect the innocent, to save lives. And here he was in the same room where his own father lay dying and there wasn't a damn thing he could do about it. He felt frustrated, angry, alone.

And scared as hell.

He watched his father struggle for breath, working his wet mouth like a faulty valve. In the quiet room, his desperate breathing sounded like a hacksaw. They had taken away his respirator; science had finally given up and decided to let nature take its course.

The nurses called patients like his father "croakers." They were patients who weren't expected to live the night. Stone had heard the term a hundred times before, but the crass horror of it had never struck him as it did now.

Now that it was his own flesh and blood lying there helpless, dying.

It seemed brutally, stupidly impossible. But in spite of the chemo, the operations, the gradual wasting away, Stone never really expected his father would die. Not *really*. Death was for other folks. Yet here was the incontrovertible evidence of personal mortality right in front of his eyes.

His father, *his own goddamn father*, was a croaker.

They told Stone they were doing everything to make his father as comfortable as possible, sending the old man floating off to the Great Hereafter on a raft of narcotics and painkillers.

Yet the wasted body kept gasping for air, going on by force of habit. Not knowing how to stop. Built to keep going. To survive. At all costs.

It seemed strangely empty in the room and suddenly Stone realized why.

All of the machinery had been rolled away, all of the tubes removed, except for the one running morphine into his father's veins and the one that snaked out from under the sheets to the bag of bloody urine at the side of the bed. Stone looked down at his father's left forearm lying on the crisp white sheet: the interconnecting pattern of bruises from the needles and tubes forced into his flesh over the last several weeks formed a black-and-blue tattoo in which Stone could read the history of his father's final agony.

Colorectal cancer.

Why not call it what it really was? *Cancer of the asshole.*

Such an undignified disease for a man who so prided himself on his dignity.

His father had been diagnosed with the cancer nearly fifteen years ago and the old bastard had been doggedly battling the inevitable ever since. Every three or four years it seemed they found a new tumor. They cut away at his intestines until last

July he'd finally run out of rope. That was when they had to do the colostomy. They punched a hole in his side so he could shit into a bag slung onto his hip.

When his father woke up in the recovery room, it was Stone who had to tell him. The old man was shattered. He had stared down death six or seven times already, bore every kind of physical and mental torture modern medical science could devise, but it was the first time Stone had ever seen his father beaten.

For days the old man refused to speak, letting the nurses tend to the sack of abomination attached to his side, as if it weren't a part of him. He refused to take solid food. Each day, after his shift was over, Stone spent his free time at the hospital, trying to talk his father out of his depression. Eventually the old man did come around, learned how to tend to his own post-operative care, but driving his father home from the hospital, Stone knew that the old man had given up. He could see it in his eyes.

Stone had once thought he'd never met a man more determined to live. Or, maybe, more afraid to die than his father. And, yet, even he had had his limit.

His father lived his final months hating what his life had become, what his body had become, *what he had become*.

They never mentioned the colostomy or the bag at his hip. But the subject was always there, fouling the air between them, like the faint stench of feces and bile that Stone learned to ignore whenever he visited his father.

Now, standing by his father's deathbed in the small hours of morning, Stone wondered at the incredible fragility of human life and the cold irony of fate: that the decision to live or not to live might all depend on the importance a man placed on his asshole.

Of course, it was more than that. The disease had finally taken away the one thing that made all the pain bearable, the one thing the old man valued more than life itself: his dignity.

Death was like that; it wouldn't take you unless you came along willingly; but it coerced its recruits by stripping away everything that made life worth living—until death was the best bet between oblivion and an existence of unceasing agony.

Stone wondered if they had removed the bag now in the final hours of his father's life. He guessed they probably hadn't. They would most likely do that in the morgue. He would have to remember to remind them. It wouldn't do to have the old man buried with it, lying beside him in the coffin for all eternity, like a mother who died with her stillborn child.

Stone sat down heavily in the orange plastic chair the hospital staff provided for visitors. He felt the tears sting his eyes.

It suddenly occurred to him that he didn't remember ever telling his father that he loved him. Of course, the old man had been difficult enough to love. Before he finally ran off when Stone was twelve, he'd left behind nothing but a lot of unpleasant memories: drunken yelling in the middle of the night, the sound of dishes breaking, the sharp crack of flesh meeting flesh, the slam of doors, the huddled shape of his mother sobbing alone in darkened rooms.

It had taken years and the experience of his own wrecked marriage for Stone to understand that his father had simply been a deeply frustrated man. But by then it was too late. He already hated the man.

Now Stone wept for those lost years. For the family they had once been. For the father who was once younger than Stone was now.

He reached down between the steel guardrails at the side of the bed and covered his father's hand with his own. Once again, he received a shock. The bony hand was cold and stiff and unfeeling, almost reptilian, more like a talon than anything human.

"Pop," Stone sobbed but couldn't finish.

He realized for the first time that what he suspected was true: he really didn't love his father.

The old man's breathing suddenly grew more ragged. On the monitor's screen, Stone could see the staggered skyline of his father's life, like a city shaken by the shock of a major earthquake. He briefly considered pressing the button for the nurse and realized there was nothing she would be able to do. Nothing anyone could do. That's why he was here.

It was time to let the old man go.

He heard the sound he had heard all too often in the line of duty: holding the bloodied hand of victims at the scenes of crimes and traffic accidents as he waited for the ambulance to come. Knowing damn well that the paramedics would never make it in time. That the odds were too long. That he was backing a loser. It was an indescribable and yet unforgettable sound: a low, hard, unforgiving rattle. Like something broken. That can't be fixed. Ever.

Stone closed his eyes and sat and waited and held his father's hand. He didn't see the moment his father died.

He didn't see the figure detach itself from the pale green wall. He didn't see it as it approached the bed—a loose assemblage of molecules and energy shaped like a man—and stood over his dying father. He didn't see it reach down and plunge its arms up to the elbows in his father's lower abdomen like one of those "spirit surgeons" on television. Didn't see those arms come up shiny with gore, clutching what was left of the old man's diseased entrails, twisted around its bloody fists. Didn't see it cramming the white, polyp-studded intestines into the black hole that passed for its mouth like so many pale, bloody sausages.

Didn't see the look of pain. Of shock. Of dumb, awestruck terror on his father's face.

Didn't see the old man's eyes snap open. The pupils widen. To take in the horror of what had come to claim him.

Instead Stone felt a barely perceptible disturbance in the atmosphere, a rush of cold air that he might not have noticed except that it made the hair on his arms stand on end. Later, he would remember that sensation and, in spite of himself, think of it as the moment he felt his father's spirit free itself from his pain-wracked body, and Stone's psyche would begin to heal.

Now he heard the buzzer go off and his head jerked up to see the green line of the monitor running perfectly flat across the middle of the screen.

He heard the squeak of the duty nurse's rubber-soled shoes as she rushed in from her station. Too late.

Always too late.

For the rush of cold air Stone felt wasn't his father's spirit leaving his body.

It was death coming to get him.

4

"Why do we have to die?"

Professor Roarke stood at the front of the horseshoe-shaped classroom and stared up at the tiers of seats that rose around him, hands on hips, as if daring someone to answer.

He was a short, robust, barrel-chested man. In spite of his tweed coat and leather elbow patches, he looked more like the wrestling coach than a professor of comparative religion. Roarke cocked his bald, bullet-shaped head to one side like an inquisitive turtle listening at the side of a highway for the rumble of an eighteen-wheeler. His glance paused on Laura but Laura wasn't biting; she knew a rhetorical question when she heard one.

"Mr. Cleghorn," he suddenly intoned, startling a hulking footballer in the third row from a daydream in which the team's cheerleaders were shaking their pom-poms stark naked.

"Huh?" he said dully.

"Why is it we have to die?"

The irony of asking a question that had preoccupied the greatest minds in human history to a throwback to the Neanderthal age raised more than a few titters from the assembled students.

Laura thought it was kind of cruel to pick on the big footballer like that, and she was surprised that Professor Roarke had done so. He was usually pretty good about not embarrassing his students. Not that the footballer didn't have it coming. After all, the jocks had their own support system and pretty much lorded it over the rest of the school.

Besides, Professor Roarke made no secret of his passionate belief that the money devoted to the school's football program was ruining the academic standards of the university by driving smaller and more esoteric disciplines like those pursued in the philosophy department to the brink of fiscal oblivion. He devoted a lecture to the topic every semester during the quarterly budget forecasts.

Laura felt a sharp elbow in her ribs and Carin's voice whispered in her ear.

"Might as well have gone down to the animal husbandry lab and asked a polled Hereford."

Laura suppressed a giggle. She made an exaggeratedly wooden face and stared straight ahead to where the footballer was now squirming in his seat, his heavy brow furrowed as if trying to force a thought from between his thick eyebrows.

"Oh, Christ," Laura whispered, "he's not really going to try to come up with an answer, is he?"

"Well, Cleghorn?" Professor Roarke prompted. "What about it? Why do we have to die?"

Even from six rows back, Laura could see the sweat dotting the scalp beneath the footballer's brush-top. He gripped his Bic like a diving pilot grips an ejector lever, ready to bail out.

"Um-uh," he began.

"Come on, Cleghorn," Professor Roarke pressed mercilessly.

Laura almost hated Professor Roarke for this blatant display of pedagogical sadism.

Almost.

The other part of her enjoyed seeing the bully getting a taste of his own brutality.

"Because—because we're human?" the footballer suddenly blurted, as if the idea had just occurred to him for the first time. There was outright laughter in the classroom now and even Laura started to chuckle. Beside her, Carin was guffawing so hard tears had actually begun to leak from the corners of her eyes.

"Oh God," she moaned and leaned into Laura. "Oh God, what a fucking moron!"

The footballer turned around and glared at the laughing students, as if taking mental inventory of whose legs he would have to break after class.

Meanwhile, Professor Roarke was smiling broadly, taking in the jocularity. "Excellent, Mr. Cleghorn!" he shouted over the laughter. "Obvious. But absolutely to the point!"

The classroom fell silent at this unexpected turn of events and Laura sat up in her chair, eager to see what would happen next.

The footballer looked thunderstruck at his luck, a silly satisfied grin growing across his face, and then he suddenly looked suspicious, as if afraid that it was all some kind of joke, and that Professor Roarke was only making a fool of him. Nonetheless, he turned slowly back to the front of the classroom, trying in vain to remember exactly what he had said.

" 'Only the Gods live forever,' " Professor Roarke's voice boomed in the silence of the auditorium, " 'but as for us men, our days are numbered, our occupations are a breath of wind.' "

Professor Roarke lowered his tattered copy of *The Epic of Gilgamesh* and looked at the class over his half-glasses.

"As Mr. Cleghorn so eloquently put it, we are human and therefore mortal. Again and again in the *Epic* it is this insurmountable obstacle that the hero runs smack up against. No matter what great feats we might accomplish, no matter how heroically we might strive, we cannot overcome the limits of our own mortality. In the end, president or panhandler, saint or sinner, we all must die."

Laura shifted uncomfortably in her chair, her mind drifting back to a hospital room in Buffalo, to a pretty woman lying on a bed of pain, her long blond hair plastered to her skull with sweat, her traitorous body seized with tremors from a chill no one in the overheated room could feel but her. Laura had just turned twelve and her mother had come down with pneumonia.

Even then it was unthinkable that a healthy, thirty-nine-year-old woman could die of pneumonia. And yet, she had; the virus had eventually settled around her heart and after three long months of needless suffering, Laura's mother died quietly of heart failure in her sleep.

It would have been disastrous enough if the loss had ended there. But when Laura's father came out of shock over the unexpected loss of his wife he found the pain waiting for him on the other side simply unbearable. He drifted further and further from his young daughter, a constant reminder of the family they'd once been, and dulled his jangled nerves with alcohol. What had once been a carefully moderated habit—a drink or two every night after work just to unwind—soon became a full-fledged addiction; a form of perpetual, self-induced shock.

Only after Laura's guidance counselor threatened to bring charges of neglect did he seek help at a local chapter of AA. But by then it was too late. Laura had seen him passed out drunk once too many times, heard one too many of his embarrassing tearful confessions. Her father, once her best friend, was suddenly a stranger to her. Predictably enough, he met another recovering alcoholic at his weekly meetings, they began dating, and they were married three months later.

Nothing could have been more devastating for a twelve-year-old girl still mourning the unexpected death of her mother. Even though he was a different man from what he had been before, Laura still loved her father. She did all she could to steal back his attention, taking several school swimming medals and making the dean's list semester after semester, but he was far too taken with his new life to pay her more than passing attention. When her first stepbrother was born a year later, Laura knew instinctively that she had lost her father for good.

From that day forward, she considered herself alone in the world. Her father and the life she had lived before her mother's death was over, sealed away like a moment in a photograph, forever. And yet she continued to swim, winning race after race, but taking little pleasure in her accomplishments. She had won scholarships to several big-name schools, but in the end chose the relatively obscure state college in Groverton, New York, a mere sixty-minute drive from Buffalo, though her father had not yet made the trip for a single one of her races.

Only lately did it occur to her that she swam because it was the only thing she knew, the only link to her old world, as if by swimming she might somehow return to that parental womb of love and caring she'd known before her mother's death, when her father still loved her and all seemed right with the world.

How many times had she asked herself why? Why her mother had to die? How differently Laura's life might have been if her mother had lived.

That line of speculation always terminated in a dead end. No matter how hard she tried, Laura couldn't imagine a happy ending to the story, her mother alive . . . And this time it was no different, her trip down memory lane came to the same dead end, snapping Laura's attention back to the front of the classroom, where Professor Roarke was now lecturing about the afterlife.

Laura liked Professor Roarke. He wasn't a dry pedant like her history prof or an arrogant bore like her English lit professor, Dr. Latelle. Professor Roarke knew how to make his subject come alive, how to make it relevant to young minds. Unlike most of her other professors, Professor Roarke didn't speak as if he were teaching from a prepared script but actually seemed to be learning and thinking along with his students. It was his genuine interest in his subject matter that made him so popular with his students. His curiosity and excitement were infectious.

". . . most religions," he was saying, "deal with the existential horror of death by holding out the promise of a heaven where the righteous are rewarded with eternal life. The peoples of the old Norse sagas had their Valhalla, where fallen warriors were reunited in the great meadhalls. In the Koran heaven is a cool oasis where the dead are served ambrosia by beautiful young women called *houris* . . ."

There was a painful groan from the girls in the class and an obligatory outburst of catcalls from some of the boys.

"I know, I know"—Professor Roarke held up his hands in sympathy and smiled at the interruption—"but you have to remember that Islam is a fiercely patriarchal religion." He put his hands in the pockets of his tweed coat and winked at a boy in the front row. "I'm thinking of becoming a convert."

There were some more groans and Professor Roarke waited until they subsided before going on.

"In the Greek and Roman culture the underworld is pictured as a dim shadow of this world, as you most likely remember from your Homer and Virgil. Judaism has a similar conception of the hereafter, which they call Sheol, the place of shades. And, of course, there is the ever-popular conception of heaven where the dead float around inanely among the clouds strumming harps seemingly without regard to whether or not the deceased had any prior musical talent or not. . . ." More laughter. He looked pleased that his joke was appreciated, but then his demeanor sobered, and everyone could tell he was going to say something important, something that might be on a test.

Professor Roarke cleared his throat and fifty pens were poised over open notebooks, ready to take down what he said next.

"But in the *Gilgamesh*," he began, "there is absolutely nothing redeeming about death. There is no facile attempt to whitewash the terrible truth of our mortality. And that sense of nihilistic terror is what makes it so unique—and so modern. In the *Gilgamesh* our worst fears are confirmed: death is the ultimate horror, unmitigated by any promise whatsoever, even the promise of oblivion; instead it is a waking nightmare from which we will never escape. And the angel of death is nothing short of an executioner—a murderer—who comes to claim us when our time is at hand, with blood and suffering."

Professor Roarke flipped through the pages of his book until he found the passage he was looking for.

" 'There stood before me an awful being,' " he read, " 'a somber-faced man-bird. His was a vampire face, his foot a lion's foot, his hand an eagle's talon. He fell on me and his claws were in my hair, he held me fast and I smothered. He led me away to the house from which none who enters ever returns, down the road from which there is no coming back."

Laura felt a chill scamper up her spine and crown her scalp with a thousand tiny pinpricks. At the same time a collective shudder passed through the students in the auditorium, like the "wave" at a football game.

"And what is this 'house' to which we are taken after our mortal lives are over? What is this vision of the afterlife according to the *Gilgamesh*?"

Professor Roarke paused for dramatic effect and looked up again over the half-lenses of his bifocals. His eyes seemed to pause for a moment on each face in the classroom. He was clearly enjoying the moment, having woven a kind of spell over his captive audience with his gruesome critique.

"It is a house of dust," he said, each word spoken in a measured tone of doom, "whose inhabitants sit in perpetual darkness eating nothing but the dust and clay of the grave, through all eternity. Do you understand what the poet is saying here? Do you understand the implication of his vision of the afterlife? It is a place of unending torture, as if the cosmos itself were fueled by the torment of its creations. . . ."

Unending torture.

Laura felt an unpleasant shock and once again thought about her mother and the "happy place" her father had tried to describe to her, explaining that that's where mommy had gone to stay and where she was waiting for them to someday join her. Laura shuddered. Believing that had made it bearable. But what if there were no happy place, what if what Professor Roarke was saying were true? Laura was sure that was the way that madness lay. . . .

"And that, ladies and gentlemen, is the grim vision left us by the ancient Sumerians. Not only is there no heaven for the righteous, there is not even the peace of oblivion. Instead, there is only unending torture and pain for both good and evil alike. For no matter how bad or unfair life gets, only one thing is certain: death is far, far worse."

Just then the bell sounded but the students would not move from their seats. It was incredible; usually everyone was up and racing for the door. Now they all sat there as if waiting for Roarke to bring a happy ending to the story.

"Class dismissed," he said, but still nobody moved.

"Oh," he added, as if purposely to break the spell, "papers are due a week from Tuesday."

There was a collective groan and then the students began to gather their things and head for the door.

"And remember," Professor Roarke called out cheerily behind them, "you must live—live as much as you can. At all costs, live!"

5

"Jeeze, talk about a downer," Carin said.

They were walking across the wide green quad that separated the humanities building from the cafeteria. "He's worse than Ozzy Osbourne. What's he trying to do, anyway, drive us all to suicide?"

Laura laughed. Her friend always had a flair for the dramatic. Carin was two years behind Laura and had come to the university from a small town in Indiana on a woman's basketball scholarship. Laura's first impression of her had been that of a tall awkward-looking girl obviously away from home for the first time.

As if by fate, Carin had glommed onto Laura during the orientation meeting in the gymnasium, and the two became fast friends. Laura found Carin's warm and earnest enthusiasm a refreshing change from the jaded attitudes of most of her city-bred classmates, and Carin considered Laura—egad!—sophisticated.

"Just the opposite, I think," Laura said of Professor Roarke's lecture. "I mean did you hear what he said about the afterlife?"

"Yeah, so?"

"Well, if there is no heaven, only unending torture, why would anyone want to kill themselves? They'd only be jumping from the fat into the fire."

"Don't remind me," Carin said, patting her stomach.

32

"You're not *fat*," Laura said. Carin's weight was an ongoing concern. While it was true she wasn't fat, she wasn't exactly thin, either, and only the constant exercise she got playing basketball kept her weight within an acceptable range.

"Yeah, yeah," she said dismissively. "And I've got a pretty face."

"You do have a pretty face," Laura said. "You're just pissed off because Roarke gave you a C on that Kubler-Ross paper."

"You'd be, too. You're not the only one who needs a B average to keep a scholarship."

"Yeah, but I would have worked harder on that paper instead of spending the night trying to outdrink half the junior varsity. You forget, I was there the morning you wrote it. I was the one pouring black coffee so you could keep your head off the desk."

Carin shook her head, amazed. "What a hangover I had."

"You wrote that paper in three hours."

"Warp time," Carin laughed.

"Hammer time!" they said in unison, and slapped each other the high-five.

It was only eleven-thirty but the cafeteria was already half-filled. The crowd seemed to be divided between those who'd had early-morning classes and others who had just rolled out of bed and were grabbing a quick cup of coffee before their afternoon schedules began. Laura and Carin grabbed two brown trays and took their place at the end of the service line.

Laura bypassed the display of shrink-wrapped bologna sandwiches and plastic containers of tuna salad without a second glance. Experience had taught her that they had been sitting there in a state of suspended animation for months. Instead she waited until she reached the serving station, where two women who looked like they had just stepped out of a *Far Side* cartoon stood guard over three aluminum bins each filled with a thick, gravylike goop in which floated anonymous chunks of what was presumably meat.

The only difference Laura could see between the offerings in the three bins was their color: red, yellow, and brown.

"I'll have a hamburger, please," she asked one of the servers.

The two women stared at Laura with bovine impassivity for a good five seconds before one of them turned and slowly made her way back to the grill. She threw a thin frozen meat patty on the hot surface and after two minutes of fitful frying handed the hamburger over the counter to Laura on a small paper plate.

As they steered their trays along the metal track, Carin stopped in front of the tiers of pie wedges, pudding cups, and jiggly plates of Jello-O. While Laura carried her tray around her on the way to the register, Carin took a large wedge of banana custard pie topped with whipped cream and shaved chocolate.

"Isn't it kind of early for that?" Laura asked, trying to be tactful.

"Wouldn't be for sale if it were too early," Carin offered with a shrug.

Laura shook her head. "Wise ass."

They made their way to an empty table by the window overlooking the mathematics building and sat down. Carin buttered a roll, stuffed half of it in her mouth, and sprinkled salt on a bowl of yellow mush that was supposed to be chicken à la king. She popped the rest of the roll in her mouth and carefully troweled butter on a second.

"Did you ever hear of cholesterol?" Laura finally said, unable to resist.

"Yeah," Carin laughed, and patted herself on the thighs. "Whatcha think I'm carrying in these saddlebags, pardner? Chopped liver?"

"Very funny," Laura said. "We're supposed to be in training, you know."

"*We* are," Carin said slyly. "Does that mean you're still on the team?"

Laura flipped up the top half of her hamburger roll and stared down at the blue-gray patty of meat inside. She opened a packet of catsup and squeezed out the watery red liquid onto the burger.

"Well, does it?" Carin pressed.

"I don't know," Laura mumbled. "I haven't decided yet."

"Well, you better decide in a hurry. The trials are only three months away, you know."

"Yeah, yeah, I know."

"Jeeze, Laura, you can't quit now. It's what you've been working for all these years. You can't just throw all that away."

"You sound just like Coach Morgan."

"Is that the problem? I mean I know he rides you pretty hard sometimes, but that's only because you've got what it takes. He's just trying to push you to be the best you can. I just wish I had half your talent . . . not to mention a mentor like Coach Morgan. What a hunk—"

"No. That's not it. Not really. It's just that I'm beginning to wonder if I really care that much about swimming after all."

Carin looked up from her chicken à la king, her eyes wide. "Not care about it?"

"You know that girl killed in the motorcycle accident—"

"Is that still bugging you?"

"Yeah, well, it just got me to thinking, that's all. There must be more important things in life than an Olympic medal. I spend up to five hours a day training in that damned pool, and for what?"

"So that dyke bitch Terry doesn't make the trials, that's what," Carin said with a grin.

Laura frowned. "I'm serious."

"That's part of the problem," Carin said. "You need to get out and let your hair down a little. A night on the town. Hey, why don't you come with me and Butch tonight."

"That second-string varsity forward you've been talking so much about?"

"Yeah." Carin grinned sheepishly.

"Congratulations are in order."

"It's not a date, really," Carin said dismissively, but Laura could read the hope in her friend's eyes. "Just a bunch of us getting together. We're going to the Horse. There's supposed to be a new band playing down there tonight."

"I don't know," Laura said. "I've got a trig test the day after tomorrow."

"Oh come on!" Carin urged. "You remember what old Roarke said." She raised her voice to imitate the professor's resonant baritone. A few students at nearby tables turned around, looking half-amused. " 'Live! Live while you can!' "

"Okay, okay," Laura said, "I'll think about it. Just keep your voice down." She bit into her burger, her face registering her disgust when she saw the bloody flakes of oatmeal filler spilling from inside the meat like sawdust.

"Yecch!" Carin said as Laura shook the burger over her plate, letting more flakes fall from inside the half-cooked meat.

Laura dropped the uneaten hamburger on the plate, her appetite hopelessly spoiled. All she could think of was Professor Roarke's description of the house of dust, where the dead were gathered, eating the clay and dust and earth of their own graves throughout all eternity.

6

TODAY WAS THE DAY Lisa Rivera decided to die.

It was not a decision that she had made lightly. What had preceded it had been nothing short of the worst month of her twenty-one-year-old life. It had all started when she'd missed her second period in a row. She ran right out to the drugstore and bought one of those at-home pregnancy tests. The next morning, sitting on the toilet, holding a small cup of urine and watching the chemically treated end of the applicator turn an unmistakeable pink, her worst fear was confirmed.

She was pregnant.

When she told her boyfriend Ted, he got mad and drunk and acted like it was all her fault. Like he hadn't been the one to tell her not to worry, that they didn't need the condom, that he would pull out of her before he came.

Of course she shouldn't have believed him: he was as selfish and untrustworthy a man as he was a lover. And besides, it was *her* body and she would be the one to pay the price. Still, in the heat and passion of the moment she had given in, afraid to make him angry, and now look where it had all gotten her.

The bastard wouldn't even agree to pay for half of the abortion. He wouldn't return her calls, and when she went to visit him at the garage where he worked, he'd embarrassed her by calling her a whore in front of the other mechanics and telling her never to come back. She hadn't heard from him since. Eventually Lisa had had to borrow money from her roommate Pam, and when the time came it was Pam who drove her over to the clinic.

The clinic was a small brick building inconspicuously located in a professional complex of similar buildings and subtly called the Groverton Women's Clinic. Lisa must have passed it a thousand times without even knowing it was there. Pam had known about it because she'd had four abortions already. She described to Lisa the hose, the suction, the mild sense of discomfort, trying to allay her fears. "It's nothing," she'd said. "It's no worse than having a bad period."

The waiting room was small, clean, and well lit. In each corner there was a real plant so green it looked fake. The air conditioning was set too high. Even the nurses were wearing sweaters. The Muzak piped into the room—reworked versions of old Barry Manilow and Paul Williams hits—made her sick to her stomach. The room was filled with girls, mostly young, mostly with girlfriends, and most of them were crying.

Lisa filled out a form that absolved the clinic, the doctors, and the nurses of any responsibility in the event that something went wrong, and returned the clipboard to the receptionist behind the desk. Lisa's hands were white as chalk.

When it was her turn a hard-eyed nurse took her into the back room, had her undress, put on a paper gown, and sit on the examination table. A few minutes later a doctor with bad breath and cold hands came in and hurriedly explained what he was going to do and then started complaining to the attending nurse about the slice in his tennis backhand.

The cramps were a lot worse than Pam had described, and she lay there in the cold room, shivering, nearly naked, hearing nothing but the gulping sound of the machine that was vacuuming the blood and clotted tissue from her womb and the sound of her own quiet sobbing.

When it was over, Lisa felt horrible and dirty and just plain guilty, even though she knew it had been the right thing to do. She knew she couldn't go to school and care for a baby at the same time. She didn't want to wind up like her mother, who'd gotten pregnant at sixteen, or like her sister Rosa, who was only a year older than she was and already living alone with three babies of her own.

Still, she couldn't stop imagining what her mother would say if she knew. Estella Rivera was a good Catholic; to her, abortion was murder, plain and simple, just like the Pope said it was. And then there was her father. Poppa, she knew, would be furious. He had been so proud of her when she was accepted into the university; Lisa was the first one in the family ever to go to college. He did not speak much but Lisa could see the pride beaming from his eyes when he spoke to his friends about his "college girl."

Whereas Rosa had always been the wild one, getting into all kinds of trouble, Lisa had always been the good one, her father's pet. Worse than his anger, which Lisa would willingly weather to absolve her of her sins, would be what she knew lay beneath it: his deep and inconsolable disappointment in his "perfect little girl." To see that hurt in his soft brown eyes—that, Lisa couldn't bear.

And finally there was the image of Rosa herself with one of her chubby brown babies suckling contentedly at her breast. It was a set of twins, the insensitive doctor had remarked offhandedly as Lisa dressed.

Less than a week later Lisa got the letter in the mail. It had come from out of nowhere, like the retribution of God himself. The budget funding her grant had been cut for the next semester. There was no way Lisa would be able to afford the tuition herself. Nor could she ask her parents. Her father, who had worked all his life driving a delivery truck for the local paper, simply didn't have that kind of money. She wouldn't even embarrass him by asking. Lisa was already working two part-time jobs to cover her living expenses. She would have to quit school, or see if she could apply for yet another student loan. That same week her friend Julie was killed on the back of Ben Harlow's motorcycle.

Today she'd been coming out of the social sciences building and found that someone had stolen her bicycle. The plastic-covered chain she had secured it with lay unbroken at the base of the tree; the lock itself was undisturbed.

Lisa stared up at the tree, nearly thirty feet away, and couldn't imagine how they had gotten the bicycle. She walked all around the tree, staring at the unbroken chain, as if it were some kind of logic puzzle. Or a practical joke.

Why would anyone have wanted to steal her bike, anyway? It wasn't one of those expensive new mountain bikes everyone was riding around campus. It was just an old, secondhand Schwinn ten-speed, painted flat black to conceal the scratches and rust rot marring the original finish. She had bought it from a graduating upperclassman for twenty-five bucks.

Lisa sat beneath the tree and started to cry. But it wasn't really the loss of the bicycle she was mourning. It was everything that had happened in the last month. The stolen bicycle was only the last straw.

Lisa walked the twelve blocks home to her off-campus apartment. It was a beautiful sunny day, uncharacteristically warm for early autumn. There were birds singing. Kids playing Frisbee. Students studying under trees or lounging on the grass of the quad under the sun.

But the fair weather did little to soothe Lisa's pain. If anything, it seemed to mock her and made her all the more depressed, as if she were somehow out of kilter with the fundamental nature of things. It was then that she made the final decision to end her life.

Once she'd made up her mind it was as if a great weight had been lifted from her shoulders. *To be or not to be.* The question had been at the back of her mind for weeks, hovering just below the level of consciousness. Now, seemingly overnight, the answer had bloomed, like a velvety black flower on the floor of a vast primeval jungle. And it was beautiful.

She felt . . . almost *happy.*

Just then a carload of freshmen in a red Geo convertible pulled up alongside her at the curb.

They leaned out, shouting something lewd, bigoted, suggestive of her short skirt, dark hair, and brown skin, as if she were a common streetwalker. Ordinarily it would have made Lisa angry and she would have fired something straight back, something calculated to shrivel their balls inside their jeans like a bucketful of ice water.

Instead she twitched her buttocks suggestively, making the short skirt dance, and gave them her brightest, most provocative smile.

The freshmen, not knowing what to do, hooted and hollered like Indians, peeling off down University Boulevard.

It was ironic.

Lisa never felt freer or more alive in her entire life.

Now that she had decided to die.

7

STONE STOOD by the side of the open grave.

The last two hours had been the most excruciating of his life. Even worse than the deathwatch at the hospital.

His father's funeral had brought relatives crawling out of the woodwork. Aunts. Uncles. Cousins. Stone never knew his father's family was so big.

Bald old men and clucking old women he didn't even recognize came up to him to shake his hand or kiss his cheek, telling him what a shame it was, that if he needed anything to just call.

So much bullshit.

Where were they when his father left home to start a new life? Leaving his wife behind with two kids and nothing to support them on but a part-time secretary's salary? Where were they when Stone had to go to school with sneakers worn through at the bottom or clothes from the bargain table at the local Woolworth's? Where were they when he went hungry at lunch hour because he was too proud to use the free meal passes his mother had applied for through the township welfare office?

What the hell did they imagine he'd need them for now?

Fucking emotional support?

A heavyset old woman with a silver goatee shambled toward him and gave him a kiss, claiming to be his grandmother. Stone looked at her in amazement. He thought she had died years ago. Stone couldn't think of a thing to say to her. Finally someone led her away, sobbing like a hog.

When Stone had called his hotshot brother in California to tell him their father had died, he'd said nothing for a long time and then "I'll send flowers" and hung up. He never did send the flowers.

These people didn't know him. Had never known him. They were just going through the motions.

He savored the indignation on their faces when they found out there wasn't going to be a wake. No free food and booze after all that driving. It was the first honest expression they'd displayed throughout the entire proceedings.

Stone stood silently through it all. Dressed in his one good suit. His dry eyes hidden behind black Wayfarers. Afraid that if he removed the glasses the "fuck-off" look in his eyes would give him away.

The service at the church was brief and to the point. One of Stone's uncles delivered the eulogy. The priest was probably the only person in the room who didn't know that this was the first time that Vince Stone had spoken to his brother since 1958.

Afterward, Stone drove himself to the little cemetery on Route 9. He thought he'd made good time, but somehow the hearse had beaten him there anyway. Stone found the site easily enough: it was located under a gaily striped yellow-and-white tent, as if they were all gathered for a family picnic. Beside the tent, the polished mahogany casket gleamed in the sun, sending off bolts of blinding light.

Stone noticed that only a handful had bothered to come to the cemetery. That suited him just fine.

As luck would have it, the day was unusually warm for September. Too warm for the overdressed old people who fanned themselves with church flyers, sweat running down their pasty wrinkled faces. They gratefully retreated to the air-conditioned interiors of their idling cars at the earliest opportunity.

Leaving Stone alone at last.

At the edge of the pit.

Standing beside a huge mound of displaced earth.

Drying in the sun.

The sound of birds came from over the rolling, too-green lawns. Hard to forget what passed for fertilizer here.

Stone stared down into his father's grave. Later, when he had long gone, a crew of drunken workmen would lower the casket down. But, for now, the hole was empty.

Roots from nearby trees dangled from the earthen walls. The exposed rocks bore white scars where they were struck by the backhoe.

Six feet deep. It might just as well have been a bottomless abyss. Sunday school aside, Stone had never heard of anyone climbing out again.

Sudden movement. From the corner of his eye.

Stone turned to the mound of dirt. Took off his sunglasses. Leaned closer.

There, wriggling in the earth, was a white grub.

Something had disturbed its slumber. Forced it out into the light before its time. Now it was blindly trying to push its way back into the cool darkness of the earth.

Stone plucked it out of the dirt and held it between his fingers.

It was moist, ribbed, a row of small vestigial legs lining its underside.

A cicada, maybe. Or an earwig.

Stone studied its black face. Its ugly mouthparts.

The worm curled defensively around his finger, as if ashamed of its nakedness.

How long would it be before the polished wood of his father's casket gave way to the elements? Softened? Rotted?

Gave way to the moles and graveyard rats?

How long before he would be food for larvae such as this?

With cruel deliberation, Stone sliced the grub in two with the nail of his forefinger. A cold, pulpy yellow mush burst out.

Like squeezing a pimple.

Stone flicked the remains off his thumbnail.

Put his Wayfarers back on.
"Fuck you," he muttered.
To the trees. To the earth. To the dead worm.
To death itself.
Lord of everything.

8

WHEN LISA GOT HOME the first thing she did was pull down all the blinds. She wanted to shut out the sun that had perversely insisted on shining on this, the last day of her life. Even now it winked through the gaps in the blinds, mocking her, striping her like some fragile, exotic animal on the edge of extinction.

She turned on her roommate's CD player and dug out her favorite disc. Grimm's *Scary Tales*. It was real headbanger stuff. The kind of music mothers were always protesting, saying that it contained satanic messages and prompted teen suicides.

She checked her watch. Pam had classes all afternoon; she wouldn't be home for another hour.

Lisa laid the disc in the drawer and watched it slide into the machine with a satisfying mechanical whir. She set it to replay her favorite track: "Deliver Us from Life."

As the music keyed up, Lisa walked back to her bedroom and did a slow striptease in front of the mirror on the back of her closet door. She imagined hundreds of horny skeletons watching her undress, lusting for the young brown flesh that would soon be theirs.

Naked, she padded across the hall and into her roommate's bedroom. She pulled open the top drawer of Pam's bureau, hearing the excited chitter of the little brown pill bottles. She found the secret cache under her roommate's silk panties.

Pam was the Ecclesiastes of pills. She believed there was a pill for everything. A pill to fall asleep. A pill to wake up. A pill to lose weight. A pill to put weight on. Her drawer looked like a miniature medicine cabinet.

Lisa read the labels on the bottles carefully: it wouldn't do to take an overdose of Pam's water-retention pills. After all, she didn't want to dehydrate herself to death.

Like most people, Lisa had given quite a lot of thought to how she might commit suicide at various times in her life. Guns were out of the question. Even if she had one, she would be too repulsed by the idea of disfigurement to use it. She had thought several times about cutting her wrists; it was the Roman way, she remembered from her ancient history class, and supposedly a not unpleasant way to go.

Only the day before in the tub while she was shaving her legs, Lisa thought how easy it would be to nick one of the narrow blue veins lying just under the skin, letting the dark blood flow into the warm water. She had scraped the cheap Bic disposable razor over the inside of her wrists, feeling the dull blade pull at her wet flesh.

But it wasn't the way she wanted to die.

Not the way she wanted to be found.

Lying naked in a cold broth of her own blood.

Lisa found a bottle of Valium that still contained a few lonely pills. But even she knew that five 2.5-mg valium pills weren't enough coinage to book her passage to the other side. She continued rooting around through her rooommate's underwear until she found what she was looking for.

Near the back of the drawer, she found a large white bottle of pills marked Charisporidyl. She was pretty sure they were the muscle relaxers Pam had coaxed from the doctor when she'd been complaining about that sore back she'd gotten from lying on the gear lever of Matt Brodsky's Corvette. She shook a few of the pills out in her hand. They were chalky, white, and nearly as big as mint Rolaids.

But the best thing was that the bottle was nearly full.

She took the pills and padded back out to the kitchen. She

pulled open the refrigerator door and found the bottle of white wine she had bought a few days before. She remembered standing in the liquor store and looking over the selection of bottles. Remembered the look on the husky young clerk's face when he asked, flirting, if he could help her and she asked him, smiling fetchingly, what went best with an overdose of tranquilizers.

She held up the bottle now and purposely read the label. Gallo, 1992. A very good year to die.

She took a wineglass from the cupboard, opened the bottle, and poured herself a glass of wine.

"Here goes nothing," she said.

Then she popped two of the big muscle relaxers into her mouth, raised the glass in an imaginary toast, and drained the contents in one studied gulp.

She carried the pills and the wine into the bedroom. Once again she stood in front of the mirror, swaying in time to the music, which had just started up again from the beginning.

Dying times have come . . .

Slowly she began to dance, watching her tight brown body in the glass: the short, shapely legs and slightly heavy hips, the dark black bush and flat stomach, the small pert breasts, each tipped with a large dusky aureole.

For the first time in her life she was able to really see herself. Without judgment. Without expectation. It was as if she were already out of her body. Looking at herself as another might see her. She blew a kiss into the mirror, imagining again that crowd of horny skeletons, reaching toward her with cold skeletal fingers, as she danced just out of reach.

She spun around on tiptoe and lost her balance, falling backward on the bed. She grabbed the bottle of wine and washed down a couple more pills. She was out of breath and suddenly very tired. She took another swig of wine and decided to close her eyes for just a minute. Just a minute . . .

A half hour later she woke up. To her surprise, she was still alive.

Outside in the living room, Grimm was still singing. She wondered why none of the neighbors had called to complain.

The music was so loud she could hear the bedroom windows rattling.

Her head was pounding; her heart beat loudly in her ears.

She looked at the wine and the pills on the nightstand. Her stomach rolled and she knew that if she tried to down any more she would vomit.

She swung her legs off the bed and lurched unsteadily to her feet, nearly pitching herself headlong into the wall. She rummaged in her book bag until she found the suicide note she had written in her notebook during Shakespeare class the week before. She laid it on the night table, under the bottle of wine.

If she were going to go through with her plan it was now or never. On her way out of the bedroom she pulled the belt out of the terry-cloth robe that hung on the back of her door.

In the living room there was a large hook, from which hung a thick macramé flowerpot holder and in it a heavy ceramic flowerpot with a luxuriant growth of shiny green leaves spilling almost to the floor. The weight of the pot and earth had necessitated that Pam screw the hook directly into the ceiling beam. It would be more than sufficient to hold the weight of a 105-pound woman.

She had heard on a talk show once—either Geraldo or Sally Jessie Raphael—that hanging was supposed to give you an orgasm. It had something to do with the constriction of blood in the throat. The show had been about teen suicide. Supposedly a lot of apparent teen suicides were the botched result of the pursuit of such dangerous thrills.

They had a fancy name for it, but she couldn't remember what it was now. Lisa wondered if it only worked for men—or if it worked that way for women, too. She hoped it did. That would be a nice surprise. It seemed to her that it would be the perfect way to die.

Lisa dragged a kitchen chair into the living room and positioned it under the hook. She stepped up and removed the heavy potted plant, carrying it carefully to the coffee table, knowing that the plant was Pam's pride and joy. Then she climbed back up in the chair, wound the terry-cloth belt around the hook, and tied it off tightly. She gave the belt a few hard yanks to make sure it was secure.

It was.

She wrapped the terry-cloth belt around her neck, fashioning a noose of sorts, and tied the knot snugly under her left ear. The music now seemed to be playing inside her own skull. Certain phrases rose out of the endless throbbing, splashing themselves across the inside of her forehead like revelation.

> *Take a sip of poison*
> *Lovers do it every day . . .*

She thought of Ted, that bastard. And thought of Pam, who would find her there. She thought of her mother and father, and her sister, Rosa. She thought of all the kids at school. Even the ones who didn't know her. They would all be sorry.

> *He comes like a dream there's no waking from*
> *With his fingers of eternity*
> *He cuts the throat of his chosen*
> *And brings to them sweet ecstasy. . . .*

Serves them right, she thought self-pityingly. And realized tears were running down her face.

Come on baby, don't be afraid, the music coaxed. *Kneel before him. He will take you away. . . .*

And with the image of her sorrowful and repenting acquaintances fixed firmly in her mind, Lisa calmly stepped off the chair.

The noose instantly tightened, snugly and yet not entirely unpleasantly, around her throat, crushing her windpipe shut and making it impossible for her to breathe. Lisa would have strangled there, quietly and without incident, within three minutes, more or less as she'd planned, except for the fact that she panicked.

There were three things she hadn't fully realized when she decided to hang herself.

One was that what made hanging a tolerably quick and efficient way of killing someone was the fact that professional hangmen took special care to weight the body of the victim to make sure that the drop from the scaffold would be abrupt enough to snap his or her neck. The worst thing that could happen was that the victim dangled there, his own weight on the end of the rope slowly strangling him.

And that was exactly what was happening to Lisa.

The second thing she hadn't realized was that the terry-cloth belt she had used to hang herself, under the weight of her body, would stretch.

It had stretched so far that the tips of her toes nearly touched the floor. Nearly.

And that led her to the third, most shocking revelation of all.

It had been implicit in nearly everything she'd done. The fact that she hadn't taken the whole bottle of pills at once. The note she had left in her guidance counselor's in-box. The fact that she had waited until now to actually hang herself. Fifteen minutes before she knew Pam would be coming home from lab.

Only now as the blood thundered in her temples, each word punctuated by the pounding of her heart, did she realize the truth.

I . . . do not . . . want to . . . die.

Only now it was too late.

Lisa reached desperately for the belt above her head, but the pills and the alcohol, not to mention the lack of oxygen, made her too weak to pull up her own weight. Her brain felt as if it were swelling inside her skull, as if the steadily increasing pressure were about to force it out of her ears and nostrils.

She blacked out momentarily. She came to seconds later, but her consciousness was fading in and out like a light bulb hooked up to a failing generator. Her legs kicked spasmodically, knocking the chair on its side and out of reach. Her toes twitched desperately for the floor that wasn't there.

Her last conscious act was to try to scream for help, but all that came out was a tiny pitiful gargling sound totally drowned out by the music from the stereo, and then she struggled to draw one last breath through her crushed windpipe as an icy blackness exploded in her brain.

And from out of the old silver-on-white patterned wallpaper a figure disengaged itself. It moved smoothly across the room, swift and top-heavy, like the shadow of someone carrying a coffin past the window, and stopped in front of the dangling girl.

In an instant it had measured the far-off siren of the ambulance racing to the apartment, the faint click-click of Pam's heels as the dead girl's roommate made her way unhurriedly around the corner at the head of the block, the three fateful inches that would forever separate Lisa's rigid and freshly painted toes from the safety of the floor.

It came to her then.

When she was almost too far gone to feel it.

Touched her. On the breasts. The lips. The belly.

Between her legs.

Wet. Willing.

Her eyes bulged, her body shuddered, and she shit herself in ecstasy.

9

DR. HENRY KENT hated death. With a passion.

He pressed the paddles on the dead girl's chest and yelled for everyone to stand clear.

"Hit me!" he yelled.

He felt the vibration of the electricity running into the paddles; it made his elbows numb.

The dead girl flopped on the gurney like a fish, her rubbery limbs animated with the brief illusion of life. She had been brought in dead, an apparent suicide. The paramedics had wanted to bring her straight to the morgue, but Kent had insisted that they bring her to the ER first. He wanted to take a crack at her.

Beside her on the gurney, he saw the stretched and bloody terry-cloth belt she had apparently used to hang herself. The paramedics had cut it from her throat at the scene when they tried to revive her. Now it would follow her around until the crime lab people came to bag it as evidence in their routine investigation of her death.

They would determine that she'd died at her own hand and that would be that.

But *why*?

She was too young to die. Pretty. Once.

Not anymore. Most people didn't realize that strangulation, like most violent death, was horribly disfiguring.

Her face, mottled and dark like spoiled eggplant, was twisted in a horrific rictus of grinning terror. Her tongue, swollen and gray, emerged from her mouth like a monstrous wad of bubble gum. Kent could see the blackened wound where she had nearly bitten it in two. Her rising blood pressure had caused the arteries in her brain to burst. Tracks of dried blood ran from her nostrils and ears. Her eyes bulged from the sockets, like pressure valves about to blow.

"Hit me again!" he yelled.

Once again the lifeless body jerked. The voltage was cranked up so high Kent could smell the faint scent of the lifeless flesh burning under the paddles. When he lifted them away he saw the large red circular burns on the dead girl's skin, as if someone had carelessly laid two teapots of boiling water on her chest.

He leaned over the girl. Sweat dripped from his face onto her cold flesh. He stared into her blind eyes, the pupils dilated to take in forever.

Kent looked up at the monitor.

In the embarrassed silence of the ER he saw what the rest of the interns and nurses in attendance had seen from the start.

The girl was dead.

Kent straightened and handed the paddles to one of the paramedics. He wiped his dripping face on the sleeve of his scrubs.

"All right," he said hoarsely, trying to control the emotion in his voice. Trying to sound *professional*. "That's it. We gave it our best shot. Send her downstairs."

Kent felt their eyes on him; noticed the way they averted their gaze when he looked at them, like cockroaches scurrying in the light. He wondered what they suspected. That he was crazy, or on drugs, or some kind of pervert. They would never guess the simple, mundane truth.

He cared too goddamn much.

And he hated death.

Unlike most doctors, Kent had no neat psychological cubbyhole in which to fit death. He didn't see it as the natural end of all life. That was the kind of crap you told the patient's family when all else failed. Nor was he able to depersonalize death like any of his more scientific-minded colleagues, who simply regarded the end of a human life as some kind of mechanical failure, a breakdown in the system of normal biological function the layman calls a life.

No. Dr. Henry Kent flat out hated death.

He hated the messy, inconvenient way it came. He hated the blood, the pain, the stench, the terror, and the sorrow. He hated the bureaucracy that came afterward and all the loose ends that needed tying. Most of all, he hated the lies, the hypocrisy, the priests, and the greatest myth of all: It's all for the best.

Whenever he saw a diseased heart, its vessels clogged with yellow fat, or held in his hands a smoker's lung, charred and shriveled like a burned football, or removed with his scalpel a cancerous ovary dwarfed by the deadly tumor to which it had given birth, he felt a nameless rage that choked him with frustration.

Many were the times he stood over some luckless soul wheeled into the emergency room at three in the morning and, feeling the life ebb away between his trained hands, cursed the limitations of medical science.

Maybe it was because he was still relatively young. Maybe it was because he had never had anyone close to him die. Whatever the reason, Kent had no use for the mindless platitudes and the empty promises of the hereafter. To him, death was the enemy, plain and simple: it was a terrorist who struck you when you least expected, mining the body with cancer, heart disease, aneurisms. It set up ambushes, accidents, muggings.

It killed without conscience; it killed indiscriminately. Men. Women. Children. Young and old alike. It struck without warning—and without mercy.

And there was no making peace with it. Ever.

And while others hoped to live long enough to arrange the terms of their surrender through philosophy or religion, Kent planned to wage his one-man war with every ounce of his strength right up to the bitter end, until the black commando itself came to him one dark night, slipped behind the cot where he often slept after a thirty-six-hour shift, and garroted him, too, with eternity.

Maybe that was why he'd chosen emergency room medicine. He wanted to be on the front lines of the war. Because that was what it was. War. The eternal war between life and death.

Kent made his way down the hall, passed the usual hustle-bustle of nurses, patients, and cops. Some guy in a denim vest and no shirt was arguing drunkenly with a nurse at the admitting desk. Next to him stood a skinny woman holding her bleeding arm in a sheet of newspaper. The nurse shrugged, "No insurance card, no admittance." She repeated this equation over and over with the unyielding patience of a pocket calculator. Nearby a cop stood against the wall, sipping coffee and watching indifferently.

Kent walked numbly past. He'd been up for nearly twenty-four hours straight and he was exhausted. He made his way back to the doctor's lounge, yanked open his locker, and then decided he was too tired even to strip off his sweaty, bloody scrubs. He grabbed a Coke from the refrigerator in the corner, thumbed open the top, and let the carbonated caffeine pour down his throat.

He dropped down on one of the cots along the wall and closed his eyes, waiting for the sugar rush to revive him.

He could still feel the numbness in his arms from the electric paddles.

Death had beaten him. Again.

Behind his closed eyelids, he saw the lifeless body, the bloated purple face.

And the terror returned. Suffocating him. Engulfing him.

As if he were drowning.

He struggled against it, battling his way through the darkness, trying to make it to the surface, but it was no use. In a matter of minutes, he was asleep.

He slept fitfully. His dreams were filled with the anguished cries and writhing limbs of every patient he'd been unable to save. Each of their voices, joined in one howling tempest of agony, damned him for having failed.

In a few hours, he would get another chance.

10

THERE WAS SOMETHING SPOOKY about the pool at night. It seemed like the shrine to some forgotten ancient goddess— all concrete and quiet—the blue chlorinated water illuminated from below and yet forever concealing some cold, heartless mystery in its inscrutable depths. Laura never came to the pool room after hours without feeling a strange sense of unease, her very footsteps sounding somehow too conspicuous in the awesome silence.

She had missed practice again that afternoon. Instead she had purposely gone to the library clear across campus to bone up for an American history final she knew she had already aced. Anything to stay away from the pool.

For four years now she hadn't missed a single practice. In every kind of weather, regardless of any crisis she might have had at the time, she always made it to the pool. It had become a kind of ritual for her. And now that she was trying to make a point of staying away, she realized that it had also become something of an addiction.

When she had returned to her apartment that afternoon, Laura had found no less than six messages on her machine from Carin, each one more frantic than the one before. Carin had just been pledged into Lambda Psi and she wanted someone to celebrate with. For the sixth time Laura listened to Carin beg her to call her back. She was just about to pick up the receiver to call when the next message played.

Though he had never spoken to her on the phone before, Laura recognized the voice immediately.

It was Coach Morgan.

"So the Great Man has decided to call me Himself," Laura snorted when the message ended. She pressed the replay pad and had to listen through all of Carin's messages again to hear it once more.

Apparently he too was worried when Laura hadn't shown up to practice—worried that she was *serious* about quitting the swim team. With the northeastern collegiate championships less than a month away, he must be pulling his hair out. If she didn't win, it would all but kill her chances of making it to the Olympic trials. Not to mention his hopes of coaching an Olympic athlete.

Selfish bastard, Laura thought.

She tossed her towel angrily onto one of the benches, slipped off her flip-flops, and padded over the grainy concrete to the edge of the pool. She stared past her pale feet and into the clear blue maze of water. Down there it was always so quiet, so peaceful, so cool. Even in the middle of competition, it was like being in your own private world.

No matter what her problems were, Laura always felt as if she had left them at the side of the pool with her clothes once she dived into the water.

It was strange when she thought about it: how she had been so afraid to dive as a kid. It was instinctual: the fear of throwing yourself forward. Even now, if she thought about it enough, she could psych herself out. There were always accidents around the pool and there were enough stories around about how some kid or other had broken his or her neck and wound up paralyzed after a dive.

Of course, if you weren't horsing around and paid attention to what you were doing, the dangers were minimal: certainly less than the risks one took every day driving a car, for example.

It was a matter of trust, really. Trust in your own body and the benevolence of the water.

But still there was always the chance that something could go wrong. A slight miscalculation in the angle of the dive . . . It was a chance that always factored into the equation whenever you took a leap of faith.

Laura breathed deeply a couple of times, letting the chlorinated air fill her lungs. The chlorine made her feel slightly light-headed and made her ears ring; still it wasn't a completely unpleasant sensation.

Without another thought, she bent over, tensed her legs, and dived full-length into the pool.

Everyone had his or her own method, but Laura liked to visualize herself as a knife—a switchblade, to be exact—springing open from its protective sheath. She was the naked blade flashing through the air and slicing into the water with a seamless zip.

It seemed like an eternity—though in truth it took only a couple of seconds—before she entered the water, but it was those few seconds that made all the practice and aching muscles worthwhile. For during those moments, Laura thought she might have glimpsed something akin to the freedom of flight.

There was no feeling quite like it in the world.

Her lungs filled with the air of her last held breath, Laura buoyed quickly to the surface, her arms pulling the water behind her in broad, clean strokes. She swam easily, without rushing, not against the clock or the competition, but simply for the pure sensual joy of the whisper of the cool water along the sleek length of her well-conditioned body.

She swam several laps, crossing and recrossing the pool until she began to feel the frustrations of the last several days seeping from her body. It felt good to just be swimming. Not trying to beat the other girls or trying to please Coach Morgan. For the first time in months she remembered something of why she had ever liked to swim in the first place.

When the first glow of fatigue finally settled into the sockets of her arms, Laura slowed down and let herself hang in the pool, treading the water lazily with her arms, just enough to keep her head above the surface, the water lapping gently against her chin.

She was just hanging there, the depth of the water holding her up, when she first heard the noise.

It sounded like someone wrenching on pipes.

"Hello?" she called. The acoustical combination of water and concrete made her voice sound unnaturally clear and resonant.

"Hello?" she said again, louder this time.

There was no answer. Just the omnipresent dripping sound one always heard in indoor pools.

Laura suddenly felt cold, the warmth draining from her muscles, bleeding away into the blue water.

She hadn't seen anybody in the building on the way in. And the maintenance crew would have been out of here hours ago. As far as she knew, Coach Morgan hadn't given a key to anyone else but her. Now she desperately tried to remember if she had locked the outside door when she came in.

She stayed like that, frozen in indecision, like a giant jellyfish, floating in the middle of the pool, until she heard the unmistakable sound of rubber kissing concrete.

Someone was coming!

Laura shook herself from her trance. She ducked her head into the water, kicked, and swam as hard as she could for the side of the pool. All the while, her imagination ran wild. She could almost feel the black-gloved hand hovering over her shoulder, ready to push her head under and hold it there. Spurred on by fear, she made it quickly to the side of the pool.

She felt her heart thudding wildly in her chest as she reached for the concrete edge and hauled herself up from the water. Even as she did so she heard the heavy door to the pool room open behind her.

Laura spun around, her flesh goose-pimpling with fear and cold.

Standing in the doorway on the other side of the pool was Terry Myers.

11

STONE HIT THE LIGHTS.

A dozen cockroaches froze in the white glare of the naked bulb overhead. They stood on the linoleum counter, sleek and brown and wet looking, waving their long delicate feelers in the air as if they were drunk on the light. Something about the way they didn't scatter struck him the wrong way: bugs should at least have the decency to run when they're found out.

Without even thinking, Stone pulled off his left shoe, raised it in the air, and in one seamless motion made almost fluid by long repetition, slammed the heel down on the counter.

The roaches took off like sprinters on a track, disappearing into the nooks and crannies of the kitchen linoleum in the blink of an eye.

Slowly, Stone lifted his shoe and saw the ruins of the roach he just smashed. Two eyelash-thin legs trembled in the air from the middle of a liquid brown smear.

He was about to reach for a paper towel when he remembered something he'd read somewhere about how roaches were repelled by the pheromones released by one of their own crushed dead. He doubted whether it were true or not, but Stone left the dead roach there all the same.

Somehow it made him feel better.

It had been that kind of day. He had wandered around the grounds of the cemetery for hours, aimlessly following the paths between the neatly spaced rows of stones and plaques, trying to lose himself in the country of the dead. Eventually, though, he had come back to the empty black pit where his own grief began and ended: the freshly turned grave of Neal Stone, Sr.

Unable to go home just yet, he had taken in a movie downtown, one of the "Friday the 13th" sequels; he couldn't recall which number. He just wanted to be somewhere cold and black and empty. He left the theater just after dark and drove to a go-go bar in the next town. One of the bad things about being a cop was that there was virtually no place you could go in your own backyard—no matter how seedy, especially if it was seedy—where you wouldn't be spotted by someone you knew.

Stone sat on a stool at the end of the bar soaking up beer and watching the tired, bored-looking girls shaking their long rubbery tits and bruised thighs to the music. He left just before closing. A whore in a peek-a-boo T-shirt and short-shorts who'd spotted him as a cop offered him a freebie. She was a cute kid. Maybe all of fifteen. With the makeup.

Stone considered it for a moment, felt the floor moving under his feet, and declined. He was so whacked not even his dick knew up from down.

He pulled open the door of his old refrigerator and scanned the barren shelves for something to eat.

Tough luck.

Aside from some crusty jars of unidentifiable condiments there was nothing in the refrigerator but a half-killed twelve-pack and a loosely wrapped package of deli meat. He didn't even bother pulling open the vegetable bin at the bottom. The last time he did he'd discovered a leaking head of lettuce black as a pygmy's head and a pair of cucumbers that had grown a thin layer of electric blue fur.

God only knew what they had grown into by now.

The vegetables had been a legacy from Marcie. Back in the days when he ate things like vegetables and thought of himself as a real person.

Marcie.

Just her name brought back her image before his mind's eye.

Tall. Blue eyed. Long legged. Norwegian blond hair that hung to the crack of her ass. And a smile that could have sold secondhand tampons to the Pope.

She had left him for her drama teacher at NYU. A pallid, blond effete without a hair on his chest and so good looking Stone himself might have raised a hard-on for him if given half a chance. He'd fucked him over pretty well as it was, barging into his apartment one night when he and Marcie were going at it and jamming his .45 down the bastard's throat right in front of her until they could all smell the load filling his bikini shorts.

Stone might even have killed him if the faggot had shown so much as an ounce of courage. Ironically it was the man's cowardice that had saved his life. Stone had left the two of them there—Marcie and her big baby lover—on the bed, shocked, trembling, and weeping. The next day he was called into the chief's office and put on paid suspension pending psychological examination.

Marcie had filed a report. But Stone didn't care. He had purged himself in one savage moment of feelings of anger and betrayal that would have taken years to "talk" out. It felt good. So damn good it sometimes scared him.

Later he learned that Marcie and her professor boyfriend had broken up shortly after the incident. Stone had so humiliated the man in front of her that she could no longer live with him. Of course, she didn't come back, but that didn't matter. He could let go now.

Stone was suddenly aware of the frigid air from the refrigerator rolling in a light steam over his arms. He grabbed the beer and the package of deli meat and kicked the door closed with his knee.

In the drawer he found a reasonably fresh loaf of bread and proceeded to make himself a bologna sandwich.

The salty smell of the bologna made his salivary glands tingle. He didn't realize how hungry he was. He hadn't eaten in nearly thirty-six hours.

Stone searched carefully through the loaf until he found two slices of bread relatively unstained by mold. He unwrapped the wax paper from around the bologna and peeled a couple of freckled slices off the sodden pink lump of meat. As he laid the bologna on the bread he idly wondered if the horror stories they told about hot dogs were also true about bologna. He didn't care. He was hungry. Not even rodent droppings, chicken claws, rat's tails, fur, pig intestines, and human piss could spoil his appetite.

Suddenly he remembered the mayonnaise.

Shit.

He was so damn hungry he was tempted to eat the sandwich without it, but the best part of a bologna sandwich was eating it with mayonnaise. In his shit-faced condition, the question assumed philosophic importance. What to do?

Eventually willpower won out over the grumbling in his stomach. The answer was simple.

Stone carefully peeled off an extra slice of bologna from the package, folded it neatly in two, and popped it into his mouth. Thus he was able to take the edge off his hunger.

As he chewed, he retrieved the mayonnaise from the refrigerator.

He struggled with the crusted top for a few moments but finally twisted it open. With a dirty butter knife, he smoothed a large greasy dollop of the yellowing mayonnaise over the inside of the bread.

Grabbing what was left of the twelve-pack, he carried the sandwich into the living room.

He clicked on the TV and found the Knicks game, taped earlier, on one of the more obscure cable channels. The Knicks were playing the Bulls, and Air Jordan and the boys were soundly trouncing them. Stone watched the Knicks' gangly back-up center and forward, a seven-footer with the unlikely name of Kiki Vandeweghe, loping up and down the court, flailing his arms awkwardly like some kind of endangered species of flightless bird.

In fact he *was* an endangered species: a white guy in the NBA.

Stone took a big bite out of the sandwich. He was glad he'd waited to put the mayonnaise on; it had been worth it, after all. It tasted so much better that way. Patience, Stone concluded, is a luxury even the hungry could afford.

He thumbed open one of the beers and sucked down half the can before coming up for air. On the screen, Jordan had just breezed passed Vandeweghe as if the big guy were a windmill.

Until recently, Stone never understood why people became drunks. Like most straight folks, he just assumed they liked that fuzzy, sloppy, insulated feeling more than was good for them. Only lately had he come to understand alcohol as a kind of medicine that could make you feel almost normal again.

He finished the rest of the can, belched, and opened a second. By the fourth he was staring glassy-eyed at the television. In the middle of the sixth, he passed out.

12

Terry moved with the malign grace of a panther.

She was dressed in motorcycle leathers and heavy, rubber-soled boots. A chain ran from her belt loop to the wallet in the back pocket of her oil-stained black jeans. Another, shorter chain held the ring of keys that slapped against her thigh. Her short, spiky hair, greasy with pomade, was slicked back on her head. She was probably on her way out to cruise the dyke bars downtown when she decided to make a short detour to the pool.

From the look in her eyes Laura could tell that she was already on something.

"Well, well, well," she said, and smiled tightly, pulling heavily on the last of a roach she pinched between resin-stained fingers. "What have we here? I thought you quit the team?"

"I did."

"So what are you doing here? Can't stay away from Coach Morgan's joystick?"

Laura tried to keep her voice firm. "What do you want, Terry?"

The big girl snorted, flicking the last of the joint into the pool, where the cool blue water extinguished it with a small sizzle. She jabbed her finger at Laura.

"I want you, bitch," she hissed.

"You can cut the butch crap," Laura said with more assurance than she felt. "It may impress your friends downtown, but it doesn't do anything for me."

She was sure that Terry could see through the lie. Laura was painfully aware of the difference in their size, her discomfort increased by the contrast in their clothing. Dressed only in a soaking-wet one-piece Sporto bathing suit, Laura saw the other girl openly appraising her body, trying to intimidate her with her aggressive sexuality.

Terry stepped forward, the keys jangling at her waist.

"You're shivering," she sneered.

"It's cold in here," Laura snapped.

"Bullshit."

Their eyes locked for what seemed like minutes until Laura finally forced herself to turn away, trying to pretend it wasn't a contest of wills, that she only wanted to grab her towel.

Terry's hand was on her upper arm in a flash, clutching, yanking her back, leaving red finger welts on the white, goose-pimpled flesh.

"Don't turn your back on me, cunt," she growled. Her finger-less black gloves were working themselves into fists.

"What do you want?" Laura said, her composure rapidly deteriorating. She was genuinely frightened now. For the first time it sank in just how alone they were. Terry had a wild look in her eyes, no doubt the effect of whatever she'd been drinking in addition to the pot she smoked. She looked like she was capable of anything.

"I told you already, bitch," she said, poking her finger painfully into Laura's left breast. "I want you!"

"Leave me alone," Laura said, hating the pleading tone that had suddenly crept into her voice. "Why are you bothering me?"

"You know damn well why. I had a talk with Dean Mealy Worm this afternoon. You convinced Coach Morgan to have me thrown off the team, didn't you?"

Laura was looking toward the heavy steel door of the pool room, estimating her chances of getting past Terry and making it outside before the bigger girl had a chance to react.

"Answer me!" Terry bellowed. "You ratted me out, didn't you?"

"I don't know what you're talking about," Laura said softly, hoping it would calm the larger girl. She took a step to the side. Terry blocked her path.

"The hell you didn't. I'm suspended. Two months. Off the swim team. Out of school. Everything. You think you're hot shit, think you've got rid of me. But it ain't that simple, babe. Nobody fucks with me. Nobody. From now on your pretty ass is mine, and I'm here to collect the first installment."

Terry's arm shot forward, the heel of her hand catching Laura high in the center of her chest, knocking her a step backward.

"Hey!" Laura protested. "Don't you dare touch—"

Terry was on her before Laura could get the next word out of her mouth. She drove her shoulder into Laura's midsection, knocking her backward, and sending her sliding across the floor. Laura felt the abrasive concrete tearing away the flesh at the backs of her thighs. Looking down, she saw that her bathing suit had ripped open on one side, exposing her left breast.

Terry stood over her, hands on her hips, eyes fixed on the naked breast. "Get up, bitch," she growled.

Instinctively, Laura's hand went up to cover herself, holding the torn flap of material over her breast. She climbed slowly to her feet, adrenaline pumping through her veins, momentarily erasing the pain of her torn flesh.

"I'm warning you," she said, between clenched teeth, "keep away from me!"

Terry lunged forward and Laura threw a wild punch, which caught Terry on the side of the face. It was a lucky punch, thrown more in defense than anything else, a simple reflex to ward off her charging attacker, but it somehow found its mark and momentarily stunned the bigger girl.

Terry staggered back a couple of steps, a look of dumb surprise on her broad, flat features. She probed her teeth with her tongue and gingerly touched her face. When she took her fingers away from her lip, they were smeared with bright red blood.

"You cunt," she screamed. "You'll die for that!"

She lunged forward again and this time there was no holding her back. She grabbed Laura around the waist, her momentum driving them to the edge of the pool, where the two women grappled for position, staggering in each other's arms like a pair of drunks. Laura could feel the steroid-pumped muscles squirming under Terry's clothes as if she were wrestling a leather equipment bag full of heavy snakes.

Laura tried to push Terry away, while the other girl concentrated on punishing Laura's body with a series of short, hard jabs to the ribs that had Laura gasping for air. She could smell the nauseatingly greasy pomade on Terry's head, which was right beneath her chin.

Terry was larger and stronger and had anger on her side. The fight would have been short and brutal except for the fact that Terry's reactions had been slowed by the alcohol and pot, and that helped equal the odds. By now the pain in Laura's ribs was excruciating, but she knew she had to hold on. If she could knock Terry off balance long enough to work free of her arms she could still make a break for the door.

Even now she could feel the larger girl was tiring, her blows carried less force, her breath was coming in short, labored gasps. Terry sensed it too and, infuriated, began stomping down hard on the floor, trying to catch one of Laura's defenseless bare feet under her heavy boots. For her part, Laura kept her feet moving, the two of them locked in a bizarre-looking dance at the side of the pool.

Laura could sense that the time had come to make her move. Terry had stopped throwing punches and was all but hanging on her now, exhausted, her hand covering Laura's face, fingers reaching for her eyes. Laura dropped her hands to Terry's leather-clad shoulders and pushed—

—just as Terry sunk her teeth into Laura's exposed left breast.

A white blindfold of pain covered Laura's eyes. She lost her grip on her opponent. For a split second, she just stood there, shocked, her hands rising reflexively to protect her injured breast.

It was all the time Terry needed.

With a savage cry of victory, she struck Laura hard across the throat with her forearm.

To Laura's stunned senses, everything seemed to be happening in slow motion. She felt herself being driven backward, felt her left foot waving at the empty air, her weight slowly shifting behind her, until, finally, even with the furious motion of her flailing arms, she could not keep herself balanced, and she fell helplessly backward into the pool.

Sometime just before she hit the water, her brain registered an ugly, dull thud. As she drifted slowly to the bottom of the pool, Laura idly wondered exactly how long one could go without air.

LAURA WATCHED THE LIGHT above her grow smaller and smaller.

She was falling backward, her legs over her head, staring up past her feet, through the quiet underside of the pool's undisturbed surface.

She felt nothing, neither panic nor pain, as she sank to the bottom. It was as if the diminishing light above her were everything she once was, or longed to be, as if the battered, semiconscious woman drowning in the water were not her at all.

If anything, Laura felt a profound sense of contentment.

She flicked her eyes to the side and saw the dark stain of blood that came from her bruised head. It hung in the water like a scarlet pennant, rippling gently in the ambient current.

A moment later, she lay on her side at the bottom of the pool. The concrete under her naked flesh was smooth as glass; unspoiled by human feet, it was as deserted as the surface of the moon. Her hair rose gracefully from her head like sea grass.

Laura had been closer to the truth than she had imagined when she thought of the pool as a shrine to some forgotten goddess. Lying unconsciously at the bottom of the pool, she had the unmistakable sense that she was in a holy place, an inner sanctum of mystery seldom visited by mortals—a place from which, quite naturally, there was no return.

Still she didn't panic. Here there was no such thing as panic. Or fear.

There was only wonder.

And gratitude.

With great humility, Laura slowly pulled her knees to her chest. It was the closest gesture she could make to kneeling.

Above her, through ten feet of blue water, she saw the bright light of Laura Kane, growing ever smaller, narrowed to a burning pinpoint.

Paradoxically, Laura's pupils slowly dilated.

Sightlessly, she stared up at the now unreachable light, as distant as a star.

She sighed.

But not with sorrow or regret. Rather she sighed with pity for the long-suffering body, lying pale and alone a few feet away. She sighed for the struggles it had endured in the name of life. She sighed for every living, suffering creature on the face of the earth.

And then a sound like rushing wind filled her ears. And the light was suddenly racing toward her. And from out of the shallow end of the pool a coffin-shaped shadow approached; propelled by hunger, it moved smoothly and purposefully through the calm water like a shark.

And then even the pity was gone, leaving only joy, the pure unalterable joy of release.

As Laura Kane's last breath bubbled merrily to the surface.

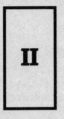

II

BLUE
MAZE

Just glide along the concrete bottom
  of the pool
as far as you can go.
Just glide along the bottom
and then come up—
holding your life between your teeth
like a knife.
> —Michael Alessandro, "Drowning"

Fear death by water.
> —T.S. Eliot

13

DR. KENT WOKE UP shouting, hoping to scare death back a step.

When he opened his bloodshot eyes, he saw it wasn't the Grim Reaper come to claim him after all. It was only one of the ER nurses, the cute one with the red hair, who'd come to wake him up. Still his heart was galloping, as if he'd just been running the Boston marathon. He reached up and held his chest, as if to keep the convulsing organ in place.

"Jeeze, Doctor," the nurse said, alarmed. "Are you all right?"

"Yeah," Kent said, propping himself up on one elbow and rubbing his temples. "I'm fine. What is it?"

"A drowning. In the university swimming pool. No one knows how long she's been under. They got her breathing but . . ." The nurse shrugged. "They'll be here in about five minutes."

Kent swung his legs off the cot. He saw the nurse—he seemed to remember her name was Lansing—wrinkle her pretty nose at the sour body odor that rose from his wrinkled clothes. How long had it been since he'd last had a shower? He really should have taken one after his last shift.

"Sorry," he muttered.

"We'll get Room Three ready, Doctor," Nurse Lansing said. "I'll tell them you're on your way."

She turned and walked briskly out of the room, her butt twitching beneath the tight, starched uniform.

Kent ran his hands briskly through his thinning hair and stared down at his feet. Christ, he hadn't even bothered to take his shoes off when he'd lain down.

He grabbed the open Coke on the nightstand beside the cot. He swallowed what was left in the can. The soda was flat and warm, but he hoped the caffeine might give him a rush.

He drew a deep breath, feeling about as awake as he was going to get. He placed both hands beside him on the cold metal edge of the cot.

He felt like a fighter, slumped in his corner, before the last round.

He was beat all to shit.

Tired. Cut.

Losing on points.

Needing a last-round knockout.

On the other side of the ring, his opponent was grinning, dancing, cutting the air with punches crisp as an abdominal incision.

His opponent all bone and gristle. Lean and mean.

Black-and-silver trunks.

Grinning skull.

Death-His-Own-Self.

Fucking Heavyweight Champion of the World.

"All right," Kent said, to no one in particular, "Let's do it."

As HE STRODE DOWN the green-walled corridor toward the emergency room, Kent ran through the standard ER procedure for drowning victims in his mind.

It was like the visualization techniques that trained athletes used before competition.

Kent wanted to know exactly what he was going to do before he did it. He didn't want to find himself uttering the five words fatal in any ER.

What do I do now?

In the distance, he could hear the faint whine of the ambulance racing toward the hospital.

Most likely, it was the ambulance carrying his floater.

He pictured the whole procedure from the moment they wheeled the unconscious patient into the ER until he'd revived her and sent her to intensive care.

The nurse had said that no one knew how long she'd been under. That meant that even if he got her stabilized, she might still wind up with all the faculties of a boiled eggplant.

Shit.

Kent entered the ER and saw the nurses and med techs waiting for him. He glanced around quickly, checking to see that everything was in order. He was just about to ask Nurse Lansing a question when the emergency room's doors slammed open and three paramedics rolled the stretcher into the room like a bobsled.

As Kent peeled the thin rubber gloves up his arms he stared down at the unconscious woman on the stretcher.

She was wearing a one-piece yellow-and-green bathing suit torn on one side. The ripped flap had been carefully replaced over her left breast. Her hair was still confined inside a rubber bathing cap.

She couldn't be any more than twenty or twenty-five. It was always hard to tell. Trauma tended to age a person.

The paramedics lifted her somewhat roughly onto the table. Her body had all the consistency of a dead mackerel.

"Someone get that suit off her," Kent yelled.

A nurse stepped forward with a pair of long-nosed scissors and expertly cut the fabric away from the girl's damp blue skin. In less than ten seconds, she was lying naked as the day she was born.

And the day she died.

If Kent didn't hurry.

He turned to one of the paramedics who'd brought her in. The paramedic was standing out of the way, back by the sink, but you could tell by his body language that he wasn't leaving until he saw the outcome. Paramedics were usually like that. Possessive.

"Did you get an airway?"

"Yes," the paramedic said.

"How long?"

"About three minutes."

"Shit. Who found her?"

"I did."

A man stepped forward from the doorway. Tall. Blond. Wearing red university gym shorts. He was soaking wet.

"How was she lying when you found her?"

"At the bottom of the pool. On her side."

"Curled up, like a foetus?"

"Yes."

Kent yanked the bathing cap off her head. Skeins of gold hair spilled out. He turned her face to the side. In the back he found what he had expected, the hair was matted with blood.

"Probable concussion," he said.

If this girl comes out of this without brain damage, he thought, it'll be a miracle.

"All right," he shouted, "everybody that doesn't belong here, get out!" He turned back to the paramedic. "Help me get this room cleared, will you?"

"Sure thing, Doc." The paramedic seemed relieved to be given something to do.

"Do we have a reading?" Kent snapped at the nurse working the blood pressure cuff.

"Seventy over forty, Doctor," she said, a note of concern in her voice.

Kent pressed the stethoscope under her blue left tit. The heartbeat sounded like a record skipping.

Suddenly the record stopped.

Kent felt his own heart stop.

"Dammit," he shouted. "She stopped on me."

A second later Kent heard the flat monotone from the monitor behind him.

Death's theme song.

He dropped the stethoscope around his neck.

Placing the heel of his right hand under her sternum, he pushed upward, waited a beat, and pushed again.

He leaned forward, covering her blue lips with his own, and breathed shallowly into her lungs.

He repeated the process again. And again.

"Nurse!" He motioned with his head.

Nurse Lansing removed the stethoscope from around his neck and put it around her own. She placed the silver dot beneath the girl's tit. In the center of her chest. Over her right tit.

She shook her head. "Nothing."

Kent pushed, breathed, and came up for air.

"Pressure?" he gasped breathlessly.

"No pressure," the nurse pumping the cuff said tonelessly. "We're losing her, Doctor."

Kent cranked his head back, caught the eye of a first-year intern. "Get the syringe ready, one cc."

The intern just stared at him, cow eyed.

"Get the shit out of your pants, Doctor. Move it!"

The intern broke from his trance and turned to unlock the cabinet containing the syringe and the adrenaline derivative. If Kent couldn't restart her heart, he would use the needle to pierce her chest cavity and inject the Adrenaline right into the heart muscle.

Hell, if he couldn't get it started, he would rip the fucking heart out of her chest and massage it back to life.

He was not going to lose another patient. Not today. No fucking way!

He could feel it, opening above him, like the unforgiving light hanging over the examination table.

A hole, white and bald.

God's eye.

Merciless. Blind and omniscient at the same time. Because it saw through everything. Or, rather, pulled everything into itself.

Devoured it.

And he felt all the energy in the room being slowly drawn through that hole. Like the drain in a sink.

It swallowed all the hope from those gathered around the table, trying to save the life of this anonymous girl.

Leaving them in darkness, cold, and despair.

Leaving them with a corpse.

"Goddammit," he shouted, his arms sore from exertion. "I won't let you have her!"

His heart slammed in his chest; the hair stood up at the back of his neck. And Kent knew he was here: the Opponent, the Adversary, Death. He was here in the emergency room fighting over the body of this unconscious girl.

"Give me the paddles," Kent yelled.

Someone handed them to him and he placed them on the girl's chest. "Stand clear!" he shouted.

The girl's body flopped.

Kent looked up at the nurse with the stethoscope. She laid it down on the girl's chest. Shook her head.

If it doesn't work the first time it usually doesn't work at all.

"Stand clear!" he shouted again.

Once again the girl flopped clumsily on the table. Kent handed the paddles back to the tech and once again started CPR. Suddenly, he saw it: a faint fluttering of the eyelids.

The blue lips parted and the girl drew a breath.

Another. And then another.

Almost immediately, her color began to grow normal.

"Doctor, I've got a pulse," Nurse Lansing said, as if she'd just caught a fish on her line. "I've got a pulse."

There was an awkward silence. Something strange had just occurred. It was as if everyone were trying to absorb in their own way the miracle they had just been witness to. Then the room burst into spontaneous applause.

Dr. Kent didn't acknowledge the appreciation of his colleagues. Instead he stared up at the ceiling of the ER.

Not in prayer.

Not in relief.

"Beat you that time, you bastard," he muttered under his breath.

But he knew it wasn't exactly true.

For the hole that had opened to accept the soul of the young woman on the examination table hadn't closed. If he had the eyes to see such visions, he would have seen the bloody volcanic wound it had left on the ceiling.

As it was, Kent felt it hanging over his head like a halo.

Or an open manhole cover.

Breathing the fetid breath of raw sewage.

14

RANDY CLEGHORN SAT on the examination table and touched the bump on his head with the tissue the nurse had given him.

Wincing at the pain, he stared at the red stain on the tissue.

Shit.

His eyesight was a little fuzzy and a couple of times he'd felt like puking. Before, when the nurse was taking his name, it sounded as if she were alternately whispering through a mouthful of cotton and shouting through a bullhorn. He squinted at the chart across the room and the skeleton depicted there seemed to be floating in a light red fog.

He wondered if he had a fucking concussion. He'd had a concussion once. Two years ago during the game with State. He'd taken a forearm on the back of the helmet from some All-American nigger defensive end after the whistle. It was a cheap shot, and to add insult to injury the fucking referee had penalized Randy for holding!

He had wrapped his pickup truck around a telephone pole on a deserted stretch of Route 79. The damn thing was totaled. He hated to think what his father was going to say. The old man was just going to shit a royal gold brick.

Luckily, Randy had the presence of mind to get out of the truck, hobble the half mile down the road to the nearest gas station, and use the telephone booth to call one of his buddies on the football team. About twenty minutes later, Eddie's black Trans Am pulled up. Inside, Eddie looked pissed off. He had just been working the meat inside good old Betsy Roland when Randy had called. Randy apologized but, after all, what are teammates for?

Eddie had insisted on driving Randy to the hospital. "You're *bleeding*, man," he'd said when Randy protested that he didn't need to go to the hospital, he just wanted to go home. Randy argued some more, once even trying to wrestle Eddie for the steering wheel, until Eddie thumped him a good one to the temple with his elbow. Randy stuck to his debating skills after that and, at one point, actually seemed to have Eddie almost convinced, when he suddenly broke out into a recitation of the "Brady Bunch" theme song. Hearing that, Eddie made straight for the ER.

"If I'm charged DWI again," Randy slurped through a mouthful of blood, "Coach says he can't do nothing to keep my license."

Eddie told him that the police couldn't charge him with drinking and driving if they didn't actually catch him in the car.

Sitting on the crinkly paper of the examining table, Randy Cleghorn sure hoped his friend knew the law better than he knew how to cross-block.

God almighty, it was cold in here.

It felt as if he were sitting directly underneath a fucking air-conditioning vent.

He looked up at the ceiling, risking another bout of dizziness, to see where the cold air was coming from.

There was no vent in the ceiling.

He hugged his arms around his body for warmth.

Outside the door to his room he could hear the nurse talking to someone in the hall.

He strained his ears to hear what they were saying.

"Can I help you, sir?"

"Yeah," he heard a man's voice say. "I'm Detective Neal Stone."

Randy felt as if someone had just yanked his stomach out of

his asshole. His head cleared instantaneously. His eyes darted around the room, like small gray mice, instinctively looking for a way out.

Aside from the door, there was nothing but three impenetrable walls of painted cinder block.

"Oh, you must be looking for the Kane girl," the nurse said.

"Yeah," the gruff voice came back. "The drowning victim."

"We moved her out of here. She's in ICU," the nurse said, sounding all cheerful. "I'll take you there."

He heard their footsteps retreating down the hall and breathed a long sigh of relief.

If they gave him the Breathalyzer, he was finished. He had so much Bud sloshing around in his body all they had to do was stick a spigot in his navel and he could pass for a keg.

Even if he did beat the DWI charge, he was finished playing football for the season. It didn't take a fucking Marcus Welby to see that.

Randy stared down at the raw, misshapen lump of mashed meat that used to be his right knee. The pain was coming right through the alcoholic haze, stabbing his brain like shards of broken glass.

He wished the nurse would come back, the pretty one with the red hair. He wouldn't mind making a grab for her tight ass while she stuck him with a needle full of some kind of mindless, spaced-out bliss.

He'd been shot with plenty of those kind of needles by the team trainer before big games in order to play through minor, nagging injuries. He liked the long, loose, floating feeling they gave him. He always played better after one of those shots.

Randy looked up.

Someone was standing outside the door to his room.

Rather, someone was standing *inside* the door to his room.

Randy shook his head, trying to clear his vision. He hadn't seen anyone actually *open* the door.

It was as if he were seeing a movie in which every fifth frame had been cut out.

Jeezus, he thought, wonderingly, maybe I really am hurt.

For the first time he was afraid.

Thinking it was the red-haired nurse come back to check on him, Randy swallowed his fear and did his best to grin wolfishly. Then he realized that it wasn't the red-haired nurse, after all.

Too tall.

Black clothing.

No doctor, either.

The detective, Randy thought. The grin froze on his face.

"Hey, dude," he said, trying to sound casual. "What can I do for you?"

Whoever it was said nothing. Came no closer.

Just stood there. And stared.

Randy squinted through the cerebral fog clouding his vision. The figure stood, straight and still as a pin, in a whirlpool of smoke.

The grin withered on Randy's face. If this was a game, Randy didn't like it. If this guy was a cop, why didn't he just come right out and arrest him?

Randy slid off the examination table. A fresh wave of dizziness staggered him and he reached back to steady himself.

"Hey, dude . . ." he said, his tone sharpening. "I ain't in no mood for games."

He took a faltering step forward and was jolted back.

All the way across the room.

His head slammed against the wall, his already bruised skull splintering into a technicolor spiderweb. Around his neck, a hand—or something—gripped him like a steel collar. His feet kicked uselessly in the air.

He had been propelled backward with such force the breath had been sucked from his lungs. Now he gasped for air, unable to shout for help, choking on blood and broken teeth.

Randy forced his eyes open. The figure hadn't moved. It still stood across the room, just inside the door.

"Who . . ."

The answer was two excruciating bolts of pain that pierced his shoulders, shutting out all rational thought. It was as if he'd been screwed there, pinned by his shoulders to the wall behind him. Then, with maddening precision, he felt the pain burn two separate paths around the outside curve of his chest, converging at a point just below his sternum.

Gasping, Randy hung there, a giant bloody V burned into his flesh.

He wept.

Because he knew.

Instinctively he knew what was coming next.

A split second later the burning pain traveled straight down, unzipping the front of his body. It stopped at the top of his pubic bone, turning the V to a Y, and letting his soft, warm, stinking entrails spill onto the tiled floor as if Randy Cleghorn had never been anything more than a soggy garbage bag ready to bust at the seams.

15

STONE SAT BESIDE the hospital bed looking down at the unconscious girl.

Her head was swathed in a gauze bandage. Beneath the bandage, her face was nearly as white as the gauze. She resembled nothing so much as an alabaster statue. Perfect. Still. Lifeless. She was wired to a heart monitor on the ceiling above the bed and there was an IV drip going into one of her arms. But otherwise, she looked all right.

Especially for someone who'd just been dead.

It was strange. Less than a week ago he'd been keeping watch by his father's bedside, waiting for the old man to let go. Now he was here again; only this time he was waiting for someone to come back.

Her name was Laura Kane.

The call had woken Stone up out of a drunken sleep. He'd been having a bizarre, feverish dream in which the secret of the Catholic Trinity could be explained through the analogy of the bologna sandwich. In the dream, the Holy Ghost was the bread, God was the bologna, and Jesus was the mayonnaise. It had all made such perfect sense. Stone had been struck by the simple beauty of the explanation. He was sure that he'd been vouchsafed a revelation on a par with that of Moses.

God was a bologna sandwich.

Then the phone rang and Stone woke up to reality. He found

himself slumped sideways on the couch, covered in sweat and crumbs. The television sizzled with blue-gray static.

Reality was this: He had a hangover. He was alone in the world. God was *not* a bologna sandwich.

He had fumbled for the phone. Grabbed it on the seventh ring.

A girl had been pulled out of the pool at the university. There was reason to suspect she'd been attacked. Did he want to question her?

As Stone saw it, he really didn't have a choice.

It was his job.

So he'd splashed some cold water on his face, rubbed some toothpaste across his teeth, and combed his unruly black hair into place with his fingers. On his way to ICU he'd caught a glimpse of himself in a mirror and felt his stomach tighten until he realized that the disreputable man slouching toward him with his hands in his pockets was him.

He hoped he was only being hard on himself and that he looked somewhat presentable. Although, judging from some of the looks on the faces of the nurses, he kind of doubted it.

He gingerly patted his still-queasy stomach.

He shouldn't have had that damned mayonnaise, after all. It had probably been bad, just as he'd suspected.

Stone looked at the other man in the room. He was about six foot three. Blond. Ruggedly handsome. Well built. He was wearing a red university polo shirt and a pair of white corduroy shorts. He had introduced himself to Stone as Seth Morgan. He was the swimming coach at Groverton State.

Stone watched him carefully. In spite of the fact there were two chairs, Coach Morgan insisted on standing, pacing back and forth across the room, until Stone was sure he'd logged a good three miles. He was chewing nervously on the thumb of his right hand, which he held in front of his face like a meerschaum pipe.

One way or another, instinct told Stone that the guy had more at stake here than just the life of his star athlete.

Just then the girl stirred, her eyelids fluttering.

"Where . . . am I?"

Morgan nearly pulled a tendon breaking from his mechanical stride; Stone leaned forward, his forearms on the metal railing of the bed.

"You're at the Groverton Medical Center," Stone said calmly.

"Hospital?" the girl said. Her eyes darted nervously to the IV stand beside her bed, following the clear plastic tube to the yellowed gauze bandage on the inside of her elbow.

"You are going to be all right," Stone continued, conscious of the presence of the coach hulking over his shoulder. "You had an accident at the university swimming pool. My name is Detective Neal Stone."

"Laura, are you okay?" the coach interrupted, his voice cracked with strain and worry.

The girl gazed over Stone's shoulder, focusing her eyes and seeing Morgan for the first time.

"Coach Morgan?" she asked, hestitantly, as if unable to trust her eyes. "What are you doing here?"

"He saved your life," Stone abruptly answered. "He was the one who pulled you out of the pool."

Stone knew that if he wanted to find out what had happened to the girl he had to get to her fast. The first minutes after regaining consciousness were often the most lucid. He had to get her to tell him as much as she remembered before the doctors and administrators confused her memory with medical tests and insurance forms. If he waited until they were through with her, it could take months of psychoanalysis for her to piece together what had happened.

A nurse appeared at the door that very moment. Stone glared at the coach, who was holding the pencil-shaped buzzer in his hand.

"Nurse," the coach said, "she's awake. You told us to buzz you."

"I'll get the doctor," the nurse said. "In the meantime, you'll have to leave."

"If it's all the same with you, nurse," Stone said, "I have a couple of questions I want to ask the patient first."

"Please, Detective Stone," the nurse said, more officiously. "You have to leave until after the doctor has taken a look at her."

"Nurse," Stone said sternly, "you're upsetting her. Please go get the doctor. I'll look after her until you get back."

The nurse shot him a look as sharp as a hypodermic. She was fighting a losing battle. Her first duty lay in getting the doctor, not in arguing hospital policy with a detective. She turned sharply from the doorway, her rubber-soled shoes shrieking on the polished floor, and stalked down the hall to the nurses' station.

"Now listen to me carefully, Laura," he said. "I want you to tell me who attacked you. Who pushed you into the pool?"

"Terry?" the girl said, again in that odd, questioning tone.

Stone looked up at Morgan.

"Terry Myers," the coach explained. "A real troublemaker. She and Laura are rivals on the swim team. At least that's the way the Myers girl sees it."

Stone had removed a small pad from his inside coat pocket. He scrawled the name with a dried-up Bic.

"Detective, just what in the hell do you think you're doing in here?"

Stone looked up to see a man standing in the doorway. He was dressed in a white lab coat and pale green scrubs. Stone took one look at the stethoscope around his neck and made a mental note never to get himself shot at three in the morning. If this guy was a doctor in this hospital, Stone did not want to be a patient.

He looked as though he hadn't slept in days. His hair was standing up on end and his eyes had the wild, paranoid look that Stone often saw in the eyes of methamphetamine addicts. When he passed, Stone caught the unpleasant scent of boiled cabbage in his clothes.

Jeezus, Stone thought with a certain amount of awe, this guy looks even worse than me.

"I'm here to ask her some questions with regard to a possible assault," Stone said.

The doctor didn't seem to be listening. Instead, he stood, hunched over his patient, looking into her eyes with a small penlight. He clicked the light off, put it in his pocket, and picked up her right wrist, feeling her pulse.

"How are you feeling?"

"All right, I guess," the girl replied. "A little disoriented."

"That's to be expected," the doctor said. "Can you tell me your name?"

"Laura," the girl said. "Laura Kane."

"What about your birthday?"

"October 1, 1970."

"Very good," the doctor said.

Stone figured the doctor had gotten the information from the girl's coach.

"And do you know what year this is?"

"Nineteen ninety-two."

The girl seemed to be getting tired of the game. Or annoyed. Or both.

"Just stay with me a little while longer," the doctor said, and smiled. ''Can you tell me who the president of the United States is?"

"George Bush."

The doctor said nothing, but continued to count the pulse in her wrist.

"Well, do I pass?"

The doctor grinned, laying her arm back down on the bed. "With flying colors."

"When can I go home, Dr. Kent?"

The doctor froze.

He had forgotten to remove his name tag from his lab coat last week and it had gotten lost in the hospital laundry. The lab coat he was wearing did not have his name on it. The detective, trained to pick up on such inconsistencies in the interrogation of his suspects, picked up on the same. Only the coach seemed not to have noticed that anything was amiss.

And, of course, the girl herself.

"What's the matter, Doctor?" the girl asked nervously, shifting her eyes to the unpleasant-looking detective, who was looking at her with hawklike intensity, and then back again.

"How did you know my name?" the doctor asked slowly.

"I . . . uh . . . I don't know," the girl said, obviously confused. "I guess I recognized you by your bald spot."

Stone's antennae went up. The doctor hadn't turned his back on the girl since entering the room. He was sure of it. Only Stone himself had a clear view of the back of the doctor's head.

Blushing, Dr. Kent leaned forward to have a better look at his strange patient.

As he did so, his hand unconsciously patted the circle of pale skin at the back of his head.

16

PAM CONNOR LEANED over the tub and cranked off the hot water.

She straightened and turned to the bathroom mirror, which had already partially steamed over, and carefully pinned up her heavy auburn hair. She shucked off her white terry-cloth robe, hung it on a peg behind the bathroom door, and walked back to the tub full of warm, scented bubbles.

She reached down and scooped the water with her hand.

It was just a little too hot for comfort.

Which meant it was just right.

Pam stepped gingerly into the tub and eased slowly into the steaming water, feeling her nerves jump and tingle with excitement.

There was nothing quite like a hot tub to ease out the tensions of a tough day. And the past week had been murder.

It had been horrible coming home to find Lisa dead like that.

Without warning. Without any explanation.

How could Lisa do that to her? They were supposed to be friends. At the very least, they were roommates. You would think that entitled her to a little consideration.

If she lived to be a hundred, Pam would never forget that afternoon. It had been like walking into a music video nightmare. The sound of Grimm's Scary Tales thundering through the apartment. The sight of Lisa's naked, discolored body hanging from the plant hook in the living room. Her blackened, twisted features. And worst of all, her blind, soft-boiled eyes bulging accusingly at Pam the moment she came in the door.

And what had the paramedic said?

If Pam had come home only five minutes earlier, it might have been time enough to cut her down and save her life.

Damn him, too!

How was she supposed to know that was the day Lisa had decided to kill herself? How was she supposed to know that she should have headed straight home instead of stopping to talk to Keith Myers, who just happened to decide to ask her out on that particular afternoon? How could she know that those precious few minutes would mean the difference between life and death?

There was no question about it. Pam couldn't live here anymore. Lisa's cousin Alvaro had already come and cleaned out her room, but the place seemed haunted by her memory. Pam would have to move as soon as she could find a new place. In the meantime, just being in the apartment gave her the creeps. Sometimes at night she thought she could still hear Lisa moving around in her bedroom, or talking on the phone, or playing a radio.

And it was always that same damned song.

"Deliver Us from Life."

The walls themselves seemed to echo that goddamn song.

Pam slid down deeper into the tub, propping her soapy feet on either side of the faucet.

Thank god for Dr. Schoner. The new tranquilizers he had prescribed certainly helped her to relax. She was lucky to have found a doctor willing to give her the pills. Even if he did insist on giving her a full physical exam every time he wrote out a prescription. How many times a year *did* a twenty-two-year-old-woman require a breast exam, anyway?

Well, if he wanted a little extra feel in return for the pills, Pam was willing to oblige. Tit for Valium. It was a fair exchange as far as she was concerned.

She could feel the pills working already. Her body seemed to be melting into the warm water. All the tension of the last several days simply draining away. She felt warm and sleepy and sexy.

Pam closed her eyes and laid her hand over her breast, wreathing it with iridescent soap bubbles. Meanwhile, her other hand slid along the inside curve of her soft belly, down between her spread legs to the sex opened like a clam in a tidal basin.

Images shuttled behind her closed lids, the faces blending into each other, a subconscious composite of her sexual Everyman: Keith Myers, sleazy Dr. Schoner, her father (briefly), Lisa's cousin Alvaro, and then Lisa herself.

Jeez, Pam thought, that's sick!

Lisa's dead, for Chrissakes.

She had never even thought of making it with Lisa when she was alive. But now that she was dead . . .

Pam was repulsed that she could even think of such a thing. But at the same time she realized that another, stronger part of her didn't care one way or another. It didn't make any difference to her body that Lisa was dead.

Between her fingers, her nipple was still hard as a small pink stone. Between her legs, the blood had begun beating like a red tom-tom.

She had no choice but to dance.

Pam squeezed her eyes shut as the orgasm came, rippling through her like the wind through a flag.

When it passed, she sunk deeper into the now-cooling bath, the foamy water ebbing against her chin.

She lay like that for what seemed like a small eternity, weightless in the water, letting it rock her gently back and forth, like some kind of exotic aquatic plant.

She listened to the persistent drip of the faucet.

Letting it take her further and further away.

Drip. Drop. Drip.

And something *else*.

Pam's eyelids fluttered open.

What she saw was wrong. Very wrong.

Even though the bathwater had cooled, the steam in the room seemed to have grown thicker; it was so thick in fact that Pam couldn't even see the bathroom door. It was more like fog, damp and heavy, covering everything with a thin sheen of nervous perspiration.

Pam shivered in the ice-cold bathwater. Suddenly she felt naked, exposed. She hugged herself, her flesh goose-pimpling.

Her eyes were drawn to the light over the sink.

The naked bulb no more than a pale smudge in the fog.

And beneath it, the bathroom mirror.

A circle wiped away in the fog.

And reflected in the glass.

A face . . .

Pam opened her mouth to scream as the black arms telescoped from inside the mirror, hands like shackles locking around her bare ankles, as an inhuman strength yanked her body neatly under the water.

She gulped a last breath instead, the scream trapped in her lungs, aching to burst out. She knew she couldn't hold it in for long.

And then she panicked.

Her naked heels thumped uselessly against the tiles. Her wet hands groped for the side of the tub, her desperate fingers unable to get a grip on the smooth porcelain.

But the worst part was the pain riveting her shoulders to the bottom of the tub.

Holding her down.

Making it impossible for her to move.

At first all she could think of was that she was being raped. That someone had broken into her apartment and attacked her.

But it was worse than that.

Far worse.

She stared up horrified from under the water.

And saw the face, floating, like a shadow on the water.

And then the lines of pain were burning her flesh, searing her, unstitching her soft, defenseless body all the way down to the navel.

Her last breath, held until that penultimate moment of glorious release, exploded from her shrieking lungs.

Boiling the bloody water.

17

THERE WAS SOMETHING not quite right about 3C.

Jakob Weisz could sense it as he passed by the green door. He couldn't say exactly what it was, but it was there, a sense that something was out of place, like when someone has moved a chair out of a room, or rearranged the pictures on a wall.

It wasn't just the fact that she always paid him her rent on the third of the month—never a day early, never a day late—and this was already the sixth. Nor was it the fact that she usually stopped by his apartment once or twice a week for a cup of coffee and maybe a piece of babka and he hadn't seen her yet this week.

If it were only that he could have easily explained away his growing sense of unease. No, it was something more than just the interruption of a pleasant routine.

It was a feeling he got every time he passed her door. Like someone had left a refrigerator door open, only there wasn't any change in temperature.

The same feeling he'd had the afternoon the Rivera girl had hanged herself behind that same green door.

What a horrible business that was!

Jakob was not a superstitious man. He didn't believe in ghosts or golems, spooks or spirits. He didn't believe in crystals or channeling or psychic healing. He was a simple, down-to-earth, sixty-five-year-old Jewish landlord with a potbelly and a too-fond taste for herring. He owned this three-story brown-stone not far from the university and rented out nine rooms at a going rate, which provided him with just enough of an income to live out his life in relative security. He was plumber, extermi-nator, painter, psychotherapist, uncle, mother, and father to his young tenants, whom he had come to think of as his own family since he had no family of his own.

The work was good for him; it kept him young, as did his re-lationship with his youthful tenants, most of whom were stu-dents at the university. The demands of the old building were a source of constant activity, and even then his efforts were just enough to keep the old place from falling down. Still, he didn't mind. On the contrary, he had learned long ago that, if he were lucky, a man's work, like his life, was never really finished, but remained in a state of flux, always giving him something to wake up for the next day.

Even God, he decided long ago, did not create the universe perfect in six days. If he had, he would have rendered himself obsolete. No, God, if he existed at all, was the Landlord of the Universe. He'd be at it every day, tinkering with an ecosystem here, patching up a hole in the ozone there, repainting an ocean somewhere else. How else could he prevent himself from going mad with boredom throughout eternity?

Not that Jakob thought a lot about God anyway. He was not a particularly religious man. He went to temple fairly regularly, kept the Sabbath after his own fashion, sent money to Israel, and observed the high holy days, but he was not a great believer in God. Most Jews he knew weren't. Not like the *goyim* any-way, with their rosters of saints and martyrs and always going on about their personal relationship with Jesus, as if the son of God were a celebrity who moved in down the block that every-one was falling all over themselves to get to know.

Jakob knew that most Jews didn't think of God much at all. And if they did, he was only a vaguely defined entity, like the CEO of a large corporation whose name you read occasionally on interoffice memos or at the bottom of your weekly pay-check, but whom no one had ever actually seen walking the halls or frequenting the men's rooms, as if his lack of corporeal existence were a carefully guarded corporate secret.

Instead, Jews paid attention to what the prophets said, tried to take care of their families, stood up against social injustices according to their conscience, and tried to overcome as best they could their own personal resentment at the social injustices that society heaped upon them.

They were a practical people by sheer necessity and theirs was a practical religion; for when their prophets had seen God he had not come as a kindly old man in a white robe and beard full of proverbs and riddles, but in such terrifyingly irrational forms as wheels within wheels, burning bushes, plagues of locusts, leveling typhoons . . .

And Holocaust.

For Jews of his generation, there was simply no way that God would have a face and form—and not be a monster.

Better to think of him as some form of alien intelligence, superior but fallible, operating (hopefully) for the general good, even if 6 million sparrows fell along the way.

Such ideas were blasphemy—and a cold, heartless form of blasphemy at that—but that was the cost the Almighty would have to pay for allowing such evil to exist in the world. To Jakob's way of reckoning, it was small recompense for allowing the Germans to offer up his entire family in Hitler's cursed furnaces.

And that was partly why, perhaps, Jakob Weisz felt such trepidation every time he walked past 3C. He knew from firsthand experience what kind of horror existed in the world.

He had been up and down the hall at least twenty times in the past two days on one errand or another. Each time he had been tempted to knock on the door and prove to himself once and for all that he was just being a silly old man. Yet each time, at the last minute, he'd turned away, arguing that he had more pressing business elsewhere, or that he didn't want to interrupt the girl's privacy, or worse, have her think he was only pestering her for the overdue rent money.

Pam was a good girl. Maybe a little wild. A little too pretty for her own good. Too many boys, too much booze, too much of that loud heavy metal music. But she had a good heart . . .

Maybe she was running a little short this month and was embarrassed to see him until she had the money.

Or maybe the death of her roommate had forced such practical thoughts as rent payments from her mind.

He didn't believe it for a second.

Not in his gut.

Not where it mattered.

Not when every time he passed her door the short white hairs in the ring surrounding his bald pate seemed to stand up on end.

Jakob stood in front of the door and loudly cleared his throat.

He suddenly realized that he'd been standing there for at least five minutes. If anyone had been watching, they might have thought he was eavesdropping at the door. The idea that anyone should think he'd been spying on the girl made him blush and spurred him into action.

Without thinking, he reached out his hand and rapped on the door.

He waited on tenterhooks for what seemed like an eternity—almost afraid that the girl might answer and even more afraid that she wouldn't—and then he knocked again.

As he stood there, he noticed that the green paint had blistered and was peeling away from the door. He needed to scrape the thing down and repaint it as soon as possible. He had to stop himself from turning away right that minute and heading down to the small storeroom in the basement where he kept his tools.

Reluctantly, he took the heavy ring of keys off the belt loop on his work pants and found the key to 3C.

He could sense the presence behind the peeling green door. There was no sense denying it now. It was like the buildup of pressure, sucking the atmosphere out of the hall and leaving a vacuum, drawing everything into itself.

Jakob placed his hand flat against the peeling green paint and almost expected to feel the wood beneath his palm vibrating. He worked the key into the lock with trembling fingers.

He knew without any doubt that when he opened the door nothing would ever be the same again.

He also knew he had no choice. If he turned away again, the evil would only grow stronger: it would only be that much more difficult to face when the time came.

And it would come.

If sixty-five years of life on earth had taught him nothing else, it had taught him that.

Evil would have its day.

And so, armed with the unique strain of optimistic fatalism that was characteristic of his faith, he turned the key, opened the door, and saw—

Nothing.

It would have been easier if the apartment had been trashed. If the furniture had been slashed, the stuffing scattered on the floor. If the walls had been smeared with blood. If the body had been left lying right there on the living-room floor.

Instead the apartment appeared to be in perfect order. The usual disarray of normal everyday living. But nothing out of the ordinary.

He looked over to the corner where the Rivera girl had been found hanging. Someone, probably Pam herself, had put the fern back on the hook.

Nothing out of the ordinary.

That's what was so horrible.

This ordinary room with its silver-on-white wallpaper, its comfortable secondhand furniture, its knickknacks and personal effects was all just a stage, as fake as any movie set, for the true horror that existed in the world. The ordinary was a disguise under which lurked the evil we tried so hard not to see. And yet, from time to time, it would erupt, like a bloody stigmata, making it impossible for us to ignore the fact that what lay beneath life were pain, suffering, sorrow, and death.

Jakob's feet seemed to know which way to go.

Past the kitchenette.

Down the short carpeted hall toward the back of the apartment.

He didn't look in either bedroom. His eyes never wavered right or left, but remained leveled straight ahead, fixed on the door to the bathroom that stood at the end of the hall.

He felt the sweat break out across his forehead, felt his heart squeezing inside his chest, and almost hoped it would choke the life out of him before he could see what lay behind the door.

In the gloom of the hall, he could see the light shining around the doorframe. It looked almost spiritual.

Slowly he reached out, placing his hand on the knob, and immediately yanked it away, leaving flesh on metal so cold it burned.

He pulled the handkerchief from his back pocket, wrapped it around his hand, and grabbed the knob again.

This time he turned the knob until he could hear the flimsy lock mechanism crush inside his meaty fist. He was praying as he entered the bathroom; praying as he saw the blood sprayed across the tile; the shattered mirror on the medicine cabinet; the pale, torn body staring up from the bottom of the water.

His mind flashed back to the nightmarish scene inside another shower, forty years ago. Of bodies, bloated and discolored. Of the cries of the blind and dying. Of a man with a tear-streaked face and a bloodstained club.

"Death Angel," he muttered.

18

NEAL STONE REACHED the second-floor landing and stopped to catch his breath.

He rubbed his sour stomach and felt the roll of fat at his waist. Jeez, he thought, I really got to start getting some exercise.

He looked up at the next flight of stairs and shook his head. It never failed. If there were three floors or thirty-three, the corpse was always at the top of the building. No one ever got croaked on the ground floor.

He puffed his way up the final flight of stairs, and made his way down the short dark hall.

There was a uniform standing guard outside the door to 3C.

"Where is she?" Stone asked.

"In the bathroom, sir," the young cop said.

As he stepped inside, Stone took a quick mental inventory of the apartment. It was sparsely furnished; most of the pieces looked as if they'd been bought at a secondhand shop or were hand-me-downs from parents or relatives. Fashion magazines covered the tables. *Vogue. Mademoiselle. Elle.* Beer cans overflowed the trash can in the kitchenette. A typical first apartment.

Except he could already smell the blood.

Thick, cloying. Like a fresh coat of paint.

He remembered the room at the ER. The blood splashed all

104

over the concrete walls, as if someone had hosed the room down with it. At first they couldn't find the body. And then they saw it. Stuffed inside the impossibly small space of the drug cabinet. Like a sack of used, bloody rags. Face pressed against the glass.

Eyes bulging. Mouth gaping.

According to the intake sheet, the kid had come in with a possible busted knee. They sent him to the morgue ripped open from chin to crotch like a fucking mackerel.

What the hell had happened in the meantime?

No one had a clue.

Stone himself had been in the hospital, only a floor away in ICU, checking in on the Kane girl, when he heard the code over the intercom. He had questioned everyone on duty in the ER from the doctors to the janitors and no one had seen or heard a thing.

It didn't make any sense.

He looked up at the heavy-duty plant hook screwed into the living-room ceiling. An elaborate macramé plant holder hung from the hook. Inside it rested a heavy ceramic pot overflowing with a luxuriant growth of shiny green leaves.

Only a week ago the naked body of a young woman hung from that same hook.

Suicide. Cut and dried. That's what the medical examiner had said.

Now Stone wasn't so sure.

He had been around too long to believe in coincidences. There was some connection between the girl's apparent suicide and her roommate's murder. There had to be.

But what?

Stone saw the fingerprint expert from the county's crime lab dusting the windows that led out to the fire escape.

"Got anything?" Stone asked.

The fingerprint man shrugged. "Couple of partials. Can't tell till I get the victim's prints if they're significant or not."

Stone felt like telling him not to bother. That he wouldn't find anything significant on the windows. That the killer hadn't come in from off the fire escape. Or the front door. Or up through the goddamn dish drain.

What he didn't know is how he knew that.

And that scared him.

Because the only other options were too wild to consider.

The bathroom was at the end of a short hall behind the kitchenette. On his way, he passed a small bedroom on the right. He glanced in it briefly. There was another uniform coming up the narrow hall. Stone squeezed to the side to let him by. The beefy cop didn't look at Stone as he passed. His face was white as a handkerchief, his mouth set in a tight grim line.

Stone knew the expression well. It was the look of someone determined not to lose his breakfast.

Just outside the bathroom, Stone saw Al Harris leaning in the doorway, his head shaved as smooth as a milk dud, his left ear sporting a shiny gold earring. The huge black detective waved when he saw Stone and stepped forward.

"Sorry to call you on your day off, Neal," he said, not exactly sincerely. "But I thought you'd want to see this."

"Real thoughtful of you, Al," Stone said, and jerked his thumb over his shoulder at the retreating officer. "I got a feeling maybe I don't."

Harris nodded. "It's bad."

"I can tell," Stone said. "You look positively white."

"You don't look so hot yourself," he said, peering through the gloom of the hall at Stone's face. "What the hell happened to you?"

"Bad bologna sandwich a couple of nights ago," Stone said. "I've been riding the porcelain pony ever since."

"Yeah, well, I'll be sure to let you know what shade of green you're sporting when you're done looking at this," Harris said dryly. "I just hope you haven't had lunch yet."

If Harris said it was bad, it was bad. The guy had done three tours of duty in Vietnam as Special Forces. He had seen just about every kind of violence possible to be inflicted on the human body. The stories he told when he had a few glasses of scotch in him were enough to straighten out pubic hair.

"Are the ghouls here?" Stone asked, referring to the little gray guys from the coroner's office.

Harris shook his head. "No. But you better hurry if you want to beat them to her. They're on the way."

Stone nodded. "Well then, let's have at her."

Harris stepped inside, stretched his arm out, and bowed with mock humility.

"After you," he said.

The first thing Stone noticed was that the bathroom was bright.

Too bright.

Clinical.

The bare bulb over the sink reflecting off the white tiles was enough to make Stone squint.

The second thing he noticed were the two naked legs angling up from the tub.

The rest of the scene was blocked by the large, squat form of Pug O'Malley. The big Irish detective looked like a gorilla in a tweed coat. He was kneeling by the side of the tub as if it were an altar.

As if he were staring into the face of God himself.

"What have we got here, Pug?" Stone asked softly, as if afraid to break the communion.

Pug raised his head and a comma of oily black hair fell across his forehead. His broad, broken face looked like a catcher's mitt that had caught one too many fastballs.

"Aye, Neal." He nodded and whispered just as softly, "Have a look for yourself."

He scuttled to the side.

Up until now, Stone had kept his eyes discreetly away from what lay in the tub. Now he deliberately looked down, knowing as he did so that what he was about to see would burn itself on his brain like a brand, become part of his nightmares, and haunt him for the rest of his life.

The tub was full of blood.

Or rather, water mixed with blood.

A thin scum lay on the surface and around the edges of the

tub, where some of the water had evaporated over the last couple of days, leaving a residue of undissolved minerals and waste products from the body.

Under the water, the girl lay staring up at the ceiling with her eyes and mouth wide open.

But the worst part was the way she'd been cut down the center. Laid open. Her flesh peeled back on either side, the blanched flaps of skin turned inside out, waving almost imperceptibly in the ambient current of the water. Her inner organs, released from the confines of the body cavity, had filled with the gas of decomposition and bobbed at the surface of the bloody water like pale blue balloons.

"Ain't no man meant to see something like this," Pug said, almost reverently.

"No," Stone whispered, hardly able to speak. His esophagus felt like a snake trying to swallow a mouse.

"She's got the coroner's initial," Pug said, referring to the large Y etched down the front of the body. It was the same cut routinely used by coroners during an autopsy. "Same as the Cleghorn kid."

"I know."

"Think we got a serial killer?"

Stone shook his head.

Pug saw the reflection in the bloody water.

"I think it's something worse," Stone said. "A lot worse."

19

LET X EQUAL Y.

Laura stared at the algebraic formula as if she were looking at a coded message from Jupiter. It might just as well have been for all the sense it made to her. She had never quite grown out of that old sophomoric complaint that letters were for spelling and numbers were for adding and never the twain should meet.

She rubbed away her last guess with her diminishing pencil eraser and brushed away the pink crumbs. She took a gulp of black coffee and stared at the problem from over the lip of her mug as if it were a hostile dog she might somehow give the slip by trickery.

It was no use.

She just couldn't keep her attention focused.

Her mind kept going back over the events of the past three weeks.

Ever since the night of the accident.

Accident?

Terry had apparently cleared out of her apartment that night, left school, and hadn't been seen or heard from since. Which suited Laura just fine. She just wanted to forget the whole thing and get on with her life. Attempted murder or not, she would be glad if she never saw Terry again as long as she lived. Or, for that matter, the detective working the case. What was his name?

Neal Stone.

Truth was, the detective gave her the creeps.

He had interviewed her several times already, asking the same questions over and over, as if he were looking for some kind of inconsistency in her story, or waiting for her to make a self-incriminating mistake. But the worst part was his eyes—eyes that seemed to regard her as just another suspect.

Eyes the color of spiders.

Eyes that trusted no one.

Seth—Coach Morgan—told her not to let it bother her. The detective was just doing his job. Trying to jar her memory. Hoping she might remember some crucial detail.

Coach Morgan had been great through it all. Maybe too great.

Laura wondered if he had taken her resignation seriously or if he just considered it the tantrum of a prima donna athlete. He hadn't raised the subject of her returning to the pool, even though he had visited her several times in the hospital. Still, it was hard for Laura to believe that he had given up his Olympic aspirations for her that easily.

As for Laura, she had begun to wonder herself if it would really be as easy as she thought to give up a dream that she had lived with most of her life. A dream that had its genesis in the family swimming pool in Buffalo when she was barely three and her father first taught her how to do the doggy paddle.

To be sure, Dr. Kent assured her that there was absolutely no reason she couldn't begin training again. After running a complete battery of tests, both psychological and physical, and keeping her under observation for close to a week, he had released her with a complete bill of health. To his credit, he tried not to make her feel like a freak.

"People are revived after clinical death more often than you think," he'd said. "It's no more a miracle than the birth of a baby."

Both Dr. Kent and Coach Morgan did their best to keep what had happened to her quiet. Ordinarily, her story would have been big news in Groverton. Lucky for her, there had been a lot going on in town over the past three weeks.

Lucky?

She thought of the series of brutal murders that had begun the night of her fight with Terry. The first victim, poor old Cleghorn, had been killed in the very examination room Laura had been moved from only moments before. Then there was Pam Connor upstairs. Butchered. Only three weeks before, her roommate had hanged herself in the very same apartment, also, coincidentally, on the day of Laura's fight with Terry.

At first, Laura thought Detective Stone suspected Terry of the murders.

Now she wasn't so sure.

It was hard to tell what the detective was thinking.

Laura herself doubted that Terry had killed those people, not the way they'd been slaughtered.

Laura shuddered.

And found herself unconsciously tracing a large Y down the front of her T-shirt.

What did they call it? *The coroner's initial.*

Dammit.

Anyway, the nightmare was all behind her now.

Wasn't it?

There were still those strange dreams. . . .

Laura took another sip from her cup, the coffee already cold, and put it down. She had to keep her mind on the algebra. If she didn't make at least a B in the course, she knew her scholarship could be revoked.

"There, that should do it," Mr. Weisz said, pulling on the fire-escape window.

The landlord had come by earlier that morning to install the new locks he'd bought for all the windows in the building. Mr. Weisz had taken the murder of Pam Connor hard, as if he had somehow been partly to blame. Now he seemed to be taking personal responsibility for the safety of the rest of his tenants.

Laura had been aware that the old man and the murdered girl were friends, of sorts. It was an unlikely relationship made possible by the only thing they shared in common: a need for family. Mr. Weisz was a kind of second father to Pam, who, for all her wildness, had a native vulnerability that begged protection, and Pam fulfilled his fatherly instincts. The landlord seemed to have no family, no friends, no life outside this building. Laura felt a pang of sympathy for the lonely old man. No wonder he had taken her death so hard.

"Just make sure this crossbar is always down across the bottom of the window frame," he said, showing her how the special lock worked, "and no one can open the window from the outside. Unless, of course, they break out the whole pane."

"Thanks," Laura said. "I appreciate it. This is awfully nice of you."

Mr. Weisz shrugged. "It is something like closing the barn door after the horse has been stolen, I know," he said. "But why take the chance of losing any more horses, eh?"

He smiled, but he looked tired and sad. Laura could hear the pain in his voice. "I wouldn't blame you if you wanted to move out of the apartment. I couldn't possibly hold you to the lease, under the circumstances."

Actually, Laura considered it at first. A couple of the other tenants, freaked out by what had happened in 3C, had already taken Mr. Weisz up on his offer, including a couple of underclass girls whose parents arrived in a panic the minute they heard the news. In the end, Laura decided that she just didn't need the additional stress that moving would have involved. Besides, she doubted that she would have been safer anywhere else. In fact, her building was probably the safest in Groverton. After all, lightning rarely struck twice in the same place.

"I have no intention of being chased from my home, Mr. Weisz. Besides, I feel safe here."

"Thank you," the old man said.

"Would you like a cup of coffee?" Laura asked.

"Oh, don't go through the trouble. You're busy with your schoolwork."

"It's no trouble," Laura said. "I need a break anyway. I'm not making much headway with this stuff."

She got up from the table and walked back to the Mr. Coffee

on the sink to freshen her cup, pulling a second mug from the dish drainer.

When she got back to the table with the two steaming mugs, Mr. Weisz had already seated himself at the table. He had picked up her pencil and was jotting down a calculation in the workbook.

"Your answer is sixty-six," he said, tapping the equation. "You forgot to square the fraction and, here, you have to square the root to the fourth place, which gives you point six two seven nine."

"Wow. That's something. And without a calculator to boot. I've been working that problem all morning. Are you some kind of math genius, or what?"

Mr. Weisz laughed as he stirred extra cream and sugar into his coffee. "No, nothing like that. You just might say I have a passion for numbers."

"A passion for numbers?" Laura said incredulously. "How can anyone have a passion for something as bloodless as math?"

Mr. Weisz blew on his coffee and took a noisy sip.

"Mathematics is not bloodless," he explained. "It is poetry without words, the highest manifestation of beauty."

"Poetry?"

"The ancient Pythagoreans believed that the highest reality could only be expressed numerically. It is a very old belief. In Hebrew, for instance, every letter has an assigned number, and thus every word has a specific numerical value."

Mr. Weisz paused to stir more sugar into his mug. It was the sixth teaspoon he had put in already. Laura began to worry that the old man might go into sugar shock. As he stirred his coffee, he went on.

"It was thought that words having the same numerical values had an inner relationship to one another. For instance, the words *God*, *love*, and *unity* have the same numerical value, therefore the ancients deduced that each of these concepts must be identical. God equals love, equals unity. Get it?"

Laura nodded.

"Likewise, if it were discovered that the words *broccoli* and *God* had the same numerical value, that would be considered proof that a hidden, heretofore undiscovered relationship existed between God and broccoli."

They both laughed.

"It's called Gematria; the practice of finding the hidden numerical correspondence between apparently unlike things. It's practiced by cabalistic scholars."

"That's fascinating," Laura said.

Mr. Weisz shrugged. "One of the mixed blessings of an orthodox upbringing." He took another noisy sip from his mug. He was dressed in a pair of baggy overalls and a flannel work shirt softened and faded by wear, the sleeves rolled up to the elbow, exposing his thickly muscled forearms. In the hairy, tanned flesh, Laura saw what she had never noticed before: the tiny row of faded blue numbers.

Laura looked away hurriedly, feeling the way she did when she encountered someone on the street with one leg or one arm, as if she had to make a point not to look to prove it made no difference.

She looked up into Mr. Weisz's sad old eyes and saw the look of recognition there.

"I'm ... I'm sorry," Laura said, and felt the blush coloring her face.

"It was a long time ago," he said, the pain in his face belying his words. "I do not think of it much anymore. What is done is done."

"Mr. Weisz," Laura said, "you mustn't blame yourself for what happened to Pam."

Jakob Weisz shook his head; suddenly he looked ancient, like one of the old patriarchs of the Bible; Job, perhaps, lamenting the enlightenment that had come too late. "If only I had updated the window locks earlier," he said. "Pam might be alive."

"No, Mr. Weisz. You mustn't think like that. It's not your fault. Even if you had put the locks on earlier, you said yourself that they aren't foolproof; whoever did it would have just figured out another way to get in. Or it could have been someone that Pam knew. The police didn't find any sign of forced entry. In that case, there's nothing you could have done. You have to stop blaming yourself, Mr. Weisz. These things happen. Terrible things. And no one's to blame."

Jakob Weisz raised blue eyes crisp with tears, forcing a slow, resigned smile across his features.

"Yes, yes, of course you're right," he said. "I am an old fool. Who should know such lessons better than I?" He patted her arm. "Sometimes, though, it takes a child to remind you. Thank you."

He finished his coffee and rose stiffly from his chair. "Arthritis acting up a little," he said. "Thank you for the coffee. I had better get back to work. I have three more apartments on this floor to do."

The old man shuffled to the window and collected his tools. As he headed for the door, Laura called out to him. He looked up again with those sad, smiling eyes that reminded her something of the bemused, incalculably wise and suffering eyes of Einstein.

"If you ever want to talk, Mr. Weisz," she began, and stopped, suddenly feeling insufferably presumptuous. Like offering someone a Band-Aid to staunch a severed artery. Still, it was too late to turn back. "Just come on down," she finished quickly, hoping he didn't think her *too much* of a young ass.

"Thank you, dear. Just one thing," he said, the blue eyes sparkling, but no longer with tears.

"Anything."

"Call me Jakob," the old man said and winked.

Laura smiled. "Jakob."

He pointed over his shoulder to the workbook spread on the kitchen table. "And if the algebra ever again gives you a problem, you just give old Jakob a holler."

"It's a deal," Laura said. She followed the old man to the door and closed and locked it behind him. Then she returned to the kitchen table and her algebra.

The next problem stood between her and the end of the lesson with the impenetrability of a brick wall.

She read the first equation in the series.

Let $y=x$.

20

AT FIRST LAURA THOUGHT she was in the hospital again. The long featureless corridors. The painted cinder block. The linoleum cold under her bare feet.

Overhead a sterile blue light emanated from a hidden source.

She assumed she had woken up in the middle of the night, left her room while she was still half-asleep, and had somehow made it past the nurses' station unobserved. Now she wanted nothing more than to return to her room before she was found wandering around the halls. But where was her room?

She looked for a door number, a sign, anything she might use to orient herself. To navigate her way back. But there was nothing—neither door nor sign—to break up the monotony of the featureless blue walls.

Perhaps she had wandered into an area of the hospital that was seldom used. Or perhaps a restricted area where ordinary patients weren't allowed to go unescorted. An area where they kept generators or the X-ray machines.

She listened closely to the silence, trying to detect the telltale hum of the machinery.

The end of the hall came up all at once, without warning. A plain concrete wall, painted the same undistinguished blue.

Laura considered turning back the way she had come. But when she turned around, the hall stretched back as far as she could see, disappearing into nothingness.

How far had she already walked?

She stared down the endless hallway. She would never be able to retrace her steps.

She turned back to the featureless wall. On closer inspection, she saw a sign about three-quarters of the way up the blue concrete.

The sign had an arrow pointing both ways. There were no words beneath the arrow.

She looked right and then left.

The hall on both sides seemed to stretch on forever. There didn't seem to be any difference no matter what direction she took.

On a whim she decided to go to the left.

She walked forward down an identical hallway. The same concrete walls. The same tiled linoleum floors. No signs on the walls. No doors. She had walked about a hundred yards before wondering if she should have turned right instead. But when she turned around she could no longer see the intersection at which she turned, or the sign with the arrow, so she kept on walking in the direction she'd chosen.

Another hundred yards and Laura came to a second intersection. This time there was no sign on the wall. Instead the hallway ran straight ahead as well as to the right and left.

I'm in a maze, Laura thought.

She reached out to touch the wall, hoping to decipher some message from its cold sweaty surface.

Nothing.

Laura looked at her hand on the wall, cold and blue, disembodied, like the hand of a stranger.

She looked down, surprised to find she wasn't wearing the hospital tunic. Instead she had on the torn bathing suit she'd worn the night of the accident.

It was at that moment that she realized she was dreaming.

But how do I wake up?

Where is the wake-up room?

Laura looked up and found herself standing in a short hall terminating in two doors.

Exit. Enter.

Laura didn't have to think twice. She turned the knob and passed through the door marked Exit—

—and found herself standing in a ward full of sleepers. On each gurney rested a body covered with a white sheet.

Laura hugged herself.

The room was cold.

Too cold.

As she walked down the aisle between the gurneys, she noticed the row of bare feet sticking out from the bottom edge of each sheet. From each rigid, blue big toe hung a paper tag.

Suddenly Laura understood why this part of the hospital hadn't been marked.

These people weren't sleeping.

They were dead.

Laura hugged herself again. But this time it wasn't the cold.

She looked down at the toe tag on the pair of feet below her.

Her heart stopped.

Started.

Beating twice as fast.

The name on the tag was Laura Kane.

Laura stepped to the side of the gurney and looked down at the silent white form.

Could it really be . . .

She stretched her hand toward the head of the gurney, grabbed the sheet, and held her breath.

What was it they said? If you saw yourself dead in a dream it meant you really were dead.

Laura fully expected to be jolted awake the moment she lifted the sheet.

Yet something held her hand.

Did she dare to lift the sheet?

Somehow she knew she wouldn't be able to wake up until she did.

Without thinking, she pulled the sheet back.

And didn't wake up.

The face under the sheet stared up at her through one blind blue eye. The eye bulged from its socket, the flesh torn away, exposing the wet, slick bone of the skull and the jagged, broken teeth of the lower jaw, that looked like a row of bloody corn kernels.

Laura felt nauseous. Even in her sleep.

She recognized the face immediately.

It wasn't hers.

It was Julie Kincaid.

Only then did Laura wake up.

21

THE LOCKER ROOM was deserted; the long gray lockers stood like sentinels guarding the silence.

Laura sat on the wooden bench pulling off her sneakers.

She looked down the silent row of lockers. Had it really been only three weeks since she'd last been here practicing with the team? It seemed more like three years.

She had come to watch the team take practice a couple of times and they'd all been great, welcoming her back and wishing her a speedy recovery, but she hadn't actually been in the water since the night of her fight with Terry. The fact that she had been at the pool that fateful night at all told her something: that she had never really intended to quit the team for good. Swimming, for better or worse, was in her blood.

She stood up to take off her jeans, hanging them up in the locker, and pulled her sweatshirt over her head. She stepped into the new one-piece bathing suit she'd bought to celebrate her return. It was black with orange racing stripes on the sides. She peeled the tight-fitting nylon over her flesh like a second skin.

She had wanted to come back even sooner, but Dr. Kent had insisted first on evaluating a battery of tests he'd ordered to make sure she hadn't suffered any lasting neurological damage. It was scary listening to him talking about brain damage. But it

120

was a real possibility. After all, she'd been under the water for a long time.

It was even scarier when she'd learned that her heart had stopped not once, but twice!

For days afterward, she was painfully conscious of her pulse, checking it at regular intervals, worried that at any moment it could decide to stop again.

Dr. Kent assured her that her worries—he called it "heart neurosis"—were perfectly common and completely unfounded. Now that its rhythm had stabilized, her heart was no more likely to stop than anyone else's.

After her tests came back negative, Laura wasted no time getting herself back on the team. She had missed the state trials, but she was still seeded high enough to qualify for the nationals. The same afternoon she'd been given a clean bill of health, she'd gone to see Coach Morgan.

To her surprise, he'd seemed tentative at first, insisting on calling the doctor himself to ensure that she wasn't rushing things. Ever since the attack, Coach Morgan had seemed different somehow, more mellow, less driven. She had tried to thank him for what he'd done, but she had only managed to embarrass them both.

How do you thank someone for saving your life?

How about by making it past the nationals and qualifying for the Olympic trials?

It would be tough, but Laura was determined to do it for Coach Morgan.

She pulled on her orange bathing cap. The tight rubber skull cap fit easily over her shorter hair. She should have cut her hair a long time ago.

She pictured Coach Morgan leaning over her half-naked body, his hands on her breasts, his mouth on hers, breathing the life back into her drowned lungs.

She blushed every time she thought of it.

Seeing him was even harder.

They both seemed to have a hard time looking each other in the eye. What was there to be embarrassed about?

Slipping her feet into a pair of rubber thongs, she stuffed her gym bag into her locker and slammed the tin door shut. She grabbed her towel from the bench and started for the pool.

Coach Morgan hadn't arrived yet when Laura entered the pool room. It was the first time she'd been alone by the pool since the night Terry had attacked her. Something about the smell of the chlorine brought the memory of that night back in vivid relief: an inexplicable mixture of both fear and rage.

She had read that victims of rape felt the same way. Even though they were the victims, some unforgiving part of their own psyches blamed themselves for allowing themselves to be victimized.

But she hadn't *allowed* it to happen: she had fought Terry tooth and nail. She hadn't wanted to die; she had fought for life.

Terry had killed her.

Killed her.

Laura shivered.

She had died. Really died.

Dr. Kent had told her she shouldn't dwell on that. But it was hard. After all, it wasn't every day a person crossed the line between life and death. And even if she did try to push the thought out of her mind, there was always someone ready to ask her what it was like over there on the other side.

Laura told them the truth. She didn't remember anything.

Death, as she had experienced it, was nothing but a black void, a dreamless sleep, a cosmic eraser that wiped away every last trace of the individual.

Not too many people asked her to elaborate.

Instead, they walked away, looking ill at ease.

Laura figured they wanted her to tell them that she had felt a great sense of peace, that she had seen old relatives, that she had seen the white angel of light, or Jesus, or God.

But she had seen none of those things.

She had seen nothing at all.

Laura looked down at the concrete at the edge of the pool and thought she could see the dark stain in the gravelly concrete where she'd hit her head.

She was about to bend down for a closer look when the door to the pool room swung open and Coach Morgan walked through.

"Laura," he said, and smiled.

But Laura could sense the difference. It was there in the way he spoke and moved. As if he were uncomfortable just being in the same room with her.

"Hi, Coach." Laura tried to sound casual.

She threw her towel onto one of the benches.

"I think we ought to start slow," Coach Morgan was saying. "Let's concentrate on freestyle. It's your strong suit and I think it'll help you get your confidence back."

"Okay," Laura said, inserting her rubber nose plugs into her nostrils.

"Don't try to go at full speed today. Just ease into it. I don't want you pulling a muscle or developing a cramp because you're overdoing it. Nice and easy does it, understood?"

"Understood." The nose plugs made her voice sound like Tweety Bird.

"All right, let's do it."

Laura slipped out of her flip-flops and approached the edge of the pool. She took a deep breath, held her arms out in front of her like Frankenstein's monster, her toes gripping the lip of concrete, and looked down into the crystalline depths of the water.

And saw it.

A blue maze at the bottom of the pool. Just like the one in her dream. Blind alleys, passages going nowhere, halls terminating in dead ends, or doubling back upon themselves, a thousand different routes that led with tantalizing variety straight back to the place where you started.

She was looking at the floor plan to hell, a blueprint of the house of the damned, constructed for the eternal torment of lost souls.

Laura suddenly felt dizzy, nausea rolling through her like a heavy wave.

Two different wills strove within her. One urging her to jump; the other, just as strong, the fear of letting go.

She stood between the two, trembling, paralyzed.

With a cry, she suddenly threw herself backward, as if she'd just received a powerful electric shock, landing on her ass on the hard concrete, tears running down her cheeks.

Coach Morgan had seen the look of terror in her face even before she fell backward and had come running. He crouched beside her on the floor, supporting her with his arm.

"I'm sorry," she sobbed into his shoulder. "I just can't do it."

"It's okay, Laura," he whispered. "It's okay. There's always next year."

22

TED MASTERS WAS WORKING under the hood of his Ram Charger at the Exxon station out on Route 79.

The place officially closed after 9 P.M., but old man Slawson didn't mind if Ted used the garage to work on his truck. The deal was that Ted would keep the lights on and the pumps going in order to pick up a few extra bucks from lost motorists on their way to the city. But the minute he saw the taillights of the old fart's '67 Caddy disappear over the hill, Ted switched off the big bright Exxon sign, and that was that.

He reached up for the beer can on the fender of the Ram Charger, took a long swallow, and wiped his mouth on his grease-stained sleeve. He was changing the plugs in the big V-8 engine, having a little trouble removing the last two in the back, the handle of the socket wrench not quite fitting in the space between the engine and the block.

Why the hell did they always make it so fucking difficult?

Ted was in a lousy mood anyway. This afternoon some cop named Stone had come around asking all kinds of questions about Lisa. He had wanted to know what kind of relationship they'd had. Why they had broken up. If Lisa had ever mentioned suicide to him. If he knew she was pregnant.

Hell, yeah, he'd known, he felt like telling the bastard. He'd known and the first thing he thought when he heard she was dead was that he'd gotten ridden of both of them. Two birds with one stone.

Instead, he'd just shrugged. Told the cop that he knew but didn't think it was his.

That was the advice his father gave him. Just deny it until they got the blood tests to prove it.

Then deny it some more.

"'Less they got pictures," his father had sagely advised, "and you ain't no fucking Rob Lowe, ain't no way they can really prove it was you that dicked her. Don't forget, she's a spic bitch and everyone knows you got to stand in line to dick a spic."

The cop had looked at him like he'd just stepped in a pile of wormy dog shit.

He'd even asked him where he was the afternoon Lisa died.

"Right here," Ted had answered.

And the cop had gone and checked it out right then and there with some of the other mechanics.

Ted saw the way old man Slawson looked at him the rest of the day. All sideways. Like a pickerel eyeballing a baited hook.

Did they fucking think he'd murdered Lisa?

Dammit! Even dead, that bitch was trouble.

He yanked up on the handle of the wrench and the socket slipped off the fitting. His fist scraped across the sharp edge of a clamp, gouging a long ragged gash in the flesh at the back of his hand. He dropped the wrench, jerked his head up, knocking it against the trouble-light hanging from the hood latch.

The swinging light threw wild shadows over the inside of the garage.

"God fucking dammit asshole!"

Ted's voice echoed in the cavernous garage. He brought his hand up to the still-swinging light and examined the cut in the grease-stained flesh. Blood oozed from between two flaps of blackened skin.

Ted blinked back tears.

Damn, that hurt!

Just then he heard a noise in the darkness outside the garage. Or rather, it was a sudden *lack* of noise. The last of the late-summer crickets falling silent, the way they did when someone was walking past.

Ted peered hard into the night, but his eyes were unable to pierce the solid wall of black beyond the garage door.

He should have put the door down, he thought. With the light on, anyone passing by could see inside the garage. But the cool air had felt too good to resist. And if he started the engine, he needed the ventilation.

Ted straightened up, wiping his hands on his T-shirt.

"We're closed," he said.

There was no answer from the other side of the darkness. But Ted could sense a presence. Standing there. Watching.

Eyes crawling over his face like spiders.

He wiped his mouth on his sleeve. Probably some drunken nigger passing by saw the light and figured to make a couple of quick bucks knocking over a late-night gas station. He often saw them hitching rides along the highway on their way back and forth from New York City.

"Fuck off," Ted growled now. "We're closed."

He backed up to the door of the Ram Charger and pulled it open. He bent down, keeping his eyes on the night, and reached under the seat for the jack handle he kept there. He had nick-named the two-foot-long, six-pound lead baton his "coconut cruncher" from the days when he and his buddies from Groverton High used to cruise the streets of nearby Seldon looking for niggers whom they'd seen hanging at the Groverton Mall.

Now he stood in front of the Ram Charger, the pipe in his right hand, staring down the darkness. His arm muscles flexed unconsciously, his body ready for a fight. There might be more than one of them out there but by God he was going to bust him a coconut or two before they brought him down.

"Come and get it, nigger," he shouted.

Nothing happened.

Seconds passed. Each seemed like an hour.

A wild impulse to charge into the darkness and beat it with the pipe spurred him. But it was checked by a more powerful instinct: self-preservation. If he charged into that darkness, somehow he knew he would be rushing right into the arms of death itself.

So he stood rooted to the spot, as if his feet were cast in the concrete of the garage floor.

A bead of cold sweat trickled down his temple, worked its way along his jaw line, and hung from his chin without falling.

Before a minute was up Ted felt like he'd been standing there an eternity.

A half minute later he started feeling foolish. Maybe there was no one there, after all. Or perhaps, he'd scared them off.

A part of him didn't believe it for a moment. Still, he felt the muscles in his face relax, as well as the tight band across his chest. The arm with the pipe slowly lowered to his side.

He never had time to lift it again.

He stared in disbelief as the double garage doors suddenly came rumbling down their metal tracks, slamming against the floor, the locks engaging like a pair of gunshots.

"What the fuck—"

Ted felt himself lifted from his feet and hurled backward against the grille of the Ram Charger so hard the big truck rolled backward on its oversized wheels. A terrible pain riveted his shoulders to the front of the truck as if he were being welded to the chassis, like some kind of bizarre human hood ornament.

The truck's halogen fog lights clicked on, flooding the garage with a sulfurous white glow.

And then the truck's big engine woke up, rumbling like a hungry lion, its hot, raw breath on the back of his neck as his head was pushed closer and closer to the fan.

Ted struggled with all his strength, trying to raise the arm holding the heavy metal bar, but he couldn't lift his shoulder from the grille. Muscles cramping, the bar fell from his hand with a hollow clang.

The garage was filling rapidly with exhaust fumes.

Ted could hardly breathe. Smoke stung his eyes and tears were running down his grimed face.

And all the while his head was being forced back toward the fan, the blade nicking away the hair at the back of his scalp.

Ted felt the urine running down the right leg of his pants as he tried to force out the words from his constricting throat.

"Take . . . everything," he choked. "Please . . . let me go."

His neck was a thick, twisted cable of veins and straining cords as he tried to fight the irresistible force slowly pushing his head toward the fan.

The car's engine revved, as if someone were holding down the idle, and Ted felt the blade hit his skull with a sickening *thunk,* catch for a second, and then the next blade hit, *thunk.*

Blood blew into the air in a fine mist and sizzled on the hot engine like hamburger grease.

Ted's scream rose over the sound of the revving engine for a second before it was cut off by the incisions angling down both sides of his chest, meeting just below the bone shielding his palpitating heart, and then running downward through his hairy belly to the bone just above his pubis.

Through the smoke and blood and frying brain, Ted managed to glimpse one fleeting view of his attacker.

He was the biggest, blackest, meanest-looking nigger Ted Masters had ever seen.

A MOMENT LATER, the garage doors were open.

The exhaust fumes had dispersed, leaving the air clear and crisp and cool.

The Ram Charger stood silent in its bay; it was no longer running. From its open hood, however, a bloody body was draped, looking like a large drop cloth on which a ruined transmission had spilled its entire contents of red fluid.

Outside, in the darkness, the crickets had resumed their chirping.

23

LAURA COULD BARELY keep her eyes open.

Her head was resting on her hand; with her other hand she lazily drew doodles inside her notebook.

In the front of the classroom, Dr. Latelle was droning on pointlessly about the use of literary allusion in T.S. Eliot's *Waste Land*. He was reading a passage from the poem in his characteristic nasal monotone that reminded Laura of a stuck-up pig. Afterward he would begin pulling literary references from the poem like a magician pulling handkerchiefs out of his sleeve.

Generally speaking, Laura liked poetry, even T.S. Eliot, but she had very little use for the moderns. Until she'd taken Dr. Latelle's course, she never knew that one line of English poetry could ever be so complicated. It was a little maddening really. After all, if Eliot wanted to say something why didn't he just come out and say it? Poetry was supposed to communicate, wasn't it? Not be a secret language.

The Waste Land was more like a puzzle than a poem. Like those word searches they ran in the newspaper. Or that puzzle where you tried to find the president's heads in a jungle scene.

Laura tried to force herself to concentrate on Dr. Latelle's words. She quit her doodling and began to write down something he said: "What Eliot is doing is providing us with a kind of shorthand of cultural knowledge . . ." but she found her attention wandering wildly off course.

She hadn't gotten a decent night's sleep in nearly two weeks. The dreams had continued almost every night. The same blue corridors. The same sense of being lost. The same urgent need to find . . . what?

Laura had begun to dread going to sleep at night. She took to staying up as long as possible, often putting off sleep until the early-morning hours. And still the dreams found her. She would wake up terrified, covered in sweat, and even more exhausted than when she'd fallen asleep. She wondered how long she could keep herself going. How long before sheer fatigue did her in.

Her eyelids had slid down halfway over her eyes before she realized what was happening. Everyone was getting up from behind their seats, gathering their books and papers, getting ready for their next class.

Saved by the bell, she thought.

She hurriedly stuffed her notebook into her nylon knapsack, slung it over her shoulder, and made her way with the rest of the crowd to the door.

Halfway down the hallway, she heard the voice calling her name.

Laura turned and saw Carin hurrying down the hallway after her. She was carrying an armful of books, her face wearing an odd expression.

It took Laura aback for a moment. And then she realized why.

Carin looked *happy*.

"Hey, wait up," she laughed.

Carin bustled her way up the hall, holding her load of books to her chest as if they were a baby. By the time she caught up to Laura she was panting.

"I thought I was going to lose you," she said breathlessly. "Guess what?"

"What?"

"I've been accepted into Lambda Psi!"

"That's great," Laura said, hollowly. She could feel herself smiling like a jack-o'-lantern. Great big grin. Nothing inside.

"The initiation is next Thursday. But Sally says it's in the bag once you get this far."

Lambda Psi was one of the most powerful and popular sororities on campus. Its membership was comprised almost exclusively of female jocks, their friends, and other hangers-on. Laura had been a member for two years before losing interest. Eventually Laura had just grown tired of the "us-against-them" mentality, the petty bickering, and childish pranks. At least that was what she told anyone who'd asked. The truth, which she hated to admit, even to herself, was that none of that had seemed to bother her so much until Terry became the president of the sorority. Perhaps it was only her imagination, or just her outright dislike for the girl, but ever since Terry took over, the pranks and jokes seemed a little more destructive, the backbiting and gossip more vicious, the clan mentality of the sorority even more insular and intolerant of outsiders.

"Can you believe it," Carin went on. "First Butch asks me out and then I get accepted into Lambda Psi. Does it get any better than this, or what?"

Laura wanted to feel happy for her friend, share her enthusiasm, but she just couldn't. She had seen Carin several times since the accident at the pool and each time it was becoming harder and harder for them to communicate with each other. It was as if they were on two different roads traveling in a widening V, the distance between them growing ever wider with each passing moment.

The fact was that Carin's life was taking the high road; and, in an ironic reversal, her own was taking the low road. And while Laura had always been there to help Carin over the rough spots, Carin had no practice in comforting someone else. She was too caught up in the whirlwind of her own successes to see that Laura was hurting, too intoxicated by her unaccustomed good fortune. Laura didn't blame her.

"Come on," Carin suggested, "let's go to the cafeteria and grab some grub?"

"No, thanks," Laura said. "I can't. I've got an appointment to see Professor Roarke."

Laura saw a flicker of something in Carin's eyes. She probably thinks I'm jealous, Laura thought. Or just being a bitch.

"Okay," Carin said, a little too jauntily. "I'll catch you later."

"Yeah," Laura said, wishing she could explain. "Later."

The philosophy department was located in the older section of the sciences building, up a narrow passage of stairs, and down a short, dark hallway whose well-scuffed linoleum had been completely worn away in the more traveled sections. The shabbiness of the philosophy wing brought to mind Professor Roarke's constant tirades against the school budget makers. Laura couldn't help but contrast the dilapidated department with the spanking new offices of the university athletic director.

Professor Roarke's office was the next-to-the-last one on the left-hand side of the hall. His door was open, but Laura knocked before entering anyway, rapping lightly on the doorjamb.

The professor did not look up. He was bent over his desk, scrawling furiously on a yellow legal pad.

Laura didn't know what to do. She didn't want to disturb him in the middle of something important. On the other hand, she didn't want him to think she'd come late for her appointment.

She knocked again, a little louder this time.

"Excuse me," she said, and coughed self-consciously. "Professor Roarke?"

The bald, bullet-shaped head jerked up. His mind, still engaged on the problem he'd left on the pad, had left his face a total blank.

"It's me," Laura said, helpfully. "Laura Kane."

Suddenly the expression came back into his face.

"Oh yes," he said, waving to a threadbare armchair across from the desk. "Ms. Kane. Come in. Please. Have a seat."

Laura noticed that the professor was wearing his corduroy coat. It was only the middle of September and the offices were already chilly.

"I hope I didn't interrupt anything important," Laura said apologetically. "You looked busy."

Professor Roarke waved at the pad on his desk. "I'm working on a paper comparing Nietzsche's Superman to the concept of God found in the Book of Job for the American Philosophical Society. Publish or perish, you know. I just wanted to corral a thought before it galloped away forever into the cerebral mists. My wife calls me the original 'absent-minded professor.' I suppose she's right. So, what's on your mind?"

Laura hadn't really planned what she was going to say to Professor Roarke. In fact, she hardly knew why she had requested an appointment with him at all. Except that something about the straight-talking professor and his lectures on religion and philosophy had led her to believe that he might be able to help.

"I'm not sure how to begin," Laura said.

"So let me begin for you," he said, reaching for a pipe in his ashtray. "It all started the day you died."

Laura felt herself stiffen with shock.

Professor Roarke knocked the cold ashes from the bowl. He inspected the chewed stem, then set it firmly between his teeth, but did not refill the pipe. Instead he seemed content to suck on the empty bowl.

"I'm sorry to be so blunt," he said. "I'm afraid I lack Plato's soothing subtlety."

"You heard about my accident, then."

"Yes."

Of course he would have heard about it, Laura thought, angry with herself for waltzing around the subject and wasting both their time. She was determined to get straight to the point.

"Professor Roarke, I want to know if you really believe what you said in your lecture about *Gilgamesh*. I mean, that there is nothing after death but pain and suffering."

"Are you asking me my personal belief?"

"I guess so. Yes."

Roarke laid the cold pipe down in the ashtray.

"Then I have to say that I don't believe in any kind of hereafter. But I won't go so far as to agree with Gilgamesh. His fantasy was borne of the terror of death. I don't think the grave is a torture chamber or that death is a sentence of eternal punishment. I think it is merely the cessation of biological function, the shutting down of the body's bio-electrical system. Period."

"Oblivion," Laura said softly.

"Oblivion," the professor echoed, nodding.

The professor looked suddenly at her with renewed interest. As if she were a promisingly shaped piece of a puzzle he'd previously overlooked. He leaned forward in his chair.

"Laura, what did you experience on the other side?"

Laura thought for a moment. "I don't know exactly. Something happened. But I can't explain it. I feel different now. Like I'm not the same person. I don't seem to care about anything that I used to care about. School. Friends. Swimming. I can't sleep at night. Bad dreams—"

She broke off. It was the first time she'd actually spoken her feelings aloud and she found them disturbing. She had no intention of sounding like a lunatic.

"Laura," Professor Roarke said gently, "don't be embarrassed. What you are feeling is not unusual. St. John of the Cross called it *The Dark Night of the Soul*. Sartre called it *Nausea*. Remember Gilgamesh, after the death of his best friend Enkidu? He, too, could find no joy in life. The best foods failed to stimulate his appetite; the most beautiful women could not arouse his lust. Life seemed like nothing but a mouthful of ashes."

"Yes," Laura said, and thought that was exactly what it was like. *A mouthful of ashes.*

"But remember, also, the advice of the sacred prostitute Sidiri. Sit down at the banquet and take your fill. Be a glutton for life. Eat of it as much as you can. For that is our portion in eternity, Laura. To have tasted everything life has to offer so that when the end of the feast has come we may have tasted of every dish and we can go to sleep on a full belly. For there is nothing worse than going to bed hungry."

"And that's all?" Laura said, feeling somehow cheated. "We are only meant to eat, drink, and copulate like animals? And when we die—nothing?"

Professor Roarke stared at Laura with unblinkingly cool, rational eyes, weighing her in some invisible balance, as if gauging the effect his next words might have on her delicate psyche.

Laura stared back, her eyes dark and wide, determined to meet his challenge.

"Nothing else?" she repeated.

"There is something," he began.

"Yes," Laura said hopefully.

"There is one conception of the afterlife that I neglected to mention in class. It is the most recent. Some people consider it the scientific basis of a new religion. I have my doubts. More than doubts. It is called NDE. Near-death experience. Perhaps you've heard of it?"

"The stuff with the tunnels and the white light?" she said, a little disappointed. She had seen a special on the subject on television. The people who claimed they'd had such experiences had seemed a little too enthusiastic. Like they were trying too hard to believe what they were saying.

Almost evangelical. Like born-again Christians.

"A friend of mine is something of an expert in the field of NDEs. You might want to contact him."

Laura sat quietly while Professor Roarke scribbled a name and phone number on a piece of paper.

"His name is Dr. Mahler. Dr. Henrik Mahler. I can't say that I believe in the work he is doing, but he is a good man. He may be able to help. Perhaps he has what you are seeking."

Laura took the slip of paper, folded it, and put it in the pocket of her denim jacket. She thanked Professor Roarke, gathered up her knapsack, and left the office. She hurried down the dark, grimy hall, feeling out of place and vaguely embarrassed, as if she'd just been told she'd failed his course.

24

SHE WAS IN THE MAZE AGAIN.

This time Laura recognized it right away. The blue concrete walls. The long hallways leading nowhere. The abrupt dead ends.

And the infernal humming of the hidden machines.

She was also conscious of the fact that she was dreaming.

Was that even possible? To be conscious and asleep at the same time?

Possible or not, she saw herself clearly, right down to the gray sweat pants and university sweatshirt she had been wearing the night before when she sat down to watch a movie on the late show.

Perhaps she was just dreaming she was conscious of herself dreaming . . .

It was kind of like playing a video game on a computer. You knew you were not the pixilated figure on the screen, not really, but for a few minutes at a time you could become so absorbed in the game that you actually did lose a sense of yourself.

Laura was familiar with the feeling. She had often experienced it while playing Pac-Man.

By channeling all of your concentration, intellect, and dexterity into the manipulation of a digitalized alter-ego, its life or death became, for a short while at least, synonymous with your own.

The only difference was that you could turn away from a video game, shut down the computer, reset the game.

But there was no getting out of her dream.

Unless she could wake up.

And the only way to wake up was to visit that awful room where the bodies lay.

Where her own body lay.

Still. Quiet. Beneath its white shroud.

Shivering, Laura moved slowly down the hall. She could feel the cold linoleum tiles beneath her feet. She was glad she had worn a pair of thick woolen sweat socks the night before.

There was a current of chill air blowing through the maze.

Artificial.

As if they were in a bunker far below the earth. Or somewhere on the moon.

She looked for some familiar sign from her previous visits, some telltale landmark that might orient her, or might remind her of how she'd found her way out before, but she could find none.

Everything looked exactly the same. And totally different.

So she wandered aimlessly up and down the blank corridors, letting whim alone guide her, turning right or left at the faceless intersections, doubling back without protest whenever her route suddenly terminated in a dead end.

She suspected the maze was a construct of her own subconscious, a garbled mental model of the brain itself, but empty of all meaning and signifying nothing at all. The more she tried to figure it out, the more complex it would become, until she was hopelessly lost in the coils of her own brain.

She came to another intersection and stopped for a moment.

And heard something.

That wasn't supposed to be there.

An extra footstep.

Laura felt the hair tingle at the back of her neck.

She listened closely to the sterile air, trying to detect some break in the quiet hum of the hidden machinery but she heard nothing.

And then a whisper so quiet it might almost have been a shift in air current, or subtle shift in the rhythm of the machinery, or a thought inside her own brain.

Laura . . .

In the quiet of that subterranean maze, she could have heard no more frightening a sound.

Laura didn't wait for the voice to call her again.

She started running.

Trying to lose the sound of footsteps that cut away the distance behind her in precise, scissorlike strides.

The hall unrolled before her at high speed, like a film coming off its reel. Laura took the corners without slowing down, her stockinged feet sliding on the tiled floor and sending her crashing into the wall across the hall. She crouched against the wall for a moment, listening, the footsteps still coming toward her with mechanical precision.

Suddenly they stopped.

And the voice. Again.

Laura . . .

Laura's heart trip-hammered in her chest. She took off down the hall like a sprinter out of the blocks.

She gulped breath, her lungs burning.

She didn't know why she was running, who or what was behind her; perhaps it would be best to just stop and confront her pursuer. Perhaps that was the only way out of this nightmare.

No!

Something inside her screamed.

If she turned around she would die.

She was sure of it. If she looked into the face of her nightmare her heart would stop cold and she would die in her sleep. When they found her they would just assume that she'd suffered cardiac arrest. That her heart had suffered some undiagnosed damage from the accident. It happened all the time.

So she ran blindly forward, hoping that something in the real world would wake her.

A telephone.

A doorbell.

Anything.

And at the same time she knew that her only escape from the nightmare was to find the morgue room.

Horrible as it was, somehow she knew it was her only way out.

And then she turned the corner and there they were.

Standing side by side.

The two enigmatic doors.

Enter. Exit.

The footsteps sounded closer now.

There was no going back.

Laura rushed forward, grabbed the knob of the door marked Exit, and rushed into the morgue room.

She saw the rows of steel tables, the inert white forms, the tagged toes, the wall of coffin-shaped lockers.

She caught the ominous whiff of formaldehyde.

She ran to the last body in the row. Saw the toe tag with her name.

She stood at the head of the steel gurney and grabbed the white sheet. Her body was trembling.

She knew she had to look at the face beneath the sheet. But she was afraid at who she might find there.

Afraid it would be her.

And then the footsteps were outside the door to the morgue room. She heard the door pushed open. She heard the voice call her name.

And she yanked the sheet down.

And saw the face of a black-haired boy, his face frozen in an eternal scream of silent agony.

And woke up.

She was sitting on the sofa in her own apartment. The blanket was draped over her lap, just where she'd laid it the night before. On the table in front of her, a half-filled mug of chamomile herbal tea. Across the room, the television was filled with fuzzy blue static.

It reminded her of the maze.

She reached for the remote and clicked to the first broadcasting channel she found.

It was the weather channel.

Then she got up and walked across the room to the chair where she'd thrown her denim jacket the day before. She fished around in the left front pocket until she found what she was looking for.

She smoothed the slip of paper in her hand.

In the dim blue light the television cast through the room, she could just make out the name and telephone number of Dr. Henrik Mahler.

25

IT WAS THE DEAD GRANDMOTHER'S turn to speak.

For the past hour Laura had been listening to the dead speak. First some middle-aged businessman who'd had a heart attack on the golf course; then a cop who'd been shot in the face during a convenience store holdup; and finally a young mother who'd been thrown through the windshield of her Ford Escort.

Now it was the grandmother's turn.

She'd suffered a brain aneurysm while Christmas-shopping at the Groverton Mall. She was in Macy's and had just reached for a white Gund bear for her granddaughter when she felt a sharp thump at the back of her head.

At first she thought some overzealous shopper had bumped her with an errant elbow. But when she turned around to give a piece of her mind to whoever it was, she was stunned to find there was no one behind her. That's when the world did a little dance around her—lights, trees, shoppers, and stuffed animals—all spinning crazily out of control.

There was no pain. Just a strange numbing sensation. Like someone had plugged a hose in her ear and was filling the right side of her body with ice-cold water.

She sank to the floor. A small crowd of worried faces filled the space above her.

Her last conscious memory was of her field of vision rapidly narrowing to a single pinpoint of light.

Like when you turn a TV off.

And a voice in her head saying, "Show's over."

Dr. Mahler shifted in his seat. "Hmmm, auditory phenomenon. That's interesting. Very interesting. Could you recognize the voice? Was it yours?"

The old lady thought for a moment. "I didn't recognize the voice, no. But it wasn't mine. It was impersonal. Like a game show announcer."

"Very interesting," Dr. Mahler repeated, scribbling on his little pad.

Dr. Mahler was a slender, refined-looking man of around forty-five with gray eyes that matched a full head of prematurely gray hair. He was dressed, as he had been on their first meeting, in an impeccably tailored gray suit. On the ring finger of his right hand he wore a chunky gold ring. Laura noticed he did not wear a wedding ring.

In spite of his serious and professional manner, as well as Professor Roarke's endorsement, Laura couldn't help but suspect something of the charlatan about the man.

After all, he was peddling the idea of life after death.

The ultimate snake oil.

The man described himself as a Jungian analyst who had become interested in the field of near-death experience after the death of his sister from ovarian cancer six years earlier. He explained that he was writing a new book on NDEs and that he often used the experiences of his patients directly in his research. He hoped she wouldn't object. Naturally, he would disguise any information he obtained from her by changing her name and the circumstances of her experiences when he wrote up the case history.

She said she doubted if he'd get much he could use from her, as she couldn't remember a thing about what had happened. Dr. Mahler disagreed. Judging from what she'd already told him, he suspected there was a good chance she might have experienced an NDE. He suggested that she come back to sit in on one of his NDE support groups.

When she hesitated, he assured her that she wouldn't have to say anything. She could just listen, observe, and come to her own conclusions.

In the end, she'd decided to come. The dreams had grown worse. Several times her invisible pursuer had nearly caught her before she could find the morgue room, where each time a new body lay under the sheet.

As a consequence, she hardly slept in a week. Keeping herself up with diet pills and black coffee and late-night movies.

Still, once in a while, sleep crept up on her.

Her head dropped.

She dozed.

And she was back in the blue maze.

So that's why she was here. Listening to this convocation of the dead.

Hoping against hope that they might have the answer. The thread that would help her find her way out of the maze once and for all.

"There was no fear at all," the grandmother said. "It was exactly like I had been watching television and now it was time to go to bed or do something else. No big deal."

"That's right," the policeman said. He talked slowly, slurping his words. "When that punk shot me, I felt this great sense of calm." He struggled for a moment over a word with too many syllables. "Serenity," he sputtered.

The businessman nodded. "It was a relief. No more deadlines. No more client meetings. No more sales reports. I was floating."

"Next thing I remember," the grandmother continued, "was looking down at my body in the ICU unit."

She explained that she had recognized the room immediately because she had spent a lot of time there only a year before, when her husband Frank died of lung cancer. She could tell by the way the doctors and nurses were clustered about her that something was going wrong.

"But it was like it was all happening to someone else. It didn't even seem particularly interesting. Like a scene from a soap opera. I could easily have turned the channel."

Laura marveled at the old woman's description of her own death. She related every aspect of it to watching television.

The young mother was nodding emphatically. "I saw myself lying there, all twisted up on the road, blood and broken glass everywhere. I mean, it was awful and I felt bad for the person and all. But I didn't really recognize her as me. It was like I was one of the passersby that had stopped out of morbid curiosity."

She had been pretty. Once.

Her face was still pretty, but it was a glossy, artificial beauty. Her facial expressions, which were minimal, had a strange, mechanical look to them.

She looked like a talking mannequin.

The businessman snorted. "I felt sorry for the poor bastard. Lying there on the thirteenth green with his custom-made clubs and his three-hundred-dollar golf pants. When I realized the poor bastard was me, I had to laugh. Is that what I had let my life come to?"

"I could see the doctor working on me," the grandmother continued. "I knew he was trying to save my life but I was beginning to grow annoyed. They had taken off my clothes and they were—"

She coughed and cleared her throat.

"Only if you're comfortable," Dr. Mahler said.

The old lady nodded.

"They were *pumping* my chest," she said, "and my body was flopping around in the most undignified manner. I wanted the doctor to stop, to just leave me alone to die in peace. I was very happy where I was, thank you very much."

"Me too," the ex-cop said. "There were cops everywhere. Sirens were screaming. My partner was sitting on the curb crying. There was so much commotion—and for what? I was dead. It was no big deal."

He paused to wipe the spittle from his mouth with a handkerchief.

"The homicide chief was crouched over my body trying to get a description of the man who shot me. He kept saying 'We'll get the fuck, Bobby. I promise, we'll get the fuck.' I wanted to tell him that he mustn't hurt anyone. That it wasn't important. That I loved everybody. Even the man who shot me—"

He stopped, stunned by what he'd said.

"I tried to tell the paramedics not to bother to revive me," the businessman said. " 'He wasn't a happy man,' I argued. 'His was not a happy life.' But no one seemed to hear me. I was standing right there, under the flag by the thirteenth hole, yet no one seemed to see me. It was as if everyone else were in a different world than me."

"Like talking to the TV set," the grandmother said, using her characteristic analogy. "I finally got so disgusted watching them pummel my body, I left the room and walked down the hall to look for someone who might help me. I remember trying to stop one or two people to ask them where the nurses' station was but they walked right past me as if they didn't see me. I puzzled over this a moment and then I saw my son-in-law standing in a phone booth against the wall.

"For a moment I was stunned to see him there and the first thing that came into my mind was that something had happened to my daughter Patricia or one of my grandchildren. Then I realized that the hospital had probably called them and they were there to see me. I wanted to tell him that I was all right and to ask him where Patricia and the kids were. He hadn't bothered to pull shut the door to the phone booth since there was no one else around. I was just about to interrupt him when I realized that he was talking about me.

"He was telling someone that it looked like the old witch was finally going to kick off. And not a moment too soon. He could use some of the money Patricia would no doubt inherit. That is if I hadn't already spent it all on denture adhesives and hemorrhoidal jelly. In any event, mine was one name he could cross off his Christmas list."

"Whoo-ee," the businessman whistled.

"Bummer," said the young mother.

Dr. Mahler looked up from his pad. "How did that make you feel?"

The ex-cop sat forward on his chair, his one remaining eye sharp as a drill bit.

"Hurt, at first," the old lady said slowly. "And then sad."

"Sad?" Dr. Mahler prompted.

"Yes. I'd always thought of my son-in-law as my own. I'd no idea that he felt like that. I thought of my daughter and grand-children. I pitied them their lives with him."

"Did you get to see them?" Dr. Mahler asked.

"Yes," the old lady said. "I found them in the ICU waiting room. My daughter was in a chair crying. Sally, that's my granddaughter, was sitting next to her, filling in a picture in her coloring book. I was disappointed that Jimmy wasn't there, but he was just a baby at the time, and they'd probably left him with a neighbor.

"Did you say anything to them?"

"I tried to. My daughter looked so sad, so miserable. Sally was still too young to really understand what was going on but she kept looking up at her mother with this grim, earnest little face. It was enough to break my heart. I wanted to tell them so desperately that it was all right. Not to worry. That I was in a better place than the one I left. But she couldn't hear me."

The young mother nodded. "It was the same with me. I found my husband Vince in the ER and he was crying. You have to un-derstand I'd never seen him cry before. He's an ex-Marine, you see, and never one to show his feelings. But there he was bawling like a little baby. I was so touched. I never knew he re-ally cared that much. I went to tell him that it was okay, that he didn't have to be sad, that I wasn't in any pain, but he didn't even know that I was there. I couldn't make him feel my pres-ence."

"The closest I came," the businessman said, "was when I stroked my youngest son's cheek. I couldn't feel a thing, my finger passed right over his flesh, like the beam of a penlight. But he brushed the cheek I'd touched with the back of his hand. As if chasing away a fly. I still get chills when I think of it."

Laura felt chills running down her own spine.

Dr. Mahler broke the almost reverent mood that had descended over the group.

"Is this when you saw the light?" he asked the room in general. It was the grandmother who broke the uneasy silence.

"I heard someone calling my name," she said quietly. "I thought that finally someone could see me. I meant to ask them what was going on. If I were really dead. And what was going to happen to me now. But when I turned to the source of the voice I saw—well, it's hard to describe, really—"

"Just do the best you can," Dr. Mahler said.

"Well, it was like the other side of the room had been hollowed out, elongated somehow, into a kind of funnel shape. And at the bottom of the funnel I saw the most beautiful, inviting light I'd ever seen.

"I can't really explain it," she said, searching for the words. "It wasn't just a light; it was like . . . love itself."

"Yeah," the cop said gruffly, but obviously moved. "It was like every good feeling I'd ever had all rolled into one. And then some."

"I saw Jesus," the young mother said, a note of defiance in her voice, as if she expected to be challenged. "I saw Jesus Christ. But he was lit from within, all cool blue light, like a fluorescent bulb."

"Did the light speak to you?" Dr. Mahler asked.

"No—yes," the old woman looked confused. "It didn't exactly speak. It . . . *summoned* me."

She described how she was drawn to the light as if it were the answer to everything she'd ever wondered about life, the world, the universe.

The businessman agreed. "It was like after all the struggle, all the bullshit, I was finally going to understand the point of it all."

The old woman described walking further into the tunnel, seeing people from her past. Old friends, school chums, family members. They were all just as she'd remembered them the last time she'd seen them.

Only they were all supposed to be dead.

"Were you frightened?" Dr. Mahler asked.

"Not a bit," she said. "Everyone was so nice. It was like a dream. Or like watching an old movie on TV. You just forget that all of the actors are really dead."

She wanted to stop and talk to each of them, embrace them, tell them how much she loved them, but there was no time. She felt a burning desire to meet the light at the end of the tunnel and the people along the way seemed to know this. They smiled at her benevolently, understandingly.

And then she saw Frank.

"He stepped out of the light like an MC from behind the curtains. He was standing there in his good suit, looking tall and handsome, like he did on the day we were married. Not wasted and broken by disease the way he was in the hospital."

Her voice caught.

"I'm sorry," she said. "I just get so emotional when I think about this part."

"It's okay," Dr. Mahler assured her. "Take your time."

"I started toward him," she said dreamily, "but he held his hand up. He was smiling. So handsome. Like a movie star. He told me I had to go back, that it wasn't my time yet."

"How did that make you feel?"

"Terrible. I didn't want to go back. I wanted to stay there with him. I pleaded with him not to send me away."

"What did he say to that?"

"He had me turn around and look at what I was leaving behind."

"And what did you see?"

"I saw my daughter and granddaughter. And I knew right then as much as I wanted to stay, that it would be selfish. That they still needed me."

The young mother was softly crying. "Me too. I saw my babies. I knew I had to go back. I knew Vince needed me, too. Loved me. That he wouldn't be able to go on if I died."

"So you went back," Dr. Mahler asked the old woman.

"Uh-huh," she said. "Suddenly I was in the ICU room again, looking down at my body in the bed. The whole thing might have taken a second—or an eternity. The next thing I knew I was once again inside my body. I heard the doctor shout 'Got her!' and there I was."

"Were you glad to be back?"

"Jeezus, I wasn't," the businessman said. "I didn't talk to my doctor for three days. I actually blamed him for saving my life! Can you believe that?"

"I can," the ex-cop said. "It was so beautiful on the other side."

"Yes," the young mother said almost wistfully. Only one side of her face showed emotion; the other side remained frozen like a mannequin's. "It *was* beautiful."

The old woman thought for a while. "You know, the truth is that I'm not really sure if I'm glad to be back or not. That's the strange part. Naturally I'm happy to be with my family again, but it was kind of disappointing. I mean, most of the people I know—or used to know—are on the other side. I think I felt more at home among the dead."

She stopped as if surprised at what she said.

And laughed.

"I did have some fun with my son-in-law, though."

"How so?" Dr. Mahler smiled.

"Well, Paul came to visit me afterward, and after he told me how glad he was to see me feeling so well, I said it looked like he'd have to put me back on his Christmas list after all."

"What did he say?"

"He looked at me kind of funny, and then I played my trump card."

"Which was?"

"I told him what I'd like for Christmas. A great big case of Preparation H."

There were some scattered snickerings from among the group members. Even Laura couldn't resist cracking a smile.

"Egads!" Dr. Mahler exclaimed. "What did he say?"

"Well, everyone else in the room just looked at each other. I think they thought I was suffering a relapse. Everyone but Paul, that is. He had turned as white as a sheet. You'd think he had seen a ghost!"

By now, everyone was laughing.

Laura along with the rest.

26

"So what did you think of our little group?"

Dr. Mahler was hunched over the yellow legal pad on his desk. The session had ended about fifteen minutes earlier and it had taken just about that long before the last of the members of the group had finally dispersed. He had asked her to stay a few minutes afterward, and now she waited as he put the finishing touches on the notes he had taken throughout the session.

He looked up from the pad, his blue eyes sparkling expectantly through his reading glasses.

On the wall behind him, Laura recognized a framed print of Steiner's famous painting "Spirits Ascending up to Heaven" from her class in art appreciation.

"I'm not sure," she said, hesitantly. "They seemed so—"

"At peace with themselves?" he suggested.

Brainwashed, was more the word that came to Laura's mind.

For the better part of two hours she had listened to the people in the group talk about dying as it if were a religious experience. They had the same unthinking, robotic optimism as born-again Christians. They spoke of the most awful occurrences—heart attacks, car accidents, physical assault—in rapturous, almost orgasmic terms.

It was as if they had wanted to believe so badly in the after-life that they were willing to believe anything: even Dr.

Mahler's pseudo-religion of tunnels, astral bodies, dead relatives, and godlike lights.

What had Professor Roarke called it? The new contemporary mythology.

Laura looked at the man behind the desk.

His expensive suit. His chunky gold ring. His shelf of best-selling paperbacks.

Trying to sell her on the idea of immortality.

She wasn't buying it.

Like any good salesman, he seemed to read the doubt on her face.

"You don't believe any of it," Dr. Mahler said, smiling. "You think we're just fooling ourselves here."

Laura hesitated.

"You can be honest, Ms. Kane."

"Yes," Laura said at last. "I mean, I want to believe there's an afterlife, but—" she just shrugged her shoulders.

"Would it help to know that no less an authority than Carl Jung, the great Swiss psychotherapist, believed in some kind of afterlife? He'd had what today we would term a near-death experience after a heart attack. He described his experience in detail in his autobiography. Of course, he's not the only one. All throughout history men and women have been describing NDEs. You've studied Dante in school?"

"Yes."

"Well, what is *The Divine Comedy* if not a record of the greatest near-death experience of all?"

Laura said nothing.

"I can see you're still not convinced," Dr. Mahler said, conceding. "Well, a healthy dose of skepticism is important in any scientific endeavor, especially in research of this kind. Even as a doctor, I find it difficult sometimes to remain completely objective. The stories my patients bring me from the other side are so inspiring.

"That's just it," Laura said. "They all seem so contrived."

"How so?"

"Well, they're all so much the same, as if they'd gotten the idea on authority from somewhere else and were repeating it like Gospel truth."

"The Gospel according to Mahler," he said laughingly.

Laura blushed. Could he really read her hostility that easily?

"It's okay," the doctor said. "The charge has been leveled at me more than once. Actually most of my patients have never heard of me or NDEs before. So it's highly unlikely that my research could have influenced their perceptions of the experience of dying. Rather, it's more like they all dreamed the same dream independent of each other, which is a statistically more unlikely occurrence than that they've actually experienced a legitimate alternate reality. Don't you think?"

"I guess so," Laura said, not knowing if she really agreed or not.

He laid down the gold Cross pen, put his elbows on the polished desk, and steepled his fingers beneath his chin.

Laura noticed the clean pink half-moons of his fingernails. They appeared to be polished.

"Let me ask you something, Ms. Kane," the doctor said. "Are you religious? Do you believe in God?"

The question took her aback for a moment. Strange that it should, but it seemed almost as embarrassing as a sexual innuendo.

"No," she said quietly. "No, I don't."

"May I ask why not?"

Laura thought of her mother, or rather, of the gray, wasted skeletal form that was her last memory of her mother. She thought of her father, broken by grief and alcohol. And she thought of the little girl she had been, lost in the emotional wasteland of adult tragedy.

"Because I don't believe that if there were a God he could possibly allow so much suffering in the world," she said quietly.

She knew how simplistic it sounded, how childish. And yet that was the bottom line.

If there really were a God, such suffering could not exist.

"Fair enough," Dr. Mahler said. "Believe it or not, it's an opinion once shared by many who experience NDEs."

Laura looked doubtful.

"It's true. Many folks who've undergone an NDE don't believe in God. Some do, afterward. Others still don't. But all of them come back with a new sense of the spiritual reality grounding our lives, as well as the peace of mind that comes with knowing there is something after death."

"You mean they believe in Heaven?" Laura said.

"Not exactly," Dr. Mahler said. He had picked up the gold pen again, moving it between his perfectly manicured fingers like a magician. "I stretched the truth a bit when I said the reality of the NDE was less improbable than the idea that all these people were dreaming the same dream. As a matter of fact, it is quite possible that the NDE is a psychological archetype rooted deep within our psyches and released into consciousness during times of severe physical distress, such as the onset of death, to help us meet the inevitable. Jung himself entertained this possibility. Did you ever see one of those nature programs on TV where the lion brings down a gazelle?"

"Yes," Laura said, uncertain what that had to do with anything.

"Savage, isn't it?"

Laura flashed on the familiar images: the ripping claws, the red, torn flesh, the spilled entrails.

"Yes," she said quietly.

"Nature red in tooth and claw, and all that," the doctor said. "But did you know that the gazelle, though it is literally being torn apart and eaten alive, does not feel a thing? There is a natural opiate in the gazelle's brain that floods its system during its final agony, transforming what should be catastrophic pain into . . ."

Once again the doctor got that faraway dreamy look in his eyes that reminded Laura of a televangelist.

"Into rapture," he nearly whispered.

Laura flashed on the sickening image of the lion thrusting its head inside the empty, lifeless carcass of the gazelle, rummaging around inside it as if it were nothing but a bloody canvas bag, eating its insides out.

How could anyone but a madman compare that to rapture?

"You see," Dr. Mahler said, excitedly, "what my detractors have suggested is that the NDE is nothing more than a psychological opiate. A fantasy released by a dying brain to comfort the ego about to face the greatest terror of all: eternal oblivion."

Mahler held the gold pen up to make his point, a yuppie version of Moses with his staff and tablets of the law.

"But even if they're right," he went on, "the fact is that the NDE has still served its purpose. For as Jung says, even if there is no such thing as God and Heaven and the afterlife, it is best to believe in them if only for the reason that belief in these concepts is essential to psychological health."

Flushed, Mahler put his pen down and smiled sheepishly. "You must forgive me," he said. "I get a little passionate sometimes, but I feel I'm onto something truly important."

Laura shifted uneasily in her chair. In spite of herself, she found herself slowly being taken in by his fervor. There was no doubting that the doctor was extremely charismatic.

"Our society is drifting, Laura, full of violence and anger and discontent. We have lost the belief system that makes morality possible. We have lost the sense that our actions have any consequences. So why not kill? Rob? Rape? The NDE can give us back a code of ethics—and a reason to follow them. It says that our actions do have consequences. That the point of life is love. That death is not the end."

"I wish I could believe—"

Dr. Mahler held up his hand. "Not belief, Laura, but experience will set you free."

"But I died and I experienced nothing."

The doctor shook his head. "You only think you experienced nothing. Your dreams tell me differently. Laura, you went further than the others. All the way to the very end. You are repressing your memory of the experience. I don't know why. Usually we only repress what is painful. But I'd like to find out what it is you saw."

"How?"

"Hypnosis," Dr. Mahler said without preamble.

He saw the look on Laura's face.

"It's not like you think. Like it is in the movies. It is merely a form of deep relaxation. You won't lose control, I assure you. You'll only go as far as you want to go."

Laura hesitated.

"Laura, this is a great opportunity in the research of the NDE. Up to now, NDE survivors have all been enthusiastic collaborators of the experience. Converts, as you call them. I suspect your experience was more objective. If you can recall it, you may be able to shed new light on what it is to die."

"I don't know that I want to recall it," Laura said.

"Can't you see, you don't have a choice. If you don't face what happened to you in the maze, your dreams will keep returning."

Laura knew he was right.

He could be a charlatan, a confidence man, and maybe worse. He might even be somewhat insane. But what choice did she really have?

"Okay," Laura said. "I'll do it."

27

IN A FEW SHORT MINUTES Carin would be reborn.

The coffin was a simple pine box barely six feet long and two feet wide. The story was that it had been made in woodworking shop by some frat brothers a gazillion years ago and donated to the sorority in return for some long-forgotten favor. Ever since, it had been part of the initiation rites into Lambda Psi that a pledge had to spend the night inside the coffin.

She was dressed as prescribed: in a short white tunic that she had sewn herself from a bedsheet on which she'd had sexual intercourse. Even now she smiled when she remembered how surprised Butch was at her aggressiveness that first night.

And how pissed off he was on subsequent nights, when he discovered that she had resumed her semester-long vow of chastity.

She would make it up to him after tonight. . . .

Carin shivered in the cold night air, her breath coming out in small puffs of white steam. Her flesh goose-pimpled. Beneath the thin white cloth of the homemade tunic, she was completely naked.

"Take off your sneakers and socks," one of the girls said. They were all dressed in long black robes so it was hard to tell who it was, but she guessed from the voice and tone it was Terry's friend Dell.

"But it's freezing," Carin protested.

158

"Do it. Now!"

Carin put her hand out and leaned against the rough bark of a dying tree. They were standing in a small stand of scrub pines in a wooded area off the interstate a few miles outside of town. In the distance she could see the lights of Buffalo dotting the darkness like a whole new galaxy of undiscovered constellations.

She picked at the knot of her laces and pulled off her L.A. Gears, rolling up her socks, and stuffing them inside the sneakers. She stood barefoot, the carpet of dead pine needles soft under her feet, her arms crossed over her breasts for warmth.

"Get in the coffin," another girl said.

Laura had told her that they really didn't make you stay in the coffin the whole night nor did they really bury you. Just threw a few shovelfuls of dirt on top of the coffin, pretended to leave you, and after ten minutes or so of tortured silence, they let you out, a full-fledged member of Lambda Psi.

Carin scanned the dark ring of figures, trying to spot a friend or two, but their faces were no more than pale smears in the moonlight. She had begged Laura to pledge her, begged her to come to the initiation, even though Laura had little use for the sorority anymore and hardly ever attended any of their functions. Still, knowing that Laura was there would have made Carin feel a helluva lot better. She knew that to get into the most popular sorority on campus wouldn't be easy, that she would have to suffer in some way. But Carin was equally certain that her friend would make sure that nothing *too bad* happened to her.

Carin suspected that part of her friend's feelings about Lambda Psi stemmed from the fact that Terry was now the nominal leader of the sorority. But Terry had disappeared after the accident at the pool, and no one with the possible exception of Dell knew where she was and Dell wasn't talking.

Nonetheless, Laura had refused to come.

No matter how much Carin begged.

Over the past several weeks Laura had gotten to be so

damned selfish. As if she were jealous that things were just starting to work out for her. . . .

"I said, get in the coffin, bitch," Dell's voice growled.

Carin stepped gingerly into the pine box and reached behind her, settling herself down into a sitting position and then lying flat on her back. The sides of the coffin pressed in on her and once again she was reminded that she needed to lose a little weight. She crossed her arms to make more room for herself in the coffin and realized that she had inadvertently taken up the traditional position of a corpse.

A tremor ran through her body.

She sighed and stared up into the cold black autumn sky between the heaving pine boughs as she waited for the ceremony to begin.

Suddenly, one of the girls stepped forward and dropped a long-stemmed rose into the coffin.

"Loyalty," she said, and disappeared into the shadows.

"Courage," another said, and dropped a second rose onto her lap.

"Sisterhood," said a third, depositing a third rose in the coffin. Instead of disappearing into the surrounding darkness like the others she turned around and faced the crowd of robed figures clustered just out of eyeshot.

"Tonight," she said, "a girl dies and with her all girlish things. Tonight we bear witness as our sister undertakes the perilous night voyage into womanhood. May the goddess have mercy on her soul. For now we lay poor Carin to rest and say good-bye to all she once was."

Laura had prepared her for what was to happen next. Each of the girls would step forward and say something about the "deceased." No matter what it was, no matter how cruel or insulting, Carin had to lay there impassively and not say a word. The slightest protest on her part would instantly disqualify her.

Shivering slightly in the cold, Carin listened with tears in her eyes as she heard her future sisters step up one by one to deliver her "eulogy." She tried to tell herself it was just part of the initiation, that the girls were just trying to say the most insulting things they could think of to rattle her, but some of the comments just hit too close to home.

"She was all right, I guess," someone said. "Except she was too damn fat."

"Yeah, a real porker," someone else chimed in.

There was some giggling and then she heard Dell's drunken voice over the others. "The cow had a nice set of udders on her, though," she slurred.

There was some more laughter. Carin's face burned with embarrassment. She was sure they could all see it glowing like a headlight in the darkness. She squeezed her eyes closed, trying to shut out the voices of the other girls, and felt the tears rolling down her reddened cheeks.

"She was a very nice person, kind and helpful. I'll miss her."

Carin recognized the voice of Lynn Oliphant, the quiet girl who sat behind her in third-period physics. In her soft-spoken way, Lynn had tried to cultivate Carin as a friend, but Carin had never considered the shy girl a powerful enough ally in her bid for popularity. Now she was sorry she had been so cold to her and vowed to make it up when she climbed back out of this coffin.

Lynn's kind words had little effect on the others, however; on the contrary, the laughter only increased, as did the insults.

Finally someone suggested that they get on with it and bury the "corpse." A moment later, Carin heard the lid of the coffin being carefully hammered into place and then she felt them dragging her coffin roughly over the ground and dropping her into the hole.

28

MEANWHILE LAURA was about to die for the second time.

Dr. Mahler had motioned her toward the faux leather couch across from his large polished desk and sat in a nearby armchair.

"Laura," he began, "what you are doing takes real courage. I want you to know I understand that. And that I'll make this as easy as I can for you."

"I don't feel very courageous."

Perhaps Dr. Mahler was right; maybe she was denying some powerful memory of her accident—even an NDE—and her subconscious was taking its revenge.

She didn't believe it for a second. Yet she still hoped it might be true.

Like a terminally ill patient, she had no choice but to believe in the huckster offering her false hope.

No choice, of course, except madness.

"Don't sell yourself short," Dr. Mahler said. "You are a pioneer who has returned from a great unexplored territory. Every pioneer has a different story to tell, a different experience to share. Your story can help push back the frontier between life and death. It might help us reclaim some of the no-man's-land that begins where life ends. To plant a garden where death has its desert."

Laura had to admit that the good doctor certainly talked a convincing game.

"You said by hypnotizing me you could make me remember—"

"I can't *make* you do anything," Dr. Mahler said. "Not if you don't want to. Like I said, hypnotism isn't like it is in the movies. I can't make you take off all your clothes and strut around the office like a chicken, if that's what you're worried about."

Laura laughed.

But in a strange way, she was worried about something like that.

"Hypnosis," Dr. Mahler went on, "is simply a form of deep relaxation. Guided meditation, if you will."

"Okay," Laura said, still a little uncertain. "What do I do first?"

"That's easy," Dr. Mahler said. "The first thing you do is make yourself comfortable."

Great, Laura thought. Here she was taking a journey into the land of death with a guide who she suspected had all the moral sincerity of Jimmy Swaggart.

"Take off your shoes, loosen any restrictive clothing."

Laura slipped off her flats. She thumbed open the button on her jeans, as well as the button holding close the collar of her blue oxford shirt.

"Now lie back on the couch."

Laura swung her legs onto the couch, slid backward, and lay back. She stared down at her pale white feet on the fake black leather.

"Now what?" she asked.

"Just close your eyes."

"Don't I have to follow a dangling pocket watch or something?"

"No," Dr. Mahler laughed. "Just close your eyes and relax."

Laura closed her eyes, but felt anything except relaxed.

"First," Dr. Mahler said in a carefully modulated voice meant to be soothing but that kind of gave Laura the creeps, "I want

you to move the center of your consciousness to the place between your eyes."

Laura pictured a golden ball of light forming on her forehead.

"Now I want you to feel the tension draining from your face,
from the muscles of your face, like sand from a pitcher. . . ."

In spite of herself, Laura did as she was told.

Little by little, she felt her resistance giving way. She followed the doctor's suggestion, relaxing the muscles of her neck
and spine, letting her arms and legs sink into the leather of the
couch, as if her body were nothing more than a heavy bag of
sawdust. For a moment, she thought she might be asleep, but
she could still hear Dr. Mahler's voice loud and clear.

"Now I am going to count down from ten to zero," he said.
"And with each count downward, you will feel more and
more deeply relaxed. When I get to zero, you are going to
be more deeply relaxed than you've ever been before. When I
get to zero you are going to go back to the day you died. Nothing can harm you there. You are only there to observe and you
can return anytime you wish."

Ten . . . nine . . . eight . . .

Laura followed the sound of his voice down the dark well of
her own subconscious like a diver follows a line. From somewhere up above, the reassuring sound of his voice encouraged
her to go deeper.

She no longer distrusted him.

She realized she had no choice.

For he was at the other end of the line that could lead her
back to the light. To consciousness.

Seven.

Laura, open your eyes. What do you see?

Water. Blue shimmering water. Blinding white tiles.

Where are you? Tell me where you are.

With a shock, Laura realized where she was.

At the bottom of the pool.

Above her, she saw the wrinkled surface.

And a pale, frightened face looking down.

Terry.

Why did she look so scared?

Six.

What do you feel? Anger? Fear?

Nothing like that at all.

Just tired. She felt so incredibly tired.

She closed her eyes, breathing in the chlorinated water, letting it fill her lungs like a drug.

And then she was drifting. Free of her body.

Stepping out of it like a pair of old shoes.

Five.

What do you do now?

She looked back and saw herself lying on the concrete at the bottom of the pool. A skein of blood unraveled from the back of her head. She was curled on her side, knees to chest, her left foot twitching as if it were waving good-bye.

Good-bye.

There was no mistaking what had happened.

She had died.

Four.

Where do you go now?

She moved away from the sad broken body at the bottom of the pool.

She hardly knew where to go.

What to do.

The bottom of the pool seemed to stretch in every direction, the light falling through the water in random patterns, forming a maze of light and shadow.

And then she saw her.

Three.

Saw who? Laura, who did you see?

A woman. She saw a woman.

She was beautiful, even from a distance, her lithe body robed in light. She motioned for Laura to come, her arm moving as slowly and gracefully as the frond of an underwater plant, accentuating the natural undulation of the water.

Come. Laura thought the voice rather than heard it.

A beautiful voice Laura had heard once before.

Sometime.

Long ago.

And Laura went toward her, following her as she turned down a long blue corridor, the light from her robe leaving a phosphorescent trail on the bottom of the pool.

And all around her Laura saw them.

They welcomed her, reached out to her with their hands of light, touching her as she passed, reassuring her.

Smiling.

Julie Kincaid. Her boyfriend Ben Harlow.

Lisa Rivera. Ted Masters. Pam Connor.

They were all dead.

But they were happy. Joyful.

Converted.

This was no place for tears. Or sorrow. Or regret.

Tears would have been a blasphemy here.

Suddenly the woman stopped and lifted her arm, beckoning Laura to look where she pointed.

Laura lifted her eyes and saw.

Saw her mother. As she remembered her.

Or dreamed she remembered her.

The mother of old photographs and preconscious memories.

For she was young. As young as Laura was now.

And beautiful.

And in her arms she held a baby. Her right breast bared to give it suck.

And then her mother looked up, looked right at Laura, with such love and pride and joy that Laura thought her heart would break. And at that moment Laura knew the baby in her mother's arms was her.

Two.

What happened then?

The light surrounding her mother suddenly intensified, as if all the love in the world were suddenly focused on that place, as if the very sun itself were rising in the spot.

Laura shielded her eyes with her arm, afraid the light would blind her.

And she heard the voice again. Only this time it was the voice of her mother.

And the voice said, Open your eyes, Laura. Don't be afraid. Look upon me.

And when Laura looked up she saw.

Not her mother. But—

One.

Who? Laura, who do you see!

Laura saw him standing there as plain as day. And yet she could hardly believe it. She had never considered herself a religious person, at least not since she was a little girl. She had prayed that God would let her mother live and when she died she had lost all faith in God and religion.

Now she realized how selfish she had been. How foolish she was to turn her back on Christ.

She felt the tears rolling down her cheeks. She fell to her knees, hands clasped in prayer.

Rise, Jesus said. Rise and come to me.

Shakily, Laura climbed to her feet.

Don't be afraid, Jesus said.

Her hands still clasped before her, Laura staggered toward the figure, its light bathing her in love and acceptance. As she approached, Jesus spread his arms; his face glowed like a powerful beacon, drying the tears on her face.

She stood before him, naked, flushed, ready to be consumed in the pure white flame of his love when suddenly that flame went out—

And a blast of chill, fetid wind hit her.

And she opened her eyes.

And instead of the gentle face of the sacrificed lord she saw a figure with a face like a dish overflowing with bugs.

And she screamed as it raised its arms, the dark skin of its wings studded with thousands of staring eyes, and tipped with two curved scythes of surgical steel.

Zero.

Laura, don't run! Don't be scared. There's nothing to fear. What does he have to say?

She ran as fast as she could, tripping, getting up, and running again. Pushed past the woman who'd led her to the light, her face torn open as if something had been feeding there. She saw her mother, gray skin stretched over the torture rack of her twisted skeleton, clutching a strangled baby to her shrunken tit.

And as she fled, screaming madly down the corridor, she saw the others.

A girl with a face swollen like a blue football, her tongue oozing between clenched teeth. A boy with the top of his head opened like a can of Campbell's tomato soup. And the others, bodies blue and bloated, unstitched down the front, their insides uncoiled and dragging the floor as hosts of flies swarmed between their legs.

They staggered toward Laura, grabbing at her with blood-stained hands, their mouths moving with mechanical precision.

Each of them saying the exact same thing. Repeating it over and over again. Like a prayer.

Go toward the light.

Go toward the light.

Go toward the light.

29

CARIN PRETENDED that she was dead.

It seemed like the most logical thing to do under the circumstances. Her reasoning was that if she could only think of herself as a corpse—a cold lump of insensate clay—then she might be able to quell the rising tide of panic that was threatening to overwhelm her.

Above her, they were shoveling dirt onto her coffin. She could hear the heavy clods of earth striking the wood only inches above her face.

She winced each time a fresh shovelful was thrown into the grave.

They don't really bury you; it's all pretend.

That's what Laura had said. They just wanted to scare you: to see if you would break. They threw some dirt on the coffin, sat around, had a couple of beers, and waited for you to start screaming. All you had to do was stick it out, prove you were tough enough, and everything would be alright.

Carin listened as another shovelful of earth was thrown onto the coffin. How many was that now? Five? Six? Certainly more than a few. And still they kept coming, hitting the wood like gusts of wind-driven rain.

There were no sounds from the girls up above. Only the rhythmic sound of the shovel biting off another mouthful of earth and regurgitating it into her grave.

Goddamn it!

How could they be so quiet?

And wasn't it about time to dig her out? To end the joke?

In the clear night silence, Carin could hear the sounds of the traffic on the expressway. The cars seemed muffled, far away.

So far away.

She shifted uncomfortably inside the cramped coffin, trying to take the weight off her shoulder blades and buttocks. For the first time she understood the projection implicit behind that most patented of all funereal absurdities: the padded coffin.

Carin examined the darkness surrounding her. With a mild sense of shock, she realized that her eyes were wide open; that they had been open for some time. She lifted her arm from her side and held her hand in front of her face.

She saw nothing.

She closed her eyes and then opened them again. There was no difference.

Absolute darkness was all around her. Like a physical presence.

God almighty, she thought. I'm really trapped down here.

She forced herself to calm down, forced her hand back to her side, forced her eyes closed, even though it made no difference, and tried to think of other things.

It was no use.

How much longer would they keep her down here?

She had wanted to bring her watch along, but, of course, that had been forbidden. How long had she been inside the coffin anyway? Five minutes? Ten? A half hour? It was impossible to say for sure. How long could she stay buried before she ran out of air?

Perhaps it had been a mistake to pretend she was dead, after all. Maybe it would have been better to count off the seconds, to somehow try to keep time inside her own head. She started a slow count to sixty, whispering the numbers in the close air inside the coffin.

She got to twenty-seven before the first wave of panic blindsided her. For the first time, she realized just how totally help-less she was.

What if they made a mistake? What if they don't dig me out in time?

Laura had guaranteed her that she would watch out for her. But Laura wasn't out there. Laura hadn't come. . . .

Before she even realized what was happening, Carin's imag-ination overturned her common sense and sent her thoughts running wild. She itched and squirmed as she imagined spiders sidling over her naked flesh; long, wet, flesh-colored worms tangled in her hair. She could feel the nest of dark beetles be-tween her legs. A pair of delicate antennas tickled her lips.

She swiped her hand across her mouth. There was nothing there but a thin mustache of perspiration. She had to stop think-ing like this, had to stop psyching herself out. It was like shoot-ing free-throws: if you thought about it too much, you'd never put the ball through the hoop.

It was no use.

Her mind had already turned against her, assaulting her with image after image of fresh horror.

Now it was rats.

She had read somewhere once how rats built elaborate under-ground tunnel systems in graveyards, eventually eating their way through the soggy coffins. Now she wondered how long it would take before she heard the sound of their small sharp claws scrabbling at the wood over her face, how long before she heard the high-pitched twittering squeaks of excitement as the first rat broke through.

She could already feel its fat muscular body drop onto her stomach, right itself, and run deftly up her chest to the dark O of her open mouth, screaming, screaming, screaming . . .

In an instant the rat would be inside her cheeks, its sharp hind claws grappling for purchase on her chin, as it worked its heavy hindquarters past her lips, its long rubbery tail disappearing be-tween her lips like a kid sucking up a string of cold spaghetti. She could feel it biting the soft tissues inside her mouth as it made its way toward the back of her throat and the soft ribbed tunnel of her esophagus. . . .

Carin's eyes were wide in the darkness, her chest heaving. Suddenly there didn't seem to be enough air inside the coffin. Every breath took a monumental effort, like trying to suck Jell-O through a straw. Her limbs were drenched in sweat, a small puddle had formed between her shoulders, making sucking sounds as she struggled. She could smell her fear in the closed atmosphere of the coffin. She knew she was hyperventilating, but it was no use, terror filled every cell of her body.

I'm suffocating! O dear God, help me, I'm suffocating!

Carin screamed in the airless darkness, pounding the wood above her head with both fists, the weight of the earth above her immovable.

I'm dying. Someone help me, please. I'm dying!

She kicked at the coffin lid with her bare feet, her toes bleeding, not even feeling the pain.

She was still screaming, still pounding against the wood, when the lid of the coffin was lifted.

A thin layer of dirt fell to the side.

Carin felt the chill, rank air blow over her naked body. She stared up from the grave. Abruptly she stopped screaming. The tears dried instantly on her cheeks.

She sat up in her coffin and surveyed the nightmarish scene that surrounded her.

Instead of the clear, star-studded night sky, the stand of scrub pines, the circle of hooded sisters, she saw a limitless plain of rich black dirt in which countless coffins were scattered, beached there like wrecked ships, in various stages of decay. And in each coffin, a single sailor, nothing more than a pile of bleached bones, sat hopelessly adrift in eternity.

It was as if they had opened the *bottom* of the coffin and she'd been given a glimpse underneath the rolling green lawns of the cemetery.

What the fuck—

Carin felt the cold blue light on the back of her neck and turned.

And saw it standing behind her.

A figure at least eight feet tall.

In an instant she was slammed backward, her shoulders pinned to the top of the coffin. Before the scream could reach her vocal cords, the steel inside her flesh had cut her throat, her agony and terror no more than a quiet bubbling sound in the silence of the lonely, homemade coffin.

EXACTLY FIVE MINUTES after they had thrown the ceremonial six shovelfuls of earth into the shallow grave, the sisters of Lambda Psi brushed off the top of the coffin, pried open the lid, and stood back to share a good laugh at the expense of the terrified pledge lying inside.

They had all thrown back their hoods for a better look.

Around the edge of the grave they gathered, peering down at the twisted, red thing lying in the box.

And screamed.

30

LAURA WOKE UP SCREAMING.

For one excruciating moment, she was caught between worlds. She had no idea where she was. She took in the well-appointed office: the desk, the paneled walls, the gray-haired gentleman with the handsome face of a TV game-show host.

Dr. Mahler.

He had lost some of his characteristic calm. His white hair, always carefully combed back, fell into his face. The pad and gold Cross pen were on the floor at his feet. His well-manicured hand, complete with the chunky gold ring, was resting on the back of her wrist.

"My God, Laura," he cried, "are you all right?"

Laura shook her head, trying to control the shudders that wracked her body like a bad case of flu.

"Yes," she sobbed, and caught her breath. "I'm all right."

Dr. Mahler handed her his handkerchief.

He picked up his pad and pen and sat back heavily in his chair.

"Jesus," he said, trying to smile. He put his hand to his chest. "I've never seen anything like it."

He smoothed his hair back. In spite of his attempt at jocularity, he looked visibly shaken.

"Would you like something to drink? Some cold water, perhaps?"

"Yes, please," Laura said. Her mouth suddenly felt dry, cottony.

The doctor stood up and walked to the sideboard. He picked up a silver canister and poured two glasses of ice water. He handed one to Laura and kept the other for himself.

Laura nodded.

She brought the glass to her lips, her teeth chattering against the edge. She gulped the cold water until her belly ached. Then rubbed the cold glass over her feverish brow.

She closed her eyes and sank back on the couch. When she opened them again, Dr. Mahler was studying her like a specimen under a microscope.

"Well, I don't think there's any question you've had a genuine NDE," he said, thoughtfully.

"What's the matter with me, Doctor?"

"Nothing is the matter with you, Laura," the doctor said calmly.

"Then why am I seeing such awful things? I thought NDEs were supposed to be so beautiful."

"They are," Dr. Mahler said. "Generally speaking."

"Then why am I dreaming such horrible dreams?"

"Laura, I believe what you are feeling is survivor guilt."

"Survivor guilt?"

"Yes. It is not unusual for the survivor of a catastrophic occurrence to feel guilt at having escaped death. It is the exact reverse of the 'why me?' syndrome. Instead of feeling persecuted because bad things happen to you, you feel guilty because something good has happened and you feel you haven't deserved it. It's a pretty common phenomenon among survivors of plane crashes, automobile accidents, even Holocaust victims."

"I don't understand. Why should I feel guilty?"

"Because you didn't die," Dr. Mahler said simply. "Don't you see? You have repressed your memory of what happened out of guilt. The recent series of murders in town have caused you to question the fairness of your own survival."

"I don't know," Laura said uncertainly.

"For God's sake, Laura! Look at the dead peopling your NDE. With the exception of your mother, every one of them has been someone murdered within the last three weeks."

"That's just it, Doctor."

"What's it?"

"That's why I don't think it's guilt," Laura said truthfully. "Because I don't feel guilty."

"You don't feel guilty, because the guilt is subconscious."

"No!" Laura said more sharply than she intended, but it was necessary to keep the doctor from elaborating his theory, which would have been dangerous. Because what he was saying was what Laura wanted to believe.

Needed to believe.

Even if she knew it was a lie.

Dr. Mahler looked stung.

"I think it's something worse," she said in a small voice. "Much worse."

"Such as?"

What she said next was nearly impossible for her to say. Because it was the thing she feared most of all.

"I think I'm somehow responsible for the people who died."

"No!" Now it was the doctor's turn to speak sharply. "You mustn't think like that, Laura. You mustn't blame yourself for what happened. You mustn't blame yourself for denying the light."

But Laura wasn't listening.

Instead she was remembering something the doctor had said earlier.

About all the people in her dream being dead.

Because it didn't seem quite right when he'd said it. And now she knew why.

Because the woman who had led her to the light was Carin.

And she wasn't dead.

Yet.

"Carin!" Laura shouted, grabbing her shoes from beneath the leather couch.

"Laura, wait," Dr. Mahler said, reaching for her.

But it was too late.

Laura was already on her way out the door.

THE CROAKER

Who will teach them what it is to be,
and what makes them think nonbeing a
better thing to be? You, fed to the
tongues of fire, turn your faces toward
the flames, toward the divine kiss which
will yank out all your teeth with a
single pull.

—René Daumal

The coming of the Angel of Death is terrible.
His arrival is bliss.

—Old Muslim saying

31

MARCIE KARLSSON WAS TALKING into the wrong camera.

She didn't know it until she saw the set chief furiously signaling her from behind camera two. She had been talking into a dead lens for nearly two minutes.

Dammit.

She turned slightly to the left and continued talking into camera three, her face never once changing expression, not so much as a flicker of annoyance shadowing her perfect features. Inside, however, she was ready to explode.

For almost five years now she had been hoping that one of the networks would notice her work and rescue her from the oblivion of local cable news. After all, they had to get their talent from somewhere. She couldn't wait to leave this chickenshit operation behind. But she had come to realize it was going to be even harder than she thought to rise above the general level of incompetence that surrounded her at TV-1. It was almost as if they were purposely sabotaging her.

From the corner of her eye, she saw the set chief shrug his shoulders as if to say it wasn't his fault.

Marcie continued talking.

"The Coroner Killer appears to have struck again," she said, launching into a report of the mutilation murder of a young woman in a graveyard just outside of town. "What appears to have started out as just a harmless sorority prank ended in cold-blooded murder for twenty-two-year old Carin Schiller, of Groverton, last night."

Marcie went on to describe the strange story of the girl who'd been sealed alone inside a nailed coffin, lowered into the ground for barely five minutes, and, in the presence of at least nine other girls, brutally eviscerated without anyone having seen a thing. It was the kind of story that should have been in a mystery novel, not on the eleven o'clock news, but it made great copy.

"And in a related item. Here is a TV-1 scoop."

She glanced past the camera to where the set chief was throwing her a desperate, questioning look.

"I have received a letter from a man claiming responsibility for the Coroner murders."

She held up a folded piece of paper and read from the cramped handwriting.

She could see the set chief talking excitedly into his headset. Her co-anchor sat stiffly beside her, looking straight ahead and smiling, like a department store mannequin.

She hadn't told anyone about the letter because she knew that if she had, they would never have let her read it on the air. In a life devoted to getting what she wanted, Marcie discovered early on that it was always easier to ask forgiveness than permission.

Much of the letter was illegible, if not downright pornographic, the paper itself smudged with stains of a suspicious origin. But in the part she could read, the writer claimed that he was the Coroner Killer and that he wanted to turn himself in. But only if he met with Marcie personally to tell his side of the story. Only then, sure that he would get a fair hearing, would he turn himself in.

Marcie spoke sincerely into the camera.

She stared into the lens as if it were the single, dark, reflective eye of the murderer himself.

That was her strong suit and she knew it.

Making a man feel as if he were the only person in the world.

"You don't need to kill again," she said softly. "There are people who want to help you. I'll meet you as requested. There will be no police, no cameras. You have my personal guarantee. No one will hurt you."

She repeated the last phrase again, hoping it would reassure him.

"No one will hurt you."

Then she turned away.

"Back to you, Bruce."

Her co-anchor came out of his trance long enough to announce a commercial break.

Marcie held her grin for a full ten seconds just in case they fucked up again and the cameras caught her cursing someone out, or worse, scratching the side of her nose.

As the makeup girl hurried out to touch up her face, Marcie decided a strong offense was the best defense. She exploded at the set chief. "Why the hell didn't you tell me I was talking into a dead camera, you idiot!"

The set chief wasn't rising to the bait. He had just got done talking to the station owner, who was as hot as a flame-eater's hemorrhoids.

"That was Aram," he said, pointing to the red phone in the control room. "He wants to know, and I quote, 'what that goddamn crazy bitch' is doing. He's on his way down here right now. What the hell am I supposed to tell him?"

"Tell him," she said, waving the makeup girl away, "I'm making news."

She gave him her thousand-watt smile.

"Dammit, Marcie," he said, all trace of his usual lisp gone. "You've gone too far this time."

ARAM KHAZABIAN WAS WAITING for her in her dressing room after the broadcast.

He had obviously been in a great hurry to get here. He hadn't even bothered to dress. He had merely thrown his tan trench coat over his monogrammed silk pajamas. His hairpiece sat askew on his head, like a silver beret. He was still wearing his bedroom slippers.

She wondered if she had interrupted him in the middle of something; he had that pissed-off look he got whenever she told him she wasn't in the mood.

Which wasn't often.

Aram Khazabian was a rung on the ladder, a step up out of the bottomless hole she called Groverton. He wasn't the kind of man who could be ignored.

She wondered whom he'd been with tonight. Not that she really gave a shit who he was with so long as he didn't catch any diseases. Most likely he'd been with one of the girls from the "escort" services he patronized. He liked to impress them by having them watch the eleven o'clock news. It was his idea of foreplay. Her little announcement must have caused a major station break in the proceedings.

Serves the horny old goat right, she thought.

In the corner stood the station manager, Cal Marlowe. Whether he'd come in on his own or Aram had called him in, Marcie didn't know. But she could tell he wasn't enjoying being there. He looked about as comfortable as a goldfish in a piranha tank.

Khazabian was sitting in front of her makeup mirror. He stood up when Marcie came into the room.

His self-control was impressive. But she could always tell when he was mad. His face looked like a mottled ham.

"I know you're an intelligent woman," he said, and sighed, wearing a smile as phony as a three-dollar bill. "So I know you have a reasonable explanation for the most irresponsible five minutes of broadcast bullshit I've ever seen in my life. And I know you're going to tell me what it is so that we can all share a good laugh before I punt your ass across the fucking Canadian border."

Marcie sat down in front of the mirror and started removing her makeup with cotton wipes. She looked up at Khazabian's reflection in the mirror.

"Ari, I'm going to put TV-1 on the map."

"How? By making us a laughingstock?"

"By catching a killer."

She could see him thinking; it was not an expression that endeared him to her. He looked like a snake eyeballing a three-legged gerbil.

"Cal," Khazabian said.

In the corner, Cal jumped to attention. He knew if Marcie was fired, he would probably be fired, too.

"Yes, sir?"

Khazabian jerked his thumb at the door.

The station manager seemed glad to be excused. He ducked quickly out the door of the dressing room.

"Okay, Marcie," Khazabian said, coming up behind her. He put his hands on her shoulders and fixed her eyes in the mirror. His breath, tickling her ear, smelled of garlic and curried lamb.

"Let's talk," he said.

32

RED STARED at the television with glazed eyes.

She's talking to me, he thought.

Me!

He was sitting at the card table in the middle of his one-room flat in a run-down boardinghouse off Coleman Street. In front of him lay the greasy remains of two Big Macs, a large order of fries, and a milk shake he'd brought home after his shift at the McDonald's where he worked.

He hated working at the McDonald's.

Hated standing over the vats of boiling grease. Or flipping hamburgers on the spattering grill. Hated the drill-sergeant mentality of the assistant manager. Hated the nasty impatient bitches too lazy to cook who came there for food. Hated their crabby, snot-nosed brats.

But most of all he hated the kids who worked with him. At twenty-nine, Red was the oldest crew person working there. Except for the assistant manager, practically everyone else was still in high school.

They were kids who didn't need a job to live. They just wanted a little extra pocket money. To put gas in the Trans-Ams and Geos their daddies bought them. Or to buy beer on Saturday night. They laughed at him and his cheap cardboard shoes. At his acne-scarred skin. His greasy hair. His rotten teeth.

They laughed and shouted out insults as they drove past him

on their way home to their quiet, tree-lined neighborhoods while he hoofed it the nine dark and dangerous blocks to his dingy flat.

He hated them all.

They were always playing practical jokes on him, getting him in trouble.

Like the time Mr. Cheever asked Red to mop up the floor after some snot-nose puked up a fish sandwich and Billy filled the mop bucket with old frying grease so that the customers were sliding around the dining area like the fucking Ice Capades. Or the time Sandy had replaced his nametag and he worked through half his shift before discovering why every kid that came into the place was calling him "Mr. Dweeb."

As he stood behind the sizzling grill, feeling a new crop of pimples sprout along his forehead, he fantasized about getting even.

He dreamed of grabbing the checkout girl's hand and holding it down on the red-hot steel of the grill until he could smell the flesh of her palm frying. Or dunking Billy in the vat of hot oil they used for the french fries until the skin boiled off his face like cottage cheese.

As he worked his spatula under the burger and flipped over the thin gray patty of meat, he pretended it came from the flank of that bitch Joellen who had the nerve to laugh right in his face when he asked her out to a movie.

The inside of his skull was a slaughterhouse.

In each bony niche, an image of death.

Bodies, red and wet.

Submissive to his dark desires.

Behind him, on a makeshift bookshelf of particle board and old cinder block stolen from an abandoned construction site, rested his "library": old paperbacks with titles such as *The Lust Killer, Deadly Relations, The Beauty Queen Killer, Perfect Victim*, as well as books on Ted Bundy, Charles Manson, the Night Stalker, and the cannibal killer Ed Gein.

On the wall above the narrow cot, he had taped up an old

movie poster from *The Night of the Living Dead*. One corner of
the poster drooped down, revealing the cheesy plaster behind it.

Red licked the mayonnaise from the Big Mac off his fingers.

Special sauce—*shit*!

And watched the screen like a cat watches a mouse.

God, she was beautiful.

A goddess.

For a moment an image flashed unbidden through his mind:
he was kneeling before her, wearing nothing but a pair of her
red lace panties, kissing her perfect toes.

No!

He couldn't allow himself to think about that! He had to remain strong for what he intended to do.

He jabbed himself in the back of the hand with a fork and,
with a supreme act of concentration, forced himself to listen to
what she was saying.

Her co-anchor, a well-dressed department store mannequin
with a name like Bruce James or James Bruce had just finished
a story about some local kid who'd won a statewide essay contest on world peace. The two of them were grinning like a couple of idiots. He turned the next story over to her.

She switched off her grin and lowered her carefully plucked
eyebrows in a look of mock concern as she read from the tele-
prompter.

He wasn't fooled for an instant. Her heart-shaped face, her
porcelain skin, her gleaming blond hair, her pouting red mouth
just waiting to be corked shut with his cock . . .

They revealed to him her true nature.

He watched carefully as her cool gray eyes, artfully shad-
owed, widened with barely concealed excitement as she re-
counted the grisly details of the last murder.

Her nostrils ever so slightly flaring. Her small pink tongue
wetting her lips.

No, she didn't fool him for an instant.

Beneath her carefully tailored suit she was just a little love
doll urging the world to "fuckmefuckmefuckme" from a thousand television sets all over the city.

Every once in a while she would shuffle some papers on her desk and he would see her long, carefully manicured fingernails. But most of the time she kept her white, smooth hands under the desk and what he imagined she did with them there!

He wondered what it would be like to slide a knife into her soft white flesh.

It would have to be the knife.

He wanted to be sure he was ready for her. He wanted to be sure he was long and hard and lethal. He didn't want to disappoint her.

He wondered if her eyes would open wide. He wondered if she would go all limp or if she would fight it at first. He wondered what she would say when she realized it was all over. If she would tell him that she loved him or if she would just go "Oh!" in surprise.

He wondered if she would have an orgasm.

Damn, he was letting his mind wander again.

Getting ahead of himself.

He had to listen to what she was saying.

Call me, she was saying. *Call me.*

Use the name you signed your letter with so I know it's you. Call me . . .

He could hardly believe his ears.

He sat there stunned.

Sat there with the cold cream on his face and the rubber bald cap on his head, his bushy, naturally red hair sticking out on both sides.

Sat there holding his rigid penis jutting through an opening in the silky clown suit.

His palm warm and slippery.

Special sauce. Indeed.

Hee-hee.

33

Stone punched the mute button on the remote control.

He leaned back in his easy chair and tipped the bottle of beer back until he drained it, the small tail of white foam disappearing down his throat.

Damn!

That bitch was crazy. What was she trying to do anyway, get herself killed?

Didn't she know that crazies were attracted to celebrities, even minor celebrities, like flies to sugar? They became obsessed with them, developed fixations, sometimes even fell in love with them. In the past few years several actresses had been stalked, attacked, even killed by such "fans."

Now here she was talking to one of them right through the TV. Encouraging him. Leading him on.

Can you imagine what that must be doing to the poor bastard? He must be going out of his mind.

Cock-teaser.

On the screen the credits were rolling and Marcie was pretending to be talking to her co-anchor.

Smiling that thousand-watt smile.

Always aware of the camera.

Of what she was showing it. Of what she was holding back.

As if she were performing for a hidden voyeur.

As if she were performing for *him*.

Every night Stone tuned in. In spite of himself. To catch a glimpse of his ex-wife.

Sometimes he was sure she knew he was watching. Sure she was flashing him a special look, a surreptitious smile, an extra inch of thigh.

She had the ability to make you feel like you were the only person in the world.

And she didn't even know you were alive.

Bitch.

Well, he hoped she knew what she was doing because the game had changed. And she wasn't playing with a burnout alcoholic cop who couldn't get it up anymore.

The stakes were much higher.

And one mistake could leave her wearing her mystery lover's initial cut into her fine white flesh.

A large red Y.

Stone let the bottle drop from his fingers to the dirty rug. He reached under the chair and pulled out one of the skin magazines he kept there. He fumbled through the pages, his fingertips feeling numb and needly from the beer, his bleary eyes running over the pictures of the nude models, as if he were trying to pick one out of a lineup.

The one who had stolen his masculinity.

The one who could give it back to him.

But she wasn't there.

Not tonight.

Stone let the magazine slide off his lap onto the floor at his feet. His head lolled onto his shoulder.

And he fell asleep.

34

"MORNING, NEAL."

Stone flipped the smug dispatcher the bird as he hurried down the hall.

He was already a half hour late.

He had gotten the call from headquarters early that morning. The chief wanted to see him in his office at eight sharp. Stone argued that he wasn't due in until three that afternoon. He wasn't too convincing. In fact, he was barely audible. His mouth felt like it was full of steel wool.

"What's this all about, Frank?" he mumbled once he remembered how to work his tongue.

The deputy chief said he couldn't talk about it over the phone. Just to get his ass to the station ASAP.

"Can't we talk about it on the phone?" he muttered. "What the fuck is this, anyway? Mission Impossible?"

The line went dead.

Stone fumbled the phone back onto the receiver, cursed the chief, the deputy chief, and both their mothers. Then he fell sound asleep.

He woke up about an hour later and then only because of an emergency signal from his bladder.

The chief's office was already full of people. Stone noticed Harris and O'Malley right off, the rest he didn't know, until his eyes were yanked to the blond sitting in the corner.

Marcie?

His mind was still trying to process this obvious displacement when the deputy chief exclaimed, "Jesus Christ, Stone, what the hell happened to you?"

Stone tore his eyes away from Marcie like a couple of suction cups. He fixed them on the short, wiry little bastard standing by the chief's chair. Frank Schofield always stood as close to the chief as possible, like the moon revolving around the sun, hoping to reflect some of the chief's light.

"I woke up," Stone said.

He heard Harris give a short snort of laughter.

The deputy chief looked pissed. "It looks like you haven't changed that shirt in four days."

"Five."

From the corner of his eye, he saw Marcie crack a smile.

"You're a real comedian, Stone," Frank said, sneaking surreptitious glances at the chief, as if looking to see how he was doing. "I ought to send you home to change and report back looking like a reputable member of the Groverton Police Department."

"Frank," Neal said, lighting a cigarette, "how 'bout if I drop my pants so you can freshen up your lipstick."

"Stone!" Frank shouted, tongue-tied, so mad he was trembling.

"That's enough," Chief Kraemer snapped. "The both of you. We have business here."

Stone leveled his gaze at the deputy chief. He looked crestfallen. In his trial of command, he had failed miserably. And he knew it.

Stone's dress and comportment may not have been satisfactory for a member of the department, but under no circumstances was it appropriate to bring up the matter in front of civilians. Schofield had aired the department's dirty laundry—Stone's, to be specific—to outsiders, newspeople, no less, and the chief would have his flabby bureaucratic ass raked over the coals for that.

Stone followed the deputy chief's eyes as they moved all

around the room, trying to avoid Stone's gaze like someone trying to avoid checkmate.

Stone savored the man's obvious discomfort.

Meanwhile, the chief introduced a swarthy, middle-aged man in a shiny, expensive-looking suit as Aram Khazabian, the president and owner of TV-1.

"The lady," he said, his lips pursed like a puckered asshole, "I'm sure you already know."

"Yeah," Stone said simply.

She was wearing a red suede dress and a pair of red alligator-skin heels. Her legs were crossed, the hem inching up her thighs. One shoe dangled from the tip of her toes, the movement of her foot accentuating the muscles of her perfect calves.

Every last bit of it calculated.

She was as phony as a centerfold.

"Hi, Neal," she said, and smiled.

Stone felt something inside of him stir.

She was good. Damn good. He had to hand her that.

"As you may or may not know," the chief started, "Ms. Karlsson somewhat ill-advisedly read a letter on air during the eleven o'clock news last night. It was by a fan of hers who claims to be the Coroner Killer. She asked him to call her and set up a place where they could meet face-to-face. Last night, right after the broadcast, he called the station."

Khazabian cut in. "We want you and your men to back up Marcie when she goes to meet him. Chief Kraemer tells us you're the best."

"Meet him?" Stone turned to the chief. "You don't mean you're actually going to sanction this bullshit, do you?"

"Stone," the chief said warningly.

"It's a hoax, Chief," Stone said, changing his tone.

"Most likely. These things usually are."

Aram Khazabian interrupted again. "We have reason to believe this contactee is for real."

Stone looked at the man like a booger he'd just found on his fork. With his $400 Italian suit, his studio tan, and his silver hairpiece, he was nothing more than a poor man's Ted Turner.

But that was enough to make him a big man in Groverton. And he was fucking Marcie. That Stone could tell just by the way he was looking at her.

"Aram's right," the chief said. "There are enough details in the letter to lead us to believe that, even if he's not the killer, he might have firsthand knowledge of the murders that could lead us to our man."

Khazabian looked like a man holding a royal flush. Stone knew that the chief had been taking some serious heat lately from the town council. A serial killer loose in a college town was not good for business. A lot of concerned parents had already yanked their children from school. So far the media had played down the crimes, but the fact was that a man who carried as much local media clout as Khazabian did had Chief Kraemer over the proverbial barrel.

All he had to do was say the word and the chief would hand him the KY.

"He wants to meet her down in the old industrial district," Khazabian said. "In an abandoned meat-packing plant on Comstock."

Stone shook his head. "It's too dangerous."

"I agree," the chief said. "But he didn't give us any choice. That's the site, take it or leave it."

"I say we leave it."

"I thought you said it was a hoax, Detective Stone," Khazabian said, and smiled. His teeth alone must have cost him a fortune.

Stone didn't answer. He was too busy imagining what it would be like to drive all that expensive bridgework out the back of the asshole's throat.

"Look, Neal," the chief said. "I know it's a long shot but it's the first shot we've had to catch this maniac. We're going to play it by the book. Mr. Khazabian has assured me of that. No cameras, no media interference of any kind, nothing to jeopardize Ms. Karlsson's safety. Right?"

Khazabian nodded.

"She'll wear a wire and you, Harris, and O'Malley will be in a van down the block monitoring the whole thing. That's if you agree to do it. If not I can find someone else—"

"I'll do it," Stone said.

"You should know that Ms. Karlsson has already expressed perfect confidence in you and your team. If you have any personal reservations—"

"I said I'll do it."

He could sense the excitement in the room.

It was almost sexual.

Stone felt like he was going to puke.

35

LAURA HAD BEEN WALKING the streets for hours.

She felt hollowed out, as if someone had scooped out her insides. The news of Carin's death had left her in something like a state of shock. Nothing seemed real. But the worse part was she had foreseen her friend's death.

Carin had been in the blue maze.

Laura had left Dr. Mahler's office earlier that evening. He had read about Carin's death and had called her up immediately. "I think you had a genuine psychic event," he'd told her. He said that an increased capacity for clairvoyance was not an uncommon trait of NDE survivors. Sometimes it only lasted for a short while; sometimes for the rest of their lives.

He explained that the blue maze was a mental construct, a kind of stage, upon which her mind could show her the events that were going to happen. "You've been given an incredible gift, Laura," Dr. Mahler had said. But to Laura, it had seemed more like a curse.

Was it a gift to see your murdered friends in hell?

If she had only been there for Carin, maybe she could have saved her life. It was true that she hadn't had her vision of Carin until the very night she died, but if she had gone to the initiation ceremony as Carin had asked her, perhaps there was something she could have done to prevent what had happened.

Dr. Mahler told her that she couldn't hold herself responsi-

197

ble. That she'd had no chance to warn Carin of what would happen. Though she knew he was probably right, Laura still felt an aching sense of responsibility.

She had been so self-absorbed over the past several weeks. All she could think of was herself; she'd had no time for Carin. In fact, Laura had been more than a little annoyed at her friend's silly obsession with her sorority initiation at the same time that Laura herself was wrestling with issues of life and death.

Only now she had discovered that it was Carin herself who all the while had been living on the razor's edge.

It was ironic.

Dr. Mahler had tried to hypnotize her again, but it had been no use. She was too keyed up to relax, too scared of what she might see if she entered the blue maze again.

Instead, he wrote her a prescription for tranquilizers. Laura doubted she would have it filled.

The last thing she wanted to do was to go to sleep.

Make that the next-to-last thing.

The last thing she wanted to do was die.

Then there would be no way out of the blue maze.

Ever.

She remembered that lecture Professor Roarke had given on *Gilgamesh*. God, it seemed like a thousand years ago.

What had he said?

That the ancient Sumerians believed that the afterlife was a place of eternal torment. How different that idea was from the one presented by Dr. Mahler and his NDErs.

Professor Roarke's haunting reading from the *Gilgamesh* came back to her.

There stood before me an awful being, a somber-faced man-bird. . . .

The thing in the maze.

It had concealed itself in the illusion of peace and love. Had clothed itself in the image of Christ. But underneath . . .

With a start, Laura found herself standing on a corner beneath a dark traffic light.

She took a quick look around her.

The street was deserted in both directions. On either side stood abandoned buildings, most of them crumbling under the weight of neglect, their rooms now occupied by the drunk and destitute, windows dark and empty holes to solitary lives of desperation. Most of the street lamps had long been broken out by vandals or had simply burned out and not been replaced.

The only light illuminating the street was that of the full moon. It filled the damp, dark corridors with a ghostly blue glow.

Somehow, without realizing where she had been going, she had drifted into a bad section of town.

Ever since she had come to Groverton Laura had studiously avoided the area. This is where people were beaten up and robbed, where women were pulled from their cars and raped, where occasionally someone would be found the next morning stabbed or shot.

Laura looked down the cold blue hallway, seeing the dark notches of the doorways. Behind any one of them death could be waiting.

A knife sliding in between the ribs.

A blunt object to the back of the head.

A pair of hands crushing the windpipe like cardboard.

Laura stepped off the curb.

And heard it.

A step matching her own step.

She felt her heart double its beat.

It took all her willpower to keep from running. But some deeper instinct told her that would be the wrong thing to do. That it would mark her clearly as prey.

And if that happened she was finished.

She was walking quickly now, right down the middle of the street.

If only a car would come . . .

Anything.

The footsteps behind her sped up to match her pace.

Laura turned right at the next street. She broke into a trot, hoping to put a little distance between her and her pursuer before he rounded the corner, and then slowed down.

Listening.

And heard them.

Coming toward her.

Flapping on the wet asphalt.

Running footsteps.

Every cell in her body wanted to run. She wanted to run so badly she felt like she would explode.

Yet a part of her calmly reflected on the absurdity of it all.

She had stared into the face of Death itself.

Mugger, rapist, psychopath.

What could be worse than what she had already seen?

Still, she wanted to run. Even if she could only put off the inevitable by a few steps.

The dirty hand across her mouth, the cold pain of the blade in her back, the stale breath of insanity on her face . . .

I am not going to be a victim.

It took every last ounce of self-control to hold herself back.

To stop dead in her tracks.

To grab the key ring in her pocketbook.

To turn.

Her fist, studded with keys, held in front of her like a mace.

"What the fuck do you want!" she screamed, the words running together like the roar of a lion.

She felt the hairs rise on the back of her neck.

It was as if the sound weren't coming from her at all, but from someplace deep inside her she didn't even know existed.

It shocked her, scared her, even.

But not half as much as it had scared the man who'd been following her.

She watched as he ran down the street.

A crazy, nightmarish figure in a leather jacket, silk pajamas, and oversized shoes. His bald, pasty white head fringed with flame red hair.

36

DR. MAHLER LOOKED UP from the screen of his PC.

He had been typing up his notes from his session with Laura when he heard the noise coming from the other room.

"Laura?"

She had left only minutes before in a highly agitated frame of mind. He had tried to calm her down but without much success. In the end, he had written her a prescription for Xanax, a mild tranquilizer, but he already regretted doing so. She didn't strike him as suicidal, but in the state she was in it wouldn't take much to push her over the edge.

She was already convinced she was somehow responsible for the Groverton serial murders. He had tried to convince her that her feelings of guilt were irrational, but being irrational, there was nothing he could say to shake her from the conviction that those people had died because of her.

Then, to make matters worse, her friend Carin had been found murdered. . . .

Predictably enough, she wouldn't allow herself to be hypnotized. *Every time I go into the blue maze,* she'd said, *someone dies.*

The blue maze.

He hadn't quite figured that one out yet.

Obviously, it was a variation on the tunnel, but why the

frightening elements? Never, in all his years of research with NDEs, had he encountered such a thing.

Was it just a neurotic clinging to life in the face of the unknown? A physiological reaction to some drug or trauma she'd experienced in the emergency room? Or had she really had a glimpse into—

Dare he even say it?

Had Laura Kane opened the door just a little wider than anyone else and taken a peek into . . .

Hell?

Mahler shook his head.

No, he wouldn't believe it. It simply went against all his research, all the data he'd collected.

Hundreds of case histories.

Nothing like this had ever happened.

He was still debating whether or not to include her experience in his work. As a scientist, he was obliged to record all the data—positive and negative. But as a prophet of the new age, how could he tell all the bright and hopeful people who flocked to his seminars and bought his books that death might not be the heavenly bliss he had promised them?

That something darker might be awaiting them at the end of the tunnel.

No, he decided suddenly. He wouldn't tell them.

What would be the point?

There was already enough fear and suffering around the issue of death. Besides, his research had taken him beyond the realm of science years ago. He was in the business of faith as much as any minister. At least, he hoped those were his real motivations for excluding Laura's case history from his next book. Beneath them all was another, less humanitarian one.

Eternal bliss was a lot easier to sell than eternal damnation.

Perhaps that was why he was pushing her so hard. Trying to get her to remember exactly what had happened. Trying to find some reason to discount her experience as a mere aberration.

Even if he had to brainwash her to do it.

Shit.

*Where did that thought come from? I'm not trying to brain-
wash her. I'm merely . . .*

He heard the noise outside again.

Or rather, a curious lack of noise.

"Laura," he called out again. His voice sounded strangely
hollow, as if he were speaking into a bottle.

Suddenly the computer screen winked out. The lights followed a moment later. The room was black for a moment and
then only the computer screen came back on. When it did it was
completely white.

Dr. Mahler hit the return key.

Nothing.

Shit.

He'd lost his notes.

"Laura?"

He glanced around the room, illuminated only by the cold
glow of the computer screen, and suddenly populated by a col-
lection of ominous shadows. He felt the hairs rise on the top of
his forearms.

There was something going on here.

Something weird.

He pushed his chair back, stood up, and came around the
desk.

In the weird half light he couldn't seem to make out the end
of the room.

But there was someone—something—standing there.

"Who . . ."

He took a step forward and suddenly felt dizzy.

The darkness before him didn't move and yet it seemed to
come closer.

One step at a time.

One thought at a time.

The doctor felt his heart stuttering in his chest, as if it were
trying to remember a name.

"Who are you?" he whispered.

But he knew who it was.

The pain had crawled its way up his sternum like ivy, its roots crushing his rib cage.

Jesus, I'm having a heart attack.

Even now his scientific mind tried to qualify his experience.

A hallucination, he reasoned. The pain is causing me to hallucinate.

For one panicked moment, he thought about going for the phone, to call the paramedics. But the pain around his chest tightened, choking off his breath.

It's too late, he thought, I'm going to die.

All of his research told him not to be afraid.

There was nothing to fear.

And yet the nearness of death was both terrifying and irresistible; it was like standing at the edge of a high place and feeling the fatal exhilaration that comes with the urge to jump.

He stretched out his hand.

And took that one fateful step forward . . .

And screamed.

Turned.

And tried to run.

But it was too late. He had already crossed the line.

And what he had seen on the other side wasn't peace, light, love, or acceptance.

It wasn't any of those things at all.

It was horror.

And fear.

And unending torment.

It was the pain slicing him open, the stink of his ruptured bowels, the blood splashed on his computer screen, and the wet reddish brown kidney lying on his Naugahyde desk blotter.

"I WAS SORRY to hear about your father, Neal."

Stone lifted his glass and stared into his clear red depth. He had promised himself he would only drink wine tonight. No hard stuff. Though from the moment he accepted Marcie's invitation to dinner he'd wanted to plug the thirsty hole in his face he called a mouth with a fifth of Johnny Walker.

"I sent flowers. I wanted to come to the funeral," Marcie said, and shrugged. "But you know how it is. Business."

"Yeah, I know," Stone said noncommittally. "Thanks."

He cut into the slice of charbroiled sirloin on his plate and felt the cold sweat breaking out under his arms.

Boy, he could sure use a drink.

They were eating at the Barton Steak House out on Route 17A, halfway between Groverton and Buffalo. A chalet-style restaurant done up in brick and redwood with deep leather booths. Marcie had suggested the place. Stone had never been there before. It had only been open for about a year, long after they'd broken up, so it was neutral territory.

"Must have been rough."

"Huh?"

"I said, it must have been rough. Watching your father die like that. He was such a fighter."

Stone nodded, chewed.

He remembered that last night at the hospital. The horrible, desperate struggle for life those last few hours. And then the moment his father passed away. Had it only been his imagination, the sense of perfect peace that had come over the old man at the end?

"Yeah," Stone said, and swallowed. "At the end, though, I think he was relieved it was over. After fighting against it for so long, I think he wanted to die. In a way, it was a blessing."

That's what Stone had been telling himself—and anyone who'd asked—for weeks now. But did he really believe it?

At the time he did. Now he wasn't so sure.

He took another sip of wine and squinted in the dusky lighting of the restaurant over at Marcie.

She was wearing a conservative red business suit and a white blouse buttoned to the throat, the collar sealed with a cameo broach. Still, even in the mannish attire, she managed to convey an air of imminent licentiousness. She was the kind of woman who could manage to look sexy in a suit of armor.

A couple of people had already recognized her and come over with napkins for her to sign. She grinned sheepishly at Stone, scribbled her autograph, and sent them off.

"Local celebrity," she said with a sigh.

But Stone could tell how much she enjoyed it.

Especially when they told her how brave she was to be meeting the Coroner Killer.

He glanced again at her tailored clothes, her coiffed hair, her immaculately manicured nails.

What was it about this woman that still made him feel desperate? That still made him want.

To live.

To love.

His eyes traveled upward to that closed collar. To the broach guarding her perfect breasts like a Medusa.

Was she sending him a message? That this dinner was all business. Nothing more.

Or had there really been no time to change after taping the eleven o'clock broadcast, just as she'd said?

What was he doing even thinking about this shit, anyway. He

gulped the rest of his wine, feeling a little feverish. A little light-headed.

Shit. He needed something real to drink.

"I'm glad to see you finally changed your shirt," she said, smiling.

"Only for tonight. Tomorrow morning I go right back to wearing the old one."

She laughed. "I feel honored. You really let that deputy chief have it."

"More wine?" he said, and refilled her glass before she could answer. And then filled his own.

"Seriously, though, Neal," she said in the same tone she used to shift gears between news stories. "I really worry about you."

If he hadn't heard her do it a million times before, he almost might have believed it. *Mr. Ed Barrow won the annual Groverton hot-dog-eating contest by downing thirty-six of the barb-e-qued dogs. In other news, a twelve-car pileup on the interstate claimed six lives. . . .*

"You may not believe it, but I do."

Yeah. And pigs fly.

The funny thing was that he wanted to believe her.

He really did.

"Listen, Marcie—"

"No, Neal . . ."

She stopped, flushed.

"Go ahead," he said.

"I know this whole situation is a little awkward, but I'd hoped we could let bygones be bygones and work together on this. You're the only one I trust to back me up on this thing. You're a good cop, you've always been a good cop. Maybe that's what came between us."

Stone could smell that line of crap coming from about a thousand miles away.

It wasn't police work that separated them.

It was greed, ambition, and good old-fashioned lust.

And they both knew it.

"I know you think I'm grandstanding, but I'm not. This

whole thing wasn't even my idea. It's all Khazabian's. He wants the publicity for his fucking TV station. He's thinking of running for Congress next November. I only agreed to do it for one reason."

"What's that?" Stone asked.

"Because I want to catch the bastard, that's why."

Stone drained his glass and reached for the bottle.

Marcie laid her hand on his.

"I hurt you," she whispered. "Let me make it up to you. To-night."

Stone looked down at the table.

Her hand on his was so small, so white, so delicate.

Part of him wanted to pin it to the table with his steak knife.

The other part of him—the part that would always win out—wanted to fall on his knees and smother it with kisses.

38

Terry looked up from the bare mattress.

She could have sworn she heard a noise on the other side of the peeling door.

Her eyes scanned the red darkness of the room, lit only by the glow of the neon sign of the all-night liquor store downstairs. There wasn't much to the place: a stained linoleum table, a couple of rusty chairs, a sagging sofa so full of roaches it crunched when you sat on it.

Furnished apartment, the old shit of a landlord had said.

Fuck.

Anything worthwhile had been stolen from the place long ago.

Beneath her, the naked girl moaned, shifted her weight against her bonds, wondering why Terry had suddenly stopped what she was doing.

"Shut up, bitch," Terry hissed under her breath, listening to the quiet.

She brought her face up close to the girl's ear. "You weren't followed here, were you?"

The girl shook her head, mumbled something through the panties balled inside her mouth.

"You better be telling the fucking truth," Terry threatened. "You lying you dying."

She had met Lynn earlier that evening in one of the local

leather bars. The younger girl had been coming down to Buffalo regularly from Groverton with news of the investigation. After a couple of drinks at the bar, Terry would bring her back to the run-down flat to give her the kind of treatment a girl like Lynn begged for.

Sometimes it was a hassle, and Terry wasn't always up for it, but it kept the kid coming back. Besides, Terry felt so damn helpless lately, it was a nice feeling to be in control of someone—of something—if only for a couple of hours.

She'd been hiding out in the city for nearly a month now. Ever since the night of Laura's accident. And it was driving her batshit.

An accident.

What had happened with Laura was just that.

Hell, if she'd wanted to kill the bitch, she would be a sack of worms by now.

Though she didn't expect Laura—or anyone else, for that matter—to believe her.

From what Lynn was telling her, they'd already made up their minds that she was guilty of attempted murder. And, if they had their way, they would try to pin the series of killings in town on her, too.

As it was, her worst crime was stupidity. She panicked when Laura had fallen into the pool.

Panicked and ran.

Now she could kick herself for being such a goddamn idiot. If she had only kept her head and dived into the pool after Laura, she could have been a hero instead of a fucking fugitive.

Who the hell was outside that door?

Terry climbed off the dirty mattress, wincing as the broken springs creaked, and padded barefoot to where her leather jacket lay on the floor.

She crouched down, reached into the pocket, and slipped out the switchblade. Its black heft felt good in her hand.

Reassuring.

She pressed the release and the blade slid out.

Quick as a priest's dick.

If it were the cops they wouldn't be creeping around out there, they'd just break the fucking door down. Wouldn't they?

Most likely it was some fucking druggie who'd followed her up here hoping to break in while she was sleeping and rob her. She'd already had to beat off the punks a couple of times already. They roamed the streets of the neighborhood like ragged wolf packs.

Well, whoever the fuck it was, they'd come to the wrong place.

There!

There it was again.

A soft ripping sound. Like the sound grass makes when you pull it from the ground.

Or hair when a scalp is ripped from a skull.

Jesus Christ, what the hell made her think of that?

She shivered. Stop it, she told herself, you're creeping me out.

She started to stand when—

The door swung open, letting a column of smoky blue light into the dingy room.

"Who the fuck—"

Terry squinted into the light, the smoke swirling around her, cold and rank, like the air from a refrigerator full of rancid meat.

And her blood froze.

For just to the right of the open doorway the real door was closed and locked.

Another door had opened.

One that Terry knew had never existed before.

Behind it a long blue hallway that led straight to hell itself.

At the other end, she saw the figure approaching, winged, terrifying.

Striding down the hall, unstoppable.

Her first instinct was to turn and run.

To dive straight out the dirty window next to the bed.

Out onto the street below.

Even if it killed her.

Instead she straightened up and walked toward the door.

Toward Death itself.

Wearing nothing but a sneer, a switchblade, and an eight-inch plastic dildo.

THE GIRL ON THE MATTRESS SQUIRMED.

Her wrists were bound tightly to her ankles with her panty hose. Her overcoat was bundled beneath her, propping her ass high in the air.

The helplessness that had seemed so exciting only a moment ago was now causing her the most intense anxiety.

"Terry," she whimpered through the panties crammed in her mouth.

Her eyes were covered with a black Harley-Davidson motorcycle bandanna.

She couldn't see what had become of her lover.

Couldn't see the body crouched against the wall above the bed.

Defying gravity.

Bloodied.

Ripped open down the middle.

Like some perverse crucifix.

Couldn't see the figure standing above her.

Just behind her raised, defenseless buttocks.

Couldn't see it spread its wings.

The thousand eyes. The cloak of scalpels.

Or the horror that jutted up from between its legs.

But she did feel the pain.

Oh, sweet Jesus.

She would feel the pain for eternity.

39

FOR THE FIRST TIME in months Stone woke up in bed.

He had to admit it sure as hell beat waking up doubled over on the couch in front of the television set. He lay beneath the satin quilt and stared up at the dark mauve ceiling of Marcie's bedroom.

The events of the night before shuttled before his mind's eye like a porno flick.

After dinner, they had driven back to Marcie's place. To her credit, she was never one to play coy. No bullshit about coming back for coffee. They'd barely got inside the door when she pressed herself against him, her hands sliding inside his sports jacket, down the front of his pants, everywhere.

She led him back to her bedroom, a red light already burning on the headboard lamp, casting the whole room in a sexy crimson glow. Setting the stage. As if she had planned the whole thing all along.

Stone wouldn't be surprised if she had.

She undressed him and then herself, her body dusky in the light, as if painted with wild berries.

She stripped slowly, expertly, gauging the effect each article of shed clothing had on him. Not that it was all that difficult to determine. His penis was hard as a meathook.

She put her foot up on the bed between his legs, bent over,

and had started to undo the black lace garter belt holding up her stockings when Stone couldn't control himself any longer.

Garter belt, indeed. A woman only wore a garter belt when she planned to be fucked.

He grabbed her under the arms and pulled her onto the bed. He pulled off the little half-bra that concealed little more than her nipples and buried his face between her breasts. His other hand worked its way up between her thighs, tearing away the thin lace panties like a piece of tissue paper.

She pressed his head to her chest, encouraging him, moaning. But Stone needed no more encouragement.

Her body was like sugar, everywhere he licked tasted sweet. In the end, he slid into her, almost reluctantly, knowing it couldn't be for long. Each thrust was like a plunge down the tracks of a roller coaster. He came, screaming inside, his body trembling, as if afraid of the power of his own hunger.

Now as he lay on the bed, bathed in the morning light coming through the window, just thinking about last night had aroused him again. His hand moved unconsciously to his groin, resting around the base of his hard cock, stroking.

She had come, too. Stone was sure of it.

Either that or she was a damned good actress.

She had given voice to the scream he suppressed, wrapping her long Norwegian legs around his back, pulling him deeper inside her, and locking her ankles as if to keep him there forever.

Stone pulled his hand away. There were better uses for what he had going on between his legs. Where was she, anyway?

He craned his head to see the digital clock on the nightstand. Nine-thirty.

Marcie had slipped out of bed earlier to use the bathroom. When he stirred, she had kissed him, smiled, and told him to go back to sleep.

And he had.

For how long?

He swung his legs off the side of the bed, massaged his scalp, and found himself staring straight down at the head of his penis.

"I know, I know," he smiled. "Let's go find her."

He found her—or rather heard her—in the kitchen. She was whispering into the phone, apparently talking to someone at the station. Stone stood behind the wall that led from the living room to the dining room, safely out of sight, and strained to listen. He could barely make out what she was saying, but he caught enough of it to feel the knife twisting in his back.

"Good-bye, Ari," she said. "Me, too."

Ari.

Aram Khazabian.

Stone heard her hang up the phone, took a couple of quick backsteps, and started walking forward again, as if coming down the hall for the first time.

He met her between the dining room and living room. She was wearing a short terry-cloth robe, which she hadn't bothered to close in the front, her breasts and belly and part of her blond bush exposed.

"Neal?" she said, smiling.

A flicker of uncertainty crossed her perfect features.

If Stone hadn't heard her on the phone, he would never have seen it. No wonder she could play him like a fucking puppet.

Her hair, even the morning after, looked perfect.

Slightly mussed.

But perfect.

God almighty, she was beautiful.

Was it any wonder he couldn't see the worm gnawing at her heart?

"Morning," he mumbled, and yawned. He rubbed his eyes, acting as if he were still sleepy, as if something bright and hard-eyed weren't staring out at her from inside his skull.

"Good morning, sleepyhead," she said, her smile broadening, seemingly more at ease.

"Missed you in bed," he said.

He could feel her eyes roaming over his naked body, stopping at his crotch.

"I can see that," she said, sounding amused.

He stepped forward, grabbing her around the waist, and pulling her toward him. He kissed her hard, more a bite than a kiss, really, assaulting her with his tongue, and bruising the smooth porcelain skin of her face with his unshaven cheeks. He slipped his hand inside her robe and grabbed her right breast.

"Neal . . . ," she managed to gasp. "What—"

No acting now, he thought bitterly.

She sounded genuinely surprised.

Maybe even a little scared.

He pressed his red-hot cock against her thigh, as if to brand her with it.

He yanked her robe off, throwing it to the hardwood floor. Then he lifted her off her feet and laid her down on top of it. She lay beneath him on the floor, naked, his hands pinning her wrists, completely helpless.

She looked up at him, her eyes wide and clear, her face as beautiful as an angel's. She didn't say a word.

Without preamble, he entered her, roughly, surprised to find her ready.

But ready or not, it didn't matter.

She was going to get it.

For the first time in his life he was going to fuck her.

Fuck her the way she had fucked him.

His cock was full, ready to explode.

And in it, there wasn't a single drop of the milk of human kindness.

40

RED WAS NOBODY'S FOOL.

He had seen enough TV cop shows to know that they weren't going to send Marcie up to the door with a ribbon around her neck and a red carnation in her butthole. Whether she wanted them to or not, they would follow her to the warehouse, monitor her every movement, probably even have her wear a wire under her clothes.

So that was why Red had come ahead of time. He wanted to have a look around the place, find a nice cozy spot where he and Marcie could be alone for a while, just long enough for him to do what he had to do to her, before her scarlet screams brought the police running into the building.

He also wanted to make sure that no one came snooping around beforehand. For two days he sat vigil by the broken windows and watched the deserted street below. At the first sign of the police, he was going to get the fuck out of there. . . .

As the lonely hours passed, he kept himself occupied by thinking of Marcie.

Of what he would do to her.

Of how he would remove her breasts and lips and tongue.

Fun and games.

He had fantasized about it all for so long he could hardly believe it was about to happen. In his dreams he was powerful, ruthless, invincible.

Would he be able to live up to his own expectations? Would he really be able to plunge the knife into her body? To cut through her living, screaming flesh?

What if she fought him, like that woman he'd followed the other night, turning on him like some kind of wild beast?

He remembered how he had run down the street, terrified.

No, not terrified.

Just caught off balance.

He swore to himself that it would never happen again.

No. This time he would be ready for the bitch. No matter what. If she had any tricks up her sleeve, he'd cut her fucking arm off at the shoulder.

He was lying on an old rubber conveyor belt he had found in one of the rooms near the back of the building, trying to catch a couple of hours' sleep before he resumed his watch at the window, when he heard the noise—a harsh, grating noise—like an old dinosaur clearing its throat.

At first he looked back to the little window at the end of the belt separated from the room beyond by a curtain of thick rubber strips. Only when the belt beneath him jerked fitfully to life did he realize what the sound was: the conveyor belt had somehow started working.

He could hardly believe his eyes. Slowly but surely he was moving toward the little window.

The machine gave a startled cry as its rusting gears clashed together and suddenly the belt starting moving faster. Red started to his feet but the surface slipped under him and he dropped back down to his knees.

He was now halfway to the little window, its rubber strips hungrily slapping the belt in front of it, like the black arms of a poisonous anemone.

Red cried out, leaped to his feet, and started running, but the tread moving along rapidly beneath his feet kept him in the same place.

He looked down on either side of the narrow belt and saw the rusty, gnashing gears. If he mistimed his jump, he would surely lose a leg or arm in their grinding works.

Casting a quick glance behind him, Red saw the little window with the black straps had crept up closer. What lay on the other side, anyway?

Earlier he had looked but could find no entrance to the room except for the little window, and he hadn't dared to thrust his head inside the tight dark hole. Now he imagined the huge, scythelike blades of some kind of immense thresher that would shred his flesh like so much bloody hamburger.

His breath was coming in short, ragged gasps. His heart was pounding in his chest like an alarm bell. There was no way he could keep up the machine's relentless pace. For every step forward, he seemed to be taking two steps back.

The black straps were now slapping underfoot, wrapping themselves around his ankles and slipping away as desperation drove him forward, but only for an instant.

He could feel the hot, oily breath of the machine on the other side of the window against his heels.

He knew he should jump, risk the loss of a limb to save his life, but fear held him to the course.

Fear behind him.

Fear to the sides of him.

And the only hope ahead of him, receding farther and farther away with every step.

Something had to give, and when it did it was Red.

Gasping for breath, he sprawled forward on the belt, holding on for dear life as it carried him through the window. He covered his head with his arms as the black rubber straps rained down on him, beating him over the shoulders and back. His legs dangled on the other side for a moment and then he was falling through the air, waiting what seemed like an eternity for the knives to begin hacking his flesh to bits.

But when he hit the bottom he was surprised to find that there was no whir of sharpened blades awaiting him.

Just the dull, reluctant crunch of something breaking underneath his weight. And a stench unlike anything he'd ever smelled before.

He opened his eyes, peering through the dust raised by his fall.

In the dim light he saw that he had fallen onto an enormous pile of bleached white animal bones. This must be where they dumped the skeletons of all the carcasses they butchered before they processed the bones for use in lime, fertilizer, and pet food. Skulls, pelvises, femurs, hooves. Jesus, Red thought as he looked around, he had never seen so many goddamn bones in all his life.

He felt a sharp stabbing pain in his side and looked down to see his hand covered with blood.

In fact the bones all around him were splashed with blood.

Fresh blood.

His blood.

He had fallen into the remains of a cow, its enormous rib cage having shattered, one of the bones tearing the silk of his shirt and puncturing the flesh underneath. Now the broken bone, slick with blood, was sticking out of his side, set so deep in his own rib cage it looked as if it were a part of him. Red took one look at the wound and felt sick to his stomach. He knew he was dead meat. He was going to rot down here with the rest of the bones and nobody was ever going to know.

Red started crying. He was still crying when the charnel room suddenly brightened. Amongst all those bones, the harsh light made him feel as if he were being X-rayed.

Red stopped crying long enough to wet his pants.

He knew he wasn't being rescued.

In fact, he was trying to scramble backward up the huge pile of bones, away from the light, when he saw the dark figure coming toward him from the other side.

Unlike the others, Red recognized him immediately.

"It's him," Red whispered hoarsely, blood filling his lungs. *It's him.*

It was the death he had wished for in countless daydreams of rape and murder. The death he had courted in innumerable suicidal fantasies. The death he had hoped for, prayed for, longed to be.

Only the reality was far more terrifying than anything he could have imagined.

And as it rushed to take him before he could lose consciousness, he greeted the pain and the horror as he always dreamed he would.

With a red rubber nose and a painted-on grin.

41

STONE WAS HAVING a hard time concentrating.

Marcie was sitting up on his desk, blouse off, as he carefully taped the wire from the portable transmitter under her right breast. Ordinarily one of the female officers would have done this, but under the circumstances it seemed a little ridiculous to stand on ceremony. Stone had been married to the woman, for Chrissakes.

Still, he was a little surprised that Marcie had asked him to do it. After the way he had taken her on the floor of her condo that morning. Nearly raping her . . . if there was a way to rape a woman like Marcie.

Neither one of them had tried to talk about it. What was there to talk about? Both of them knew what had happened: it was the kind of thing that only became less clear with words. Stone had dressed and left without saying anything, leaving her on the floor right where he took her, bruised and naked, purposely not covering herself, his fluids leaking out of her.

He had no idea whether or not Marcie knew what had come over him. How he'd overheard her on the phone with Khazabian. The fact was that he didn't care.

He clipped the mini-mike to the inside of her bra, between her breasts, trying to ignore those perfect mounds of barely concealed flesh.

So were Harris and O'Malley. They had excused themselves

like gentlemen but Marcie told them not to be ridiculous and insisted they stay.

"After all, I'm trusting you guys with my life."

Stone realized this was her way of getting back at him.

Harris shrugged, said it would probably save time, and took up residence by the water cooler. O'Malley sat behind one of the other desks, put his feet up, and lit a cigarette. Both men were looking, how could they help it, though they were trying not to be obvious about it.

Not that Marcie was making it any easier.

The bitch was dressed to kill: or to die.

She looked like a goddamn streetwalker: tight black leather miniskirt, sequined black sweater, rhinestone dangle earrings, seamed stockings, and high-heel sandals exposing all ten of her perfect painted toes.

Stone found himself wondering if underneath the leather skirt she was wearing the garters.

He had no idea what kind of perverse sexual thrill she and her boyfriend Khazabian might be getting out of all this, but Stone wanted no part of it.

"Remember, this is only a transmitter," Harris explained, fiddling with the receiver unit. "We can't take the chance that he'll spot the earplug. We can hear you. You can't hear us."

They had been through it all ten times already but in this kind of work it paid to be thorough: one mistake could be fatal.

"What you want to do is get him to tell you as much as you can," Harris went on. "But don't spook him. Let him do the talking. If you ask too many questions, he may begin to get suspicious."

"He'll already be suspicious," Stone corrected. "You've got to make him feel comfortable. Make him think you find him interesting. Exciting. Remember, this is a guy who probably has no self-esteem. Who kills to make himself feel like a man."

"That's right," Harris offered.

Stone kept his gaze averted from Marcie's face. The knowledge in her eyes would have killed him.

"He probably has no social life to speak of. No ordinary human relationships. Try to make him think of the whole thing as a date. Closure is crucial. If he makes any sexual advances at the end of the meeting, ask him back to your apartment. Tell him you'd be more comfortable there. We'll grab him outside. If he doesn't, set a date for another meeting."

He had finished with the wire and Marcie was pulling her sweater back on. It was cut low down the front, showing a lot of cleavage, but the mike was still concealed.

"What should I say?" Marcie asked.

"Ask him out for a drive or dinner or a movie. Any damn thing. Make him look forward to something. This guy thinks in terms of climax. If he thinks your relationship is coming to an end with the evening, he is likely to kill you. Set up another meeting and get the hell out of there. We'll rush in and take him."

"Got it."

"And remember," Harris said from the cooler, "if you get into trouble, you say the magic word."

"Do you remember the magic word?" Stone asked.

"Yeah."

"Say it," Harris said.

"Cigarette."

"Jeezus," Harris shouted over the piercing shriek of the transmitter. He yanked the earphones off his head.

On the other side of the room, O'Malley was clapping his hands, red-faced, laughing.

Harris scowled. "Dammit, I think I'm deaf."

He fiddled around with the controls on the transmitter and this time he held the earphones away from his ear. "Say it again."

"Cigarette," Marcie said.

"Again."

"Cigarette."

"That's better," Harris said, satisfied. "All you have to do is use that word in any sentence and we'll be right in after you. Get it?"

"Got it." Marcie grinned and raised one well-manicured thumb.

"Good," Harris winced and returned the thumbs-up.

"Okay," Stone said awkwardly. "Let's get the show on the road."

42

"THAT LADY HAS a lot of balls."

"Yeah," Stone said, staring through the windshield of the surveillance van. "And two of them are mine."

Harris choked on his coffee.

Behind the steering wheel, O'Malley's craggy face was as still as a gargoyle's.

"Shit, Neal, this is a new tie," Harris said, dabbing at the flowered silk with a napkin.

They were watching Marcie walk down the wet street toward the meat-packing plant two blocks away. There were two more unmarked cars on the stakeout, one parked on the next block, and one disguised as a junker in an abandoned lot on Howser Street. But no one would do anything without word from the van.

This was the worst part: waiting.

Cramped inside a van with two other large men, each of them sweating, farting, swilling coffee, and pissing into jars.

Stone adjusted the headphones. He would be the first one to know if something went wrong. He would be the one to hear the innocuous word that meant everything was unraveling.

Cigarette.

Stone reached into his coat pocket and pulled out the soft pack. He shook out a cigarette, lit it.

"Jeezus, do you have to smoke in here," Harris whined.

"Man, don't you listen to the surgeon general? You're giving me cancer smoking that thing."

Stone flipped him the bird.

"Come on, gentlemen," O'Malley rumbled. "Can we get serious here?"

Stone looked over at the burly man stuffed behind the wheel. O'Malley had been uneasy about this whole operation from the start. From experience, Stone had learned to value the big Irishman's instincts. He seemed blessed—or cursed—with a fair degree of his people's legendary second sight.

Not that you needed 20/20 vision to see that there was something wrong with this picture.

Stone didn't feel right about it, either. Yet he hadn't tried to talk Marcie out of going through with the plan. He thought about how easy it had been to believe she had changed, how easy it had been to convince himself that she wanted him back again, how easy it had been for her to make a fool of him. He remembered how he'd made her pay the next morning and realized with a shock that not even then had he taken out the full measure of his hurt.

No, he wanted her to pay the full price for her ambition, her promiscuity, her greed, her duplicity.

He wanted her to get exactly what was coming to her.

Stone watched as Marcie came to the end of the half-lit street, stood for a moment, and then passed out of sight as she turned in the direction of the meat-packing plant.

Through the headphones he heard the clip-clop of her high heels on the wet pavement. And the terribly intimate sound of her heart, just below the mini-mike clipped to her brassiere, as it quickened with excitement in the presence of the ultimate aphrodisiac.

Death.

43

MARCIE COULD SMELL THE BLOOD.

Maybe it was just her imagination; after all, the plant had been closed down for years. She looked up into the cavernous interior of the building. Broken windows set high in the walls let in the bluish light of the moon. The ominous-looking works of the plant were still intact: the pulleys, chains, and hooks for dressing and hauling carcasses. They still looked as if they were operable, only waiting for someone to flip the right switch.

The place reminded her of a medieval torture chamber. Everywhere she looked she saw an instrument of death.

She hugged herself for warmth.

It was so damn cold in here. . . .

She heard a sound, spun around—

Nothing.

"Dammit!"

She remembered the mike clipped to her bra.

"It's nothing," she whispered. "I thought I heard something."

What she thought she'd heard was the lowing of cattle.

She had done a story once about a haunted house in a rural area just outside Groverton. The current residents complained of footsteps on the stairs at night, the sound of children crying, and, most disturbingly, the mysterious appearance of four spots of blood on various walls of the house. What they hadn't known was that thirty years before the house had been the scene of a savage murder. A teenage boy had murdered his entire family, including his three-year-old baby sister, with a pitchfork while they slept.

Marcie didn't believe in ghosts, but what the psychic investigator had said at the time had always stayed with her. Wasn't it possible, he'd argued, that a place where people had suffered strong emotion, especially those emotions associated with death, could be marked by a trace of those events, an echo of the tremendous energy expended there. Couldn't such places be a passageway of sorts between our world and the world beyond?

Marcie didn't think so. Still she had to admit she did feel a certain uneasiness when visiting a murder scene or the site of a fatal accident.

Who didn't?

Was it only the imagination, or something more?

Could a place that had seen the systematic slaughter of thousands of animals for so many years retain some semblance of the confusion, the fear, the pain of those poor dumb beasts?

She passed an enormous iron vat, rust peeling off its sides like skin. What could it have held?

Blood?

She tried to imagine so much blood. And what could have bled so much to fill it.

She couldn't.

She saw a conveyor belt leading to a small window. She touched its rubber surface as she passed.

He could be anywhere.

Hiding in the shadows. Waiting.

She heard a low, rooting gurgle.

The snort of a pig.

She ignored it. Her mind was playing tricks on her.

On the cement floor, her high heels clicked loudly in the silence.

She wondered what he would look like. Whether he would be tall or short, handsome or misshapen, or just your average-joe-works-at-the-office kind of guy. Maybe even a woman. No, the odds were that he would be the quiet kind of guy you never expected but you should because it was always him. . . .

She heard it again.

Closer this time.

Only this time it sounded like a sheep. A lamb.

Baah.

It was probably him. Making animal noises. His idea of a joke.

Leading a lamb to slaughter.

What the hell was she doing in here, anyway? This was insane. Suicide, pure and simple. She must have been crazy to talk Khazabian into letting her do this. Did she really want a shot at the network this badly?

"Think I have something, Neal," she whispered. She wanted to say more, but she was afraid he could be watching from somewhere in the shadows. If he saw her talking, it would be all over.

It was strange being wired like this: knowing that Neal could hear every word, every breath, every heartbeat.

So intimate.

It was as if he were inside her head, sharing her thoughts. If only he were . . .

He would know how much she still cared for him. So much so that she didn't blame him for the way he'd taken her that morning. In her own mind, she knew she'd deserved it, knew how much she'd hurt him. If only she could explain that she needed more in life, so much more than what he could give her. She was destined to hurt him.

That morning she had wanted to give him a chance to hurt her back. To give up some of the pain that he was carrying around inside him. If only she could make him understand.

She wondered if the others could hear her over the transmitter, or only Neal. In any event, they'd be making a tape of the whole thing to use in court. What the hell, she thought. *I love you, Neal,* she was about to whisper when something up ahead caught her attention.

In the gloom Marcie saw the odd, misshapen bundle hanging off one of the hooks.

At first she thought it was just a bag of old rags that had been left there years ago. Only as she drew closer did her mind begin to process what the vague shape really was. Only when she stopped, within three feet of it, did she see that the sodden bundle of silk was *dripping*.

Then she saw the white face, the red rubber nose, the bald cap with the fringe of bright red hair.

Above the big pom-pom buttons the dead white face was wearing a huge, painted-on grin.

She stood before the dead clown, speechless. Her puzzlement had spared her the terror of the situation. She didn't even think to call Stone. To tell him to come get her. The sheer absurdity of the image had paralyzed her mind.

She didn't hear the hook sliding down the long rack through the darkness behind her.

A moment later she was swept off her feet and propelled through the air, finally coming to a stop several yards away, her legs kicking spasmodically, reaching in vain for the floor.

Marcie looked down, saw the blood drenching her sweater, and the tip of the slender, rusty hook emerging just below her breastbone.

And then the silence was shattered by a hellish cacophony of cries: a barnyard symphony of bleatings, honkings, and clucking, punctuated by the enraged snorting of pigs and the stampeding of cattle hooves. It was as if the ghost of every animal that had ever been slaughtered here had been given a chance to voice its outrage one last time.

Marcie tried to say the word that would bring Stone and his men running.

She had never wanted to say a word so badly in her entire life. But she couldn't. No matter how hard she tried. She couldn't force the word out of her brain.

It felt as if her vocal cords had been tied in a knot.

Just then she saw a light, as if someone had opened a door, and a column of illuminated blue fog stretched into the room.

Marcie stopped trying to talk.

Suddenly she was calm, so calm it scared her, and she realized why.

She knew she was going to die.

She smiled bitterly, tasting the blood in her mouth, and it no longer seemed important to call Stone. What difference did it make anyway? All she wanted was to see his face. The face of the man who was going to kill her.

Suddenly, her shoes dropped from her feet, hitting the floor, one at a time, as if they each weighed a hundred pounds. Her black leather skirt split along the seams and her sweater unwove itself. Her garters sprang open and her stockings rolled themselves down her legs. Her panties were yanked rudely away. Her bra flew off, as if it had wings, and disappeared into the darkness.

Marcie hung there, naked, shivering, dying on a hook in the darkness.

Waiting for her dark lover to come.

She threw back her head, gasping, every muscle in her body pulled as taut as a violin string. Something had touched her on the shoulders. Its fingers, like liquid fire, tracing two burning lines to the center of her chest, laying open the defenseless white mounds of her perfect breasts. It continued downward, mercilessly, parting the muscles of her smooth belly, opening her as if her flesh were made of warm butter.

Her feet pawed the air, toes spread, her hands opening and closing as if grasping for flies.

The razor-sharp finger traced its fatal line through the soft curls of her sex, burning over her clitoris, through the perineum, all the way to her rectum.

Only at the ultimate moment, either out of mercy or mockery, did it loosen her vocal cords, allowing her to scream her passion once and for all for the lover who had spoiled her, forever.

44

Inside the van, Stone was screaming like a madman.

He hadn't even realized it, but the inhuman screaming coming out of the headphones had elicited his own sympathetic howl of horror and rage. He had unholstered his .38 and climbed to the front of the van beside O'Malley. The lead from the headphones had popped out of the receiver jack but Stone could still hear the screaming.

He pounded on the van's dashboard, yelling at O'Malley to start the engine. The big cop fumbled nervously with the keys, jamming the ignition.

"Start it, start it, start it!" Stone shouted at the top of his lungs.

"Dammit, Neal," Harris shouted, pushing forward. "What is it? What the hell's going on in there?"

His voice was abruptly cut off when Stone's gun discharged, shattering the windshield. Harris ducked down under the dashboard, blood running down the side of his neck, the blast puncturing his eardrum.

Somehow O'Malley got the van started, jammed it into gear, and floored it down the middle of the street, thrusting his head out the side window to steer. Meanwhile Harris had grabbed the mike from the van's radio, pressed the transmit button, and was shouting the command to activate the waiting units, trying to make himself heard over Stone's rantings.

As for Stone, he was still pounding the dashboard, his eyes bugged out of his head, staring with maniacal intensity through the sugared windshield.

"Who are you," Stone was screaming. "Who the fuck are you!"

"She can't hear you," Harris shouted from under the dashboard, his arms wrapped around his head, expecting O'Malley to veer into a telephone pole at any moment. "She can't hear you."

But Stone knew differently.

He was sure that whoever was on the other end could hear him. The same way he could still hear the screams through the headphone, even though the wire was dangling, disconnected, at his thigh.

Who are you!

In the blue static coming through the earphones he got his answer.

For a moment the screaming inside his head stopped.

The one whispered word sounded stilted, awkward.

As if spoken by a stroke victim.

Or someone unfamiliar with the English language.

"Cro—

k—

Croak—

er . . ."

The voice raised the hairs on the back of Stone's neck. It was the same quasi-mystical feeling he'd had the night his father died.

Only now the veil of illusion had lifted and Stone knew the horrible truth.

Knew what lay on the other side of life.

And that it had come through to this side.

The moment of clarity passed. The screaming in his head started up again.

It was the screaming of the damned.

As if hell itself were contained within his skull.

45

LAURA WAS WAITING for the police to arrive.

She had called the station about ten minutes ago and left a message for Detective Stone. The murders of Dr. Mahler and Terry had left no doubt in her mind. She was responsible for the deaths plaguing Groverton. How—or why—she still didn't know. But she could no longer wait to find out. Death was dogging her every step, leaving a trail of innocent victims in her wake.

"Thank you," she murmured, taking the coffee mug from Jakob Weisz.

She had come down to stay with the old landlord until Stone came for her. She didn't want to face the dour, seedy-looking detective alone. Jakob had come to the door dressed only in a plaid bathrobe, his fringe of white hair standing up around his head like a halo. Laura had begun to apologize for waking him up but he'd taken one look at the desperation on her face, waved off her apologies, and without a word ushered her into the kitchen. He sat her at the little table and fixed them both a pot of coffee.

Now as she sipped the strong, hot coffee she knew her instincts had been right to lead her here.

Jakob stirred extra sugar into his coffee, blew noisily into the cup, and slurped down a mouthful.

Laura snuck a glance at the clock on the stove.

235

It was ten minutes to three.

"I'm sorry to come so early," Laura said again. "But I needed someone to talk to."

"What early?" Jakob said. "I'm up every hour anyway."

Laura looked incredulous.

"Old men don't sleep well," he said. "Weak kidneys, bad prostate, spastic colon . . ." He shrugged. "We keep one ear open for the Grim Reaper."

"You're not so old. . . ."

Jakob sighed. "I'm old enough to wish you were right," he said. "But too old to fool myself into believing you are. Now tell me, what is troubling you?"

"It's difficult to begin. . . ."

"No so difficult if you start at the beginning."

Laura told him everything. About the accident, about the dreams, about her memories under hypnosis, about her conviction that she was somehow responsible for the deaths of those around her.

When she finished, she half expected him to tell her she was crazy or, at the very least, to tell her she was being unreasonable, like Dr. Mahler had, that she couldn't possibly hold herself responsible for the Groverton murders.

Instead he fixed her with his bright blue eyes.

Eyes of a physicist.

Ready to split an atom.

He didn't say anything. Just stared. As if waiting for just the right moment. Knowing that once he spoke, nothing would ever be the same again.

"Laura," he said softly, "I'm going to tell you something that I have never told anyone before. It is not a story that I am proud to tell, and by the time I am finished you may have come to hate me."

Laura started to protest, but he waved her to silence.

"At least you will understand me for the monster that I am. For years I have kept what I am about to tell you between me and God. Until this moment, I could not imagine telling it to another living soul. But I realize now that I must make peace with the past once and for all. You are the one I must tell my story to. I can't keep silent any longer. If I can only make you understand, it may save your life."

He pushed up the sleeve of his robe, exposing the row of faded blue numbers on his wrist.

"It has to do with this."

Laura suddenly felt cold. He was starting to scare her.

"You don't have to—"

"Yes," Jakob said, emphatically. "I do."

Laura dropped her eyes to the stygian black depths inside her coffee mug. The pain ravaging the old man's face was too much to bear.

"I got this in a place called Buchenwald," he began. "My family was sent there in the summer of 1943."

He paused and looked past her, his brilliant eyes piercing the veil of the present, as if seeing the past all over again.

"They say that hell is a place of fire and brimstone. That is what the priests and the poets say. But ask the survivors of Buchenwald, Dachau, Auschwitz and they will tell you. Hell is not fire and brimstone, it is not the bottomless pit, the torment of pitchforks, the howl of demons. No. The place that the poets and priests describe is a place of passion. And where there is passion, there is humanity, and where there is humanity there is hope. Hope that hatred can turn to love, vengeance to forgiveness, cruelty to kindness . . .

"Such a place is not hell."

Laura knew that he was right. She had gotten a glimpse of hell.

In her nightmares.

In the blue maze.

She had only visited. The old man sitting before her had lived there.

"There is no passion in hell," he said. "Hell is a bureaucracy. Cold and efficient. Where cold-blooded murder is as much a business as making sausages or bottling pickles. Such a place was Buchenwald. There the lash of a whip across your back in genuine anger, or a boot in the groin delivered with heartfelt hatred rather than official contempt, would have almost seemed like a lover's caress."

Laura was shocked by the old man's speech. She had heard other descriptions of the Holocaust before, but never anything like this. Was he mad?

"The Nazis had a genius for organization that approached the supernatural. In the concentration camps they had designed in theory and practice a working model of hell. A hell where there was no sin and no redemption, where you were sent for no reason at all except that you were a Jew, or a homosexual, or a Communist, or a Catholic, or a political opponent of National Socialism. It was completely random, totally absurd—in short, it was hell.

"I was nineteen, maybe twenty, when my family was sent there. It is impossible to tell what it was really like. There is nothing to compare it to. It was like nothing else—"

The old man interrupted himself, as if impatient with his own lack of eloquence.

"Have you ever seen the pictures, the old film reels of the camps after the Allies liberated them?"

Who hadn't seen them?

The naked bodies stacked like cordwood, the piles of human skulls beside the furnaces, the living skeletons lying on their cots, too weak to move . . .

Laura nodded.

"All the pictures, all the stories, nothing can come close to what it was really like.

"Let me tell you one detail that will give you some idea of what it was really like. They put me to work in the showers. In charge of the cleanup detail. In the pictures—"

Jakob paused, his voice faltering. He cleared his throat.

"In the pictures, the gas comes on and the people die and we carry them out to the crematorium. In hell, it was not like that.

"Not even the Nazis could achieve such perfection. Many times the gas did not kill everyone. Afterward many of the people were still alive. Naked, poisoned, screaming, blind with pain. Sometimes, even worse, they begged for their lives. It was my job to pull the living from the pile of dead bodies. Not to save them, mind you. Not to comfort them—

"To finish them off.

"To do this they gave me a large oaken club. Men. Women. Children. It was my job to kill them. A single blow over the head. To shatter their skulls. To stop them screaming. How I did this—"

He shrugged, sniffed.

"I do not know. They were doomed, sentenced to death. Many had already lost their will to live. They'd been used in medical experiments or had gotten too sick to work or had broken down mentally. It was an act of mercy. We were putting them out of their misery. That is what we told ourselves as we walked down the rows of the dying. Our clubs covered with bone, tissue, and matted hair. The Nazis watched us from the corners. They had machine guns. They could have done it themselves. But the point was to make *us* do it.

"That was hell."

"Mr. Weisz, please—"

The old man didn't hear her, and even if he had, it wasn't likely that he would stop. The words were rushing out of him now, like magma from a source deep inside the earth.

"In the pictures," he hissed, "they show us marching to the crematoriums like lambs to the slaughter. And people nowadays say 'why?' Why didn't we speak out, why didn't we fight back, why didn't we *do* something. They didn't see the courage of the mothers who died rather than give up their children, of men who were tortured beyond human endurance rather than give up their comrades, of a people who were exterminated to the brink of annihilation rather than give up their principles.

"They didn't hear the defiant shouts of the damned as they were marched to their deaths. 'Today us, tomorrow you!' we cursed the stone-faced guards as they herded us naked to the edge of a mass grave and raked us in with machine-gun fire like so much compost.

"We fought back. Perhaps not dramatically. Perhaps not suc-

cessfully. But we fought back with the only defense a defenseless people have: their faith, their spirit, and their obstinance.
Some of us younger men in camp secretly formed groups dedicated to bringing as much discomfort to our oppressor as possible. Our goals were modest; we knew we could not bring down
the whole Nazi regime. But we did what we could. Anything
that would throw a monkey wrench into the damnable perfection of their bureaucracy of death.

"We knew that if we were caught it would mean death. But it
wasn't bravery. We were no heroes, at least not most of us, as
you'll soon enough find out. It was youth. It was foolishness. It
was boredom. It was desperation. But most of all, it was fear."

Jakob lifted his mug and took a loud gulp of coffee. Laura
was still staring into her cup, her hands wrapped around the ceramic, from which the warmth had already leaked away.

"I told you that my whole family was taken to the camp,"
Jakob began again. "Well, they had separated us, sending us to
different barracks. For nearly a year we hardly saw anything of
each other, except for an occasional unexpected glimpse
through a barbed-wire fence. We communicated by sending
brief messages by other prisoners or through notes written on
stolen toilet paper. My sister I never saw again. Later I learned
that she'd been sent to Dachau to be used in a forced-
sterilization experiment. She died there."

"I'm sorry," Laura muttered. In the context of such horror,
the word seemed so insignificant, so trite. Almost like sarcasm.
But what could you say in the face of such horror. Human language hadn't invented a word to express the shock, the outrage,
the sorrow.

Because the acts themselves weren't human. . . .

Jacob nodded, acknowledging her condolence. Perhaps he
could read in her face the emotion that the words could not convey.

"Sometimes," he said cryptically, "it was more fortunate to
have died than to have survived. If only that would have been
my fate. It could have been. It should have been." He smiled

sadly. "But, alas, that was the whole problem. I was afraid to die."

"I don't understand."

"I got word through one of our informers, a prisoner who worked in processing, that my parents were about to be moved to a work farm in Poland. It was a place infamous at Buchenwald and everyone knew that being sent there was the equivalent of a death sentence. I knew that I would never see my parents again. So I—"

He stopped again, running his big hand over his face.

"I arranged with a friend of mine, a young violinist from another barracks, to take my place at evening roll call while I went to say good-bye to them. Us Jews, with our heads shaved and all dressed in the same baggy overalls, looked the same to the Nazis. It was a plan not without its risks, but it should have worked. Only that evening, when the sergeant in charge of our barracks called out my name and the young violinist answered, he was seized and taken away on charges of conspiracy. You see, my involvement in some minor acts of vandalism around the camp had been discovered. I had escaped arrest that evening only by the merest chance.

"They say that he who hesitates is lost. To do the right thing is hard because it requires us to act. Not to think. Not to deliberate. We always know the right thing to do. What takes so long to do it is that we try to talk ourselves out of doing it."

Jakob Weisz stared down at his hands, as if he were trying to recognize them, as if they weren't his hands at all.

"When I returned to the barracks, naturally I found out what had happened. My first instinct was to step forward and tell them I was the man they wanted.

"I didn't.

"I reasoned that by turning myself in it would only get us both killed. That I could do more for my people if I stayed alive. That my family needed me. I had a thousand reasons. But the fact of the matter was that I was terrified. That I didn't want to die."

Laura was still staring into her cup, her face pale and ghostly on the black surface, features hollowed out, sleepless, haunted, reminding her of the faces she'd seen looking out from behind barbed wire in photographs of the Holocaust. . . .

"Please forgive me for what I am about to tell you," Jakob said softly, his head bowed. His hands were clenched tightly together, as if in prayer.

"In our camp, there was a man we called the Death Angel. He was a brutal man, not a soldier, but a sadist. They said that he would entertain himself with some poor soul all evening, finally dispatching him or her when he grew too drunk to go on, and then sleeping it off with the corpse under his cot. It was this man's job to enforce discipline in the camp, as well as to extract information from his prisoners.

"For this he had a special method that struck terror in each of us. Whenever he decided that someone might be harboring some shred of useful information he would descend upon him without any warning whatsoever. He would always come for the man personally, in the middle of the night, usually at three A.M., for as a surgeon before the war it was his conceit that death visited more people at that hour than at any other."

Laura suddenly realized why Jakob had most likely been telling the truth when he'd said he'd been up anyway. But not because of a bad prostate or diarrhea.

He was waiting for the Death Angel.

Old terrors never die.

They just come back to haunt you.

"He had a room outfitted for just this purpose. Upon taking his victim there he would make the prisoner strip naked and then, if it were a man, he would force him to alternately submerge his testicles in two basins of water, one ice cold and the other scalding. This he would force his victim prisoner to do over and over again until the flesh began to peel from his scrotum. Then he would order one of his guards to paint the raw tissues of the victim's testicles with iodine—"

"Please, Mr. Weisz," Laura cried, feeling nauseous. "No more. I'm going to be sick—"

"You must listen, Laura," Jakob said, hissed. And now there

was nothing sad or plaintive in his voice, but something fierce and angry, that would not be denied. "You must hear. You must know what happened."

Instinctively, Laura looked up in response to the urgency in that voice.

And was instantly sorry she did.

His eyes blazed with a purpose that bordered on lunacy. She suddenly felt afraid.

A traitorous thought flashed across her mind.

Could it be him?

"I'm listening," she said quietly.

He seemed to calm down.

"Good," he said, satisfied. "Where was I? Oh, yes.

"Afterward, crippled and barely conscious, they would strap him inside a device they called the Sky Wagon. It was a kind of box on rollers which they used to simulate rapid ascent and descent to and from high altitudes. Inside the box were instruments measuring the victim's cardiac rate so that his torturers could see just how much it took to kill him. Over and over again they would force him to ride the Sky Wagon, up and down, up and down, all the time increasing the velocity until he went into heart failure, or choked on his own vomit, or simply died of fright. Sometimes they would even revive the prisoner from death, just in order to kill him again."

"Please," Laura begged, putting her hands over her ears. "I really can't listen to any more." She didn't care if he threatened her or not; anything would be preferable to listening to another word of this horror.

Jakob ignored her.

"I don't tell you this to excuse my cowardice. But so that you understand the bravery of the young man who died in my place.

"All that night and the next, I waited for the guard to come and take me from my bunk. But no one came. And then I realized why. He had not talked. I could only imagine what he must be going through, the tortures he must be enduring in my name. I couldn't eat, I couldn't sleep, and yet still I did not speak up.

"Surely he is dead already, I reasoned as one day bled into

the next. If that were so, then what would my confession accomplish but to kill two of us instead of one. My bunkmates said nothing, neither to the guards nor to me. They knew the choice I faced and there was not a soul among them who wasn't sure what he would do in the same circumstance.

"I never said a word.

"A year later the camp was liberated and I left Buchenwald with his name and his life.

"His name was Jakob Weisz.

"My own name died with him. I have never spoken it again.

"After the war I tried to locate his family, to let them know the sacrifice he'd made, but, like my own family, they had all perished. Ever since I have kept his name to remind myself that I am living another man's life. I have tried to live well by his memory, to bring honor to his name, but nothing can erase the blood on my hands. It was I that should have died and he that should have lived.

"I thought I had known hell inside of that camp, but it was nothing to the hell I have carried around in here," he said, and thumped his head with his forefinger.

"Hell is not from God; it is not from the Devil. It is from man. It is built out of the iron bars of our own fears. I could have escaped hell forever if I'd only stepped forward and accepted the death that was mine. Now I am trapped—in here—forever."

He jabbed his head again, hard, as if he were trying to push his finger through the skull itself and scratch once and for all the itch that was driving him insane.

"My life," he said sadly, "has become the death I sought to avoid."

"What . . . what can I do?" Laura asked, afraid of the answer.

"Laura, I know what it is to feel the shadow of death dogging your every step. I have lived with its presence every day of my life for nearly half a century. Listen to me . . ."

There was so much pain in the words Laura looked up, alarmed.

"You must face your greatest fear."

Laura shook her head.

"Yes," he said, almost passionately. "What happened to you in that pool opened a doorway between life and death and something slipped through. You must close the door. If you don't, your life will never be your own."

"I can't do it," Laura sobbed.

"Laura," he said, and this time his tone was more reasonable, "it is the only way.

"But I'm scared."

He placed his large, worn hands over hers. They looked like the gnarled roots of a tree, a thousand years old.

"That is why it must be done."

"I don't think I can—"

"I will help you, Laura," he said. "I will help you close the door."

Laura looked up at his face. In the cold flat light of the kitchen he looked ancient. Each line carved in his flesh the signature of the god of pain himself.

Only his eyes were still alive.

In them she saw something she hadn't noticed before.

Hope.

"We must hurry," Jakob said. "Before it is too late."

He looked at the clock on the stove.

It was three A.M.

46

STONE DROVE LIKE A MADMAN.

He ignored a red light and streaked across the intersection dividing Hope and Main, barely evading a black Trans-Am and a Volkswagen Rabbit. Behind him, the two cars veered into each other, as if they were sexually attracted.

Stone didn't notice.

His life had only one speed now—fast forward.

He was staring bug-eyed through the windshield as the night unraveled around him. On the passenger seat, his big Colt revolver lay, unholstered, fully loaded.

He hadn't even bothered to bring his service weapon. What he was going to do tonight had nothing to do with service.

Or duty.

Or even law and order.

It had to do with something far more satisfying.

Revenge.

The last three hours since Marcie's murder had been a complete blur: a hellish merry-go-round of alcohol, cops, and reporters. He had spent most of the time passed out in front of the television in the hospital waiting room, but in his few lucid moments all he could think about was the last horrifying sight he'd had of his ex-wife.

Murdered?

Slaughtered.

Her once-fine white body hanging from the hook like a side of USDA choice beef. Her flesh stripped off in bloody ribbons, leaving nothing but the blue-ribbed carcass underneath.

The doctors had sent him home less than an hour ago, telling him there was nothing more he could do for her. One of the uniforms drove him back to the flat.

Harris had called him from the station a little after three in the morning. Earlier that evening a girl named Laura Kane had called the dispatcher and left a message for Stone. She wouldn't disclose what she wanted to talk to him about, except to say that she would only talk to Stone.

Then she'd hung up.

"How long ago?" Stone had asked.

He could *hear* Harris looking at the Edwards office clock on the wall over the coffee urn.

"About an hour ago," Harris said. "I was just coming off duty and happened to check your messages in case something important came in when I recognized the Kane girl's name. Isn't she the one from the hospital? The one who supposedly came back from the dead?"

"Yes," Stone had said, hardly able to keep his voice from trailing off into the high falsetto rambling of the insane. "Yes, she is."

"I thought you'd want to know, Neal," Harris said. "I know you're on leave and all after what happened to Marcie, but—"

"Thanks, Harris, I appreciate it."

"Promise me one thing, Neal."

"Yeah," Stone had said, his eyes already darting to the closet, where he kept the big Colt. "Anything."

"You'll come into the station first. Let O'Malley and me come with you. Remember we were in that van, too. We saw what happened to Marcie. We want a piece of this, too. Neal?"

"Yeah, I'm here."

"Do this by the book, please?"

"Yeah, I'll do it by the book."

"Promise?"

"Yeah, I promise."

"Okay. See you in ten."

"See you in hell," Stone muttered, remembering the conversation.

He patted the revolver on the seat beside him, as if to reassure himself that it was still there.

It was the same gun he'd used to shove down the throat of that little prick from NYU. Tonight he'd use it to kill the woman responsible for murdering Marcie.

That damn Kane girl.

From the start, his instincts had told him there was something odd about her. Yet it was common sense that kept him from accepting the irrational truth. He still had no idea exactly how she was connected to the murders, but he would find out. He would let her talk, confess to him, and then he would put the gun to her forehead and blow her a lead kiss to oblivion.

He had already made his decision. There would be no Miranda rights, no psychological evaluations, no trial by a jury of her peers.

Just a bullet to the center of the forehead.

Stone-cold justice.

He had already decided that tonight was the end of the line.

For her.

For him.

For anyone that stood in his way.

He pressed the accelerator to the floor, wrestling the Buick around a corner, the tires screeching like a flock of vultures.

Just ahead three black kids dressed in oversized L.A. Raiders parkas were strolling down the middle of the street, as if they owned the goddamn thing, and in this part of town, at this time of night, they just about did. As he barreled down the street, Stone could see the one in front, the one carrying the big polished walking stick, glare at him defiantly.

Stone had seen that look a hundred times before.

A thousand times.

It was a look that said "Come on, you white motherfucker, you just go on and hit me, you just go on and hit this nigger and see what a sorry-ass piece of white shit you gonna be."

Any other night Stone would have swerved obediently to the side like the good white liberal he was.

But not tonight, boys.

Tonight he had an appointment to keep.

An appointment with Death.

And he was not going to keep that bad dude waiting.

Stone kept the car straight on track.

He could see the obstinate defiance stamped in their ebony faces slowly give way to stark terror as they were suddenly reminded why any black person had ever been scared of a white one in the first place.

Two of the black kids dived toward the curb. The one with the stick, still not able to believe that the guy in the car would really run him down, waited until the last possible second.

But he wasn't quite fast enough.

Stone felt the rude, heavy thud as the car hit the kid, the impact crumpling the left front fender and shattering the headlamp.

The boy's body flopped onto the hood and rolled over, his arms spread wide, as if embracing the speeding Buick. For a split second, his face was pressed to the windshield, his eyes goggling, his open lips kissing the glass.

And then he was gone, his body sucked up into the slipstream, flying up over the roof and tumbling along in the road behind the speeding car, like a dark sack of laundry tossed out the window.

A half block away Stone calmly switched on his wipers. The rubber blades slapped away the blood and teeth smeared across the windshield, clearing his view of the road ahead.

A one-way road that led straight to hell.

47

TERRIFIED, Laura stared into the pool.

She felt as if she were standing on a plank suspended over hell itself. Perched on the end of the diving board, dressed in nothing but her one-piece Speedo bathing suit, she felt completely exposed, defenseless. Earlier, as she changed in the locker room, amongst the tile and smell of disinfectant, she couldn't help but think of the showers of Jakob's concentration camp.

She shivered in the cold, chlorinated air.

How many times had she made this jump without even thinking? How many times had she risked concussion, or a broken neck, or even drowning in those deceptive waters?

Her naiveté seemed incomprehensible to her now.

How could she have been so trusting?

She stared past her pale feet into the beautiful, deceptive water below. The water glittered seductively, as if it were filled with silver coins—a countless treasure only waiting to be claimed.

But Laura knew better. . . .

Somewhere in that water lurked her own death.

Now it circled below her, invisible as a glass shark, waiting for her to take that one fateful step. . . .

"Laura, don't be afraid. Jump!"

Jakob Weisz was treading water a few feet from the diving

board. He was clad only in a pair of blue boxer shorts that billowed from around his white and flabby old man's body. He spread his arms out to either side.

"Trust me, Laura. Don't be afraid."

Laura was suddenly reminded of her father. How he had first taught her to dive, coaxing her to jump toward his arms, and how she had, knowing that he would catch her, knowing that even if the water had failed to hold her up, he wouldn't. She had learned a valuable lesson that afternoon; she had learned how to trust—to trust in others, in the world, in herself.

Now Jakob Weisz was asking her to trust again.

But could she trust him?

Could she trust herself?

But worst of all, could she trust a world where so many bad things happened. Where people grew sick and died for having sex with the wrong person? Or because they ate too much red meat, or too much sugar, or not enough fiber? Where women were raped and murdered for walking down the wrong street at the wrong time? Where going into a 7-11 for cigarettes could get you shot? Where getting a flat tire on a lonesome stretch of highway could mark you as prey for a serial killer? Where driving home from a party could put you on a collision course with a drunk driver? Where most fatal accidents occurred in a person's own home?

Who could believe in such a world?

How could such a place be anything but hell?

She stared into the pool and suddenly she saw it again.

The blue maze.

The bureaucratic corridors of doom.

What had the old man said?

If there is a hell, it is a bureaucracy.

"Laura, please," Jakob coaxed, but an edge of desperation had crept into his voice. "There isn't much time."

Could she really trust him?

How did she know he would not betray her as he did his friend so many years ago? Perhaps he was the killer himself. . . .

Suddenly the doors to the men's locker swung open.

"Laura, stop!" Seth Morgan shouted.

He was already bending over, yanking off his sneakers.

"Coach Morgan?"

It seemed unreal seeing him here, as if she were dreaming.

"Jump!" Mr. Weisz shouted from the water.

"Laura, don't!"

Seth was running toward the pool, pulling his polo shirt over his head.

Laura was frozen at the edge of the diving board, crouched, ready to jump. Part of her wanted to turn away from the water, from the nightmare of blood and death that lay at the bottom of the pool, to run back to the comfort and safety of Coach Morgan's arms. Yet another part of her knew that it was too late for that. She couldn't run away from what pursued her any more than Jakob Weisz could escape from the prison of his own conscience.

There was nothing to do but to jump.

And yet how could she get the brain, the muscles, the nerves to obey? When every cell of her body was programmed to survive?

Just then the doors to the men's locker-room banged open again and a wild-looking man in a tan trench coat came bursting into the pool room. In his right hand, he held a large silver-plated revolver. Its single, black eye searched the room and came to a stop when it found the center of her forehead.

"Now, Laura!" Jakob cried. "It's now or never."

And as the gunshot roared, reverberating through the cavernous room like a bolt of lightning, making even the water tremble, Laura leaped from the board, arms reaching, legs together, back arched, just as her father had taught her, and began the most important race of her life.

48

STONE STOOD in the ringing silence, his gun smoking.

What he had seen hadn't made any sense at all. The Kane girl on the diving board, the naked old man wading in the water, coaxing her in, as if teaching her to swim. And that crazy-ass coach suddenly streaking past him, stripping off his shirt and shoes and diving headlong into the water.

Whatever the fuck was going on here was a helluva lot more screwed up than he'd ever imagined.

He'd barely had time to snap off a shot at the girl, the bullet whizzing wide of the mark, chipping off a divet of tile across the room, before they'd all disappeared into the goddamn pool.

Stone hurried to the edge of the pool and stared into the crystal blue water, his gun trained on the foam marking the passage of the diving bodies. He stood and waited as the tiny bubbles sizzled to the surface, the water lapping at the concrete beneath his feet. He stood and waited as the water calmed, revealing its depths, until he could see the smooth blue floor at the bottom.

Stone pulled the trigger, the big gun bucking in his hand.

He pulled it again. And then again.

The reports were deafening, as if a mad god were loose in the pool room, hurling lightning bolts against the walls.

Stone was weeping, trembling, grinning like an idiot.

The bullets plunked harmlessly into the water, following

their own mad trails down the endless corridors of light and shadow.

Stone felt the sweat of delirium breaking out across his forehead.

The pool was empty.

This is it, he thought, I've lost it.

I've reached critical mass.

My brain is exploding.

He started laughing, his voice echoing off the tile walls, until the room sounded like the cell of a guy he'd once busted upstate who'd killed his wife and three kids one happy Christmas morning with a Black and Decker electric screwdriver.

Stone reached into the deep pocket of his tan trench coat and grabbed a handful of shells. Calmly, he loaded the shells into the revolver.

Then he took a deep breath.

And dived, feetfirst, fully clothed, into the pool.

49

TONIGHT WAS THE NIGHT Laura was going to get out of the blue maze.

She had been here so many times in her dreams she could have walked these halls with her eyes closed. The blue, featureless walls, the enigmatic signs, the mysterious lighting that seemed to sweat from the walls themselves no longer seemed confounding but more like familiar landmarks to someone returning home after a long time away.

The maze hadn't changed at all.

She had.

Now she knew where she was going.

Mr. Weisz had made it clear to her that there was only one way out of the nightmare. And that was to die—to die as she was supposed to die the night Terry pushed her into the pool.

She had gone too far into the tunnel, seen too much of the mystery, and had tried to come back.

But what she had seen no living person had been meant to see. It was like the unpleasant truths about mortuary science, or what happened to the human body after two weeks in the grave—all things better left hidden under the discretion of the white sheet. Once you lifted a corner of that sheet and peeked underneath, your life was changed forever.

What had Mr. Weisz said?

She had opened the door between worlds.

And *something* had slipped through.

Laura had peeked under the sheet and seen something that no one was meant to see—and live. And it wasn't going back until she paid the full price of her unwanted new knowledge.

Laura had to die.

That was what Mr. Weisz was trying to tell her.

And Dr. Mahler.

And Professor Roarke.

She had to face her fear of death once and for all.

Until she did, the killings in Groverton would continue. Others would die in her place and she would be to blame. She would wander through the blue maze for years, until life became a living hell, just as it had for Mr. Weisz.

There was only one way out.

And that was to die.

How long had Laura know that, deep down, but been afraid to admit it, even to herself?

Yet sooner or later didn't we all leave the maze the same way? What was life anyway but an intricate series of blind alleys, dead ends, and intersecting passageways, forever holding out the promise of a goal at the end but, in reality, leading nowhere except to the grave?

Ahead Laura saw the two doors marked Enter and Exit.

In her dreams, she had always chosen the latter, assuming that it offered her a way out of the nightmare. What she didn't realize was that waking up wasn't a way out at all, only another detour in the maze.

This time she knew what she had to do. She had to choose the other door. The door marked Enter.

The door that led to the afterlife.

It stood before her, both innocent and terrifying.

Anything could be hiding behind it.

Though deep down Laura knew what she would find behind it. She had seen it under hypnosis with Dr. Mahler.

Now as she walked down that last hall toward the official-looking door, she thought of the millions who had marched to their deaths in the showers of Hitler's concentration camps. She remembered how Mr. Weisz had spoken of their courage and for the first time she understood something of what he meant. She too was marching *voluntarily* toward the death she knew awaited her.

She put her hand against the cold metal plate.

Took a deep breath.

And pushed the door open.

On the other side she saw what she expected to see.

She ignored the people on either side of her. Their hands reaching to touch her, to comfort her, to reassure her. Their expressions frozen in beatific rapture. Donna, Lisa, Ben, her mother, Carin. They weren't real. Laura knew that now. She had peeked underneath their robes of light and seen the corruption, the horror, the crawling truth.

They were just an illusion—a trick to coax her toward the light.

Which itself was just an illusion.

A disguise.

Concealing the greatest darkness of all.

Only Laura no longer needed the lies, the half truths, the myths, or the fairy tales anymore. She didn't need god, Nirvana, Heaven, NDEs, or anything else that man had invented over the course of his existence to quiet the terror he experienced in the face of his own inevitable mortality.

No.

Laura would walk toward extinction on her own two feet.

At the end of the hall the light was rushing toward her.

Like the single glowing eye.

On the front of a speeding train.

STONE FOLLOWED THE TRAIL of wet footprints through the maze, reading them like an Egyptologist reads hieroglyphics.

He had no idea where he was.

One minute he was diving into a swimming pool. The next he was walking through the featureless blue corridors of—what?

A locker room?

A hospital?

Some kind of government facility?

Perhaps he had blacked out when he hit the water and had kept going out of sheer instinct, fueled by anger, until he'd finally regained consciousness in this strange maze of concrete and linoleum. He'd probably never remember what happened during the missing time. Had he found out anything important? Had he killed anyone?

He touched his trench coat: it was dry. Maybe a little damp, as if he'd just been out in a light drizzle, but not what he might have expected. He must have been crazy to jump into the pool with the coat on—it must have weighed fifty pounds soaking wet. He could have drowned.

How long could he have been out to have let the coat dry?

Two hours?

Three?

The sad fact was that he'd had similar experiences often enough to know exactly how to handle them. It was like dreaming. You take everything at face value, try to learn the rules of the world you were in as soon as possible, and then play by them without question, no matter how absurd they may be.

Stone had narrowed his game philosophy to brutal simplicity: *whatever moves, shoot it.*

It was a philosophy that had served him well on several occasions.

He stared down at the footprints, forcing himself to concentrate. He couldn't let his mind wander, not now. He might black out again.

And he wanted to be awake.

Bug eyed, adrenaline jolted, wide awake when he found the girl.

Her footprints on the linoleum were easy enough to read. Even where they had started to dry, the moisture had left a ghostly imprint of her small bare feet.

Matching his pace to hers, he could tell that she wasn't in any hurry. Nor was she tarrying.

It was the strong, determined pace of someone who knew exactly where she was going.

Stone turned the corner and stared down yet another featureless corridor. He realized that he hadn't seen a single door or window since he'd awakened inside the maze. He figured he must be underground; that would explain the lack of windows. But what about the doors? Why weren't there any doors?

It suddenly occurred to him that the line of footprints were his lifeline through the maze.

Without them he might wander around lost until he finally sat down somewhere and died. His bones little more than a small dusty pile of refuse in a corner of this vast metropolis of empty, well-lit halls.

For a moment he wondered what would happen if the footprints dried out and he couldn't find his way back.

He smiled grimly.

There was already no going back. He was following the trail like a flame follows a fuse. When he reached their source, he was going to explode.

He turned yet another random corner and saw them.

Two doors. Side by side.

Enter. Exit.

The one marked Enter swinging, almost imperceptibly, its movement dying against the inertia of its hinges.

Stone was already running, his right hand outstretched, ready to straight-arm the door.

Between his brain and the gun in his left hand there was only a single, urgent command.

Shoot.

Shoot.

Shoot.

LAURA FELT the shadow of death upon her.

Just like in the psalm.

Except that she felt the fear . . .

A whole lot of it.

She wanted to turn and run as fast as she could from the terrible light that bathed her, penetrated her like an X ray, exposing all of her flaws. And yet she knew it was no use. The shadowy thing inside the light would follow her to the ends of the earth and back again. There was no corner, no closet, no hiding place, no matter how obscure, where it could not, would not, find her.

She tried to remember what Mr. Weisz had told her.

To find courage in his words. Even hope.

But in the cold blue light of death, there was no comfort. Everything appeared stark, hard, and ugly.

In this light, there was only fear: the dumb animal-like fear of pain and annihilation.

Laura fell to her knees before the light.

She was trembling, as if she were freezing.

She looked down at her hands, folded in prayer, and saw the blue, goose-pimpled flesh.

Her lips, numb as clay, mumbled the words of the only prayer she could remember.

"Now I lay me down to sleep,
I pray the Lord my soul to keep . . ."

The prayer died on her tongue, dissolving like a bitter pill.

There was no Lord.

No God.

No hope.

Only this thing of darkness hiding in the light.

She fought the urge to look up into its face.

A face like an open grave.

Just then she felt it touch her on both shoulders, burning her, like a pair of hot brands.

Her head jerked up, involuntarily. Her breath yanked from her lungs.

Unable to scream.

She hung there, like a fish out of water, gasping.

As the gunshots thundered in her ears.

NOW I'VE SEEN IT ALL, Stone thought as he charged into the room, gun raised.

To be sure, he'd seen a lot of horrific things both dreaming and waking in his dual career as cop and drunk. In fact, until that very moment, he might even have ventured to guess that he'd seen it all. But never had he seen anything that even remotely matched what he saw behind that swinging door.

It was a man—or maybe it wasn't.

He was standing in a circle of light, radiant, like a fluorescent bulb. His robes were incandescent, his form as cool and perfectly formed as carved ice, his bearded face wearing a look of such peace and benevolence that Stone was nearly moved to tears.

"Jesus Christ," Stone muttered, without the least trace of irony.

At his bloodless feet, the girl was kneeling, head bowed, as if she were praying.

Suddenly she threw her head back, her whole body going rigid, her mouth opening in a wordless cry of ecstasy—or pain.

Stone couldn't tell which.

Slowly, she began to rise from the floor, lifted by a force that was clearly not the ordinary result of the mechanical working of muscle and bone. Instead, she seemed to be *floating*.

Rising from the floor without any effort whatsoever.

Levitating.

She hung suspended in midair, her feet leaving the ground, separated from the floor by a good five feet.

Stone might have been convinced that he was witnessing a miracle until he saw the bloody wounds forming on the girl's bare shoulders.

"Who the fuck are you?" Stone shouted.

The man of light turned and Stone fired his revolver.

Whatever force had been holding the girl from the ground had suddenly been cut off, like an electric switch, and she fell to the tile floor like a rag doll.

The bearded face showed no change of expression, the body of light no damage from the bullet that had supposedly just plowed through it. Unhurriedly, the man of light came toward Stone, the pale, bloodless feet not even touching the tiles below.

"Who the fuck are you?" Stone shouted again and fired two more times.

His senses told him he was shooting Jesus Christ, the Son of God, but his gut told him something else entirely.

Suddenly he remembered.

Remembered the broken word whispered through the headphones.

Over the static and the screaming.

"Croaker," he muttered.

And then he screamed it.

"Croaker!"

And from behind the light, behind the disguise of benevolence, he saw what he had been stalking through a hundred homicide investigations.

It was seven feet tall, maybe eight. The Christ-like face was ghost-like, a tissue-thin aura beneath which the real face could be seen: insectoid, like the skull of a mosquito, if a mosquito had a skull; it looked like a gas mask made of bone. Its arms were spread, revealing winglike flaps of skin filled with the eyes of the damned, as if the flaps were the leathery curtains concealing the legions of hell itself. On the tips of each wing gleamed a razor-sharp hook of gleaming steel.

One look and Stone knew he'd found the weapon used to carve its lethal signature into Marcie's flesh.

Stone fired again and then again.

The bullets had no effect.

Just like a dream, Stone thought grimly.

Maybe I can wake up.

By his count he had one last bullet left.

He put the gun to his temple.

"Come and get me, you fuck-faced bastard," he screamed, grinning like a lunatic. He remembered something his father had said, on more than one occasion, when talking about bill collectors, banks, or loan companies.

It was kind of a family motto.

"You can't get blood from a Stone!" he shouted.

Then he pulled the trigger.

• • •

SHE'S DEAD.

Jakob Weisz saw the girl kneeling on the floor; his first thought was that he was too late. She was naked and covered in blood and gore from head to toe. The sight of her terrified him; it took all of his remaining willpower to force his feet, bolted to the floor in fear, to shuffle toward her.

If she were dead . . .

A few feet away a man in a tan trench coat was sprawled out on the tiles, his glassy eyes turned to the floor, as if wondering what his brains, which lay in a gray puddle a few inches from his nose, were doing out of his skull.

Jakob knelt beside Laura, lifting her wrist between his fingers. The pulse was fast and thready, but she was still alive. He put his arms around her trembling shoulders, trying to warm her body with his own. He was relieved to find that the blood and gobs of gray jelly on her body weren't hers after all, but had come from the dead detective. Except for the two nasty puncture wounds on the insides of her shoulders, she appeared to be relatively unharmed.

There was still time.

But not much . . .

Already the light was rising again.

"Laura!" Jakob said sharply, trying to shake her awake. She seemed to be in some kind of trance.

"Laura, can you hear me?"

Laura nodded.

Jakob turned and saw that she was staring into the light, her eyes glazed like those of a small animal on the highway.

"Laura," Jakob said, "you must go back."

Laura shook her head slowly. "Go to the light. Must go to the light."

"No," Jakob said. "No, Laura, you must listen to me."

"It wants me," Laura said. "I have to go to it."

"No, Laura," Jakob said. "It's me it wants. I'm the one who must go."

Laura looked up at him, confused.

"It's true," he nodded.

"But I thought—"

"It will accept me in your place. Forgive me for using you, but I needed to find a way back."

He started to get up; Laura grabbed hold of his arm.

"You can't do it, Mr. Weisz."

Jakob waved off her protests.

"I, too, cheated death, Laura; I, too, have been living on borrowed time."

"But why you?"

"I'm older. I have less to lose. Someday, when you are old, you may have the chance to save someone else's life. Pay your debt then. In the meantime, make your life count for something."

The light was stronger now, Jakob could feel it on the back of his neck, across the breadth of his shoulders, burning his pale, old man's flesh. Crouching there on the bare tiles, his arms around the bloodied girl, he had never before felt so totally exposed and defenseless, or so fully or more poignantly what a poor and powerless thing was man in the face of his own mortality.

"I have to go now, Laura," he said, and stooped to kiss her forehead. "From time to time, perhaps you will remember your old friend Jakob."

"No!" Laura yelled as he slipped from her grasp.

Jakob Weisz stood up and faced the light.

It pierced his eyes like toothpicks, his corneas bleeding down his burned cheeks like tears.

But he didn't need eyes to see this light.

He walked toward it without hesitation, his shoulders squared, his jaw set.

He walked toward it without anger, without resentment, without fear.

Instead, he walked toward it with love.

Love for the girl crouched behind him on the tiles, for the life she represented, the life of every living suffering being on the planet, and last, but not least, love for a lonely Jewish landlord in a pair of baggy boxer shorts who had proven himself a hero after all.

In the end he didn't even pray.

The last word on his lips was the name he had forbidden himself to use for nearly fifty years.

"It's me," he shouted to the insensate elements. "It's Itzak Groetsch!"

That was his prayer.

And then, like everything else, he disappeared into the devouring light.

SETH WAS RUNNING OUT OF AIR.

He had already been to the surface twice to fill his lungs before descending and he knew that he didn't have much time left. If he didn't find Laura on this dive, it would be too late. That meant he was going to stay down until he found her—or until his lungs burst.

He'd been awakened at half past three that morning by that seedy homicide cop who'd come around asking all those questions when Laura was in the hospital. It had taken Seth a few minutes to shake the cobwebs out and place the name, but by the time he had he'd already blurted out the information Stone was looking for; namely, where Laura might be if she weren't home at three in the morning.

The second he hung up—or rather, the second *Stone* hung up—Seth knew he'd made a mistake.

Laura was in some kind of trouble. He didn't know what kind of trouble, but Seth knew he had to help her.

He'd raced to the university pool as quickly as he could, getting there just in time to see the bizarre drama unfolding: Laura on the diving board, the old man in the pool—and the detective himself taking a shot at Laura.

Seth had hit the water running.

Now as he frantically searched the bottom of the pool, he wondered where they all could have gone. There was no sign of any of them—Laura, the old man, or the detective. He knew that water could be disconcerting, had been in a few ticklish situations himself, but that had been in the ocean, where the vicissitudes of current and tide could confuse the most experienced swimmer. This was a standard, Olympic-size pool, for Chrissakes, full of crystal-clear, chlorinated water. Where could they possibly have gone?

People just didn't disappear in a pool!

Seth frog-kicked down toward the bottom of the pool, his powerful legs driving him to within a few feet of the floor. His lungs felt like two overinflated footballs ready to burst from his chest. Inside each, he felt his heart pounding.

Even if he found her now, Seth thought sadly, he wouldn't have enough air to make it to the surface.

The pressure in his lungs was unbearable, each heartbeat a sledgehammer to the chest. The temptation to take a breath was unlike anything he'd ever known; all he wanted to do was open his mouth.

Just for a second.

To release a little of the terrible pressure.

To breathe.

It was impossible; it would be like trying to stop an orgasm once it started. He would be unable to control himself, to keep from gasping, his whole body convulsing with the hunger for air.

Still, the temptation to let go was great, that fatal tickle deep inside his lungs . . .

And then he saw her.

Lying at the bottom of the pool.

I've got to make it.

The thought burned through his brain like neon. He was so close, so damn close. He remembered the last race of his collegiate career, against Swenson, at the Olympic trials. One race. If he had won, he would have been an Olympian. Three-tenths of a second. That was all that separated them at the finish. Yet it might well have been the distance to the sun.

For years those three-tenths of a second had haunted him. If only he had turned sooner off the wall, kicked a little harder, took one less breath of air, or one more—what minute, almost imperceptible mechanical fine tuning could have made up those fateful three-tenths of a second?

The difference between winning and losing.

Between life and death.

With a strength borne of sheer desperation and years of physical conditioning Seth kicked his way to where Laura lay crumpled in the corner of the pool, worked his arms under hers, and pushed off toward the light dancing on the surface of the water.

So far away—

He passed his arm across her chest, and with the other, pulled the impossibly heavy water down behind him. Above him the light teased, coaxed, cajoled. . . .

Just a little further, Seth told himself, as the light retreated yet one more stroke beyond his grasp.

Go toward the light

Keep going toward the light—

With his last breath escaping from between his teeth, Seth Morgan reached up and made one last grab for the light beyond. . . .

50

"WE HAVE TO STOP meeting like this."

Dr. Henry Kent stood over the unconscious patient, gazing at her still, beautiful face. She was resting under light sedation, an occasional frown, like ripples on the surface of a pond, all that marked the trauma she had recently been through. They had brought her in a little over an hour ago, barely breathing, her lungs filled with enough water to qualify them as a pair of sponges.

Apparently she had gone to the pool early that morning, hoping to overcome the aversion to water that had troubled her since the night of her first accident. She had forced herself to dive into the pool, only to suffer some kind of paroxysm of fear that had caused her to panic and begin to drown. Luckily for her, that coach had been on the scene again to pull her out of the pool.

Or was it more than luck?

The way he had clucked over her, refusing to be treated for his own injuries, Kent suspected that there was more to the relationship than merely that of coach and athlete. Or there soon would be. . . .

They had finally pried him away from her bedside, but only by convincing him that his continued presence would only keep her from getting some much-needed rest. He finally agreed to leave, abruptly collapsing from sheer exhaustion in the hall outside her room.

His EKG was a little dicey for a while there and Kent was concerned that the coach may have suffered a mild heart attack brought on by extreme, almost superhuman, exertion, but now he was sure that Morgan would be all right if he could just keep the coach in bed for a day or two.

Detective Neal Stone was not so lucky.

He was lying in a metal drawer downstairs in the hospital morgue, half his skull blown away, as if his brain had exploded. Kent had seen a half dozen wounds like that in his years as an ER doctor. He didn't need a detailed autopsy report to tell him the obvious: the detective had shot himself.

Rumor was already spreading through the hospital grapevine that he was the Coroner Killer.

It might have been a plausible theory except for what only Kent and the few others who had handled the body had seen: the bloody Y with which the Coroner Killer signed each of his unfortunate victims.

Right now a large black detective with a shiny shaved head was sitting in the lobby waiting for Kent to tell him it was okay to talk to either Laura or the coach. They always took it especially hard when one of their own got croaked.

Even if he did it himself.

Especially if he did it himself.

Well, the black detective could wait until hell froze over. Kent wasn't jeopardizing the health of his patients under any circumstances.

He stared down at the sleeping girl, two gauze bandages, rusty with dried blood, covering the wounds on her shoulders. She looked like an angel who, deciding not to die, had been cast out of paradise, her wings ripped from her shoulders as a mark of her apostasy. That's what she was, all right. His fallen angel. Twice he'd dragged her back through the tunnel from the brink of death.

He raised his middle finger and smiled grimly at the ceiling.

"Beat you again, you bastard."

There was one thing that still didn't make any sense. Both Laura and the coach had babbled something about an old man named Jakob Weisz. He had supposedly been there in the pool with them. Naturally the police were very anxious to find the old man, hoping, perhaps, to pin the murder of their comrade, as well as the other Coroner killings, on him. But even after an intensive police search, no sign of him had been found, either in the pool or anywhere on the university grounds. The old man, if he'd existed anywhere outside the fevered imaginations of the girl and the coach, had seemingly vanished into thin air.

Kent shrugged.

That was a mystery for the police to solve. He already had his hands full.

Just then he heard the code blue crackling over the hospital intercom. Someone in ICU, one of the croakers, was dying.

Kent was no fool—he hadn't fooled himself. He couldn't save them all; he couldn't save any of them, really. In the end, death would get them all, every last one of them, even this girl whose life he'd saved not once, but twice.

Even himself.

Kent felt the abyss of despair open up in front of him as it always did when he thought of the futility of his job. Sometimes the hospital seemed like a maze from which there was no escape, where every corridor led to a room that, sooner or later, would prove to be a dead end. Life is a horror story more terrifying than any fiction. In real life the monster gets us all in the end.

In the meantime all that was left was to cheat the son of a bitch.

To fight him every step of the way.

Kent had come in kicking and screaming; he was determined to go out the same way.

At the nurses' station he saw the pretty red-haired nurse. What the hell was her name?

"Please watch over that patient," he said. "She's someone special."

"Yes, doctor," the nurse said, and smiled.

Kent smiled back.

He'd ask her out after his shift. Hospital rumor had it that she'd say yes.

He made his way down the cold blue corridor toward ICU, where yet another innocent man was about to face his executioner.

The monster that would rend him limb from limb.

Croaker.

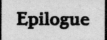

Epilogue

THE LIGHT AT THE END

What happens after death is so unspeakably
  glorious
that our imaginations and our feelings do not
  suffice
to form even an approximate conception of it.
—C.G. Jung

Death is before me today
Like the recovery of a sick man,
Like going forth into a garden after sickness.
—Egyptian hymn

My God, my God, why hast thou forsaken me?
—Jesus Christ

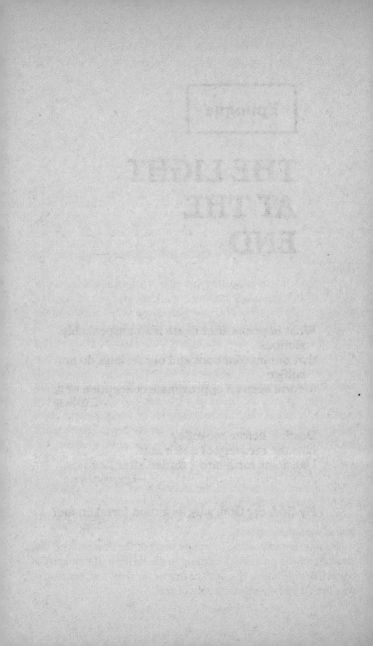

ITZAK GROETSCH WALKED that last lonely mile into the light.

He could feel it blistering his skin, raising raw blisters of blood and water, as if he were walking into a radioactive afterflash. He wiped his face with the back of his wrist and the flesh sloughed off his cheeks like soggy pink bandages, but still he kept walking, the floor hot as an electric skillet, his bare feet sticking with every step.

He could feel every cell in his body counting backward to zero, his blood turning to rusty smoke in his veins, his brain twinkling out like the lights of a blacked-out city. With every step he was dissolving into the elements of which he was comprised, the magnetic attraction that held together the particles of his being dissipating, molecule to molecule, atom to atom.

Little by little, Itzak Groetsch was giving back what he had only borrowed.

All around him he heard the eternal howl of outer space, of the black areas between the stars, of nowhere.

Except it wasn't really just the howl of empty space, was it? It was something worse.

What he heard was the incessant howl of the doomed and the damned, of the poor souls burning in the furnace of humanity's collective nightmare, the furnace that never went out, because it was fueled by an endless supply of fear.

275

Of the fear of the dead who were nowhere and no one and nothing and who burned with that knowledge throughout eternity. . . .

Even now Itzak wanted to turn and run. All that was left of him, all that was still alive, was seized with one convulsive urge: to survive. And yet Itzak knew that if he turned away now all was lost: if he ran it would be straight to hell.

On either side of him was an abyss, and he was walking in the middle, on the edge of a razor cutting him in half.

Oh what a God it was who would program life into every fiber of our being only to make the price of our redemption the overcoming of that one insurmountable desire. For Itzak understood now what he had only half understood before: that hell was the fear of death and nothing more. And eternal torment lasted only so long as we ran from our fear. The moment we turned to face it, the torment ended.

But even with that knowledge the horror remained. Terror was not susceptible to reason. The current of fear that ran through his body was as difficult to stop as water: when you grabbed it here it simply reappeared there. He might as well have tried to strangle himself with his own bare hands.

From the other end of the endless hall, Itzak heard his own death coming and knew who it was long before he saw him. The stride long and confident, chopping off the distance between them like a pair of black scissors.

He didn't need to see the coal gray uniform, the lightning SS collar patches, or the elite death's head insignia. He didn't need to see the dark and brooding face beneath the visored cap to know who had come for him.

It was the Death Angel himself.

Itzak dropped to his knees before the polished boots as if someone had slipped the pin that held his skeleton together. In the boot's perfect shine he could see his own face, pale and distorted, the tears sizzling off the hot leather, leaving only their salty residue.

Itzak had found the way out of the maze, solved the paradox of good and evil, the riddle of heaven and hell. But it was hard, so hard he would almost have suffered the eternal torment of hell rather than do what he knew he had to do. With his little remaining strength, Itzak Groetsch stretched out his neck, placed his lips against the blue-black leather, and kissed the storm trooper's boots.

He had expected something—a taunt, a curse, an acknowledgment of some kind, it had been such a long time. But there was nothing—nothing but the sudden and horrible blow of the hooks as they penetrated his chest just beneath the shoulders, yanking him up off the floor. The pain followed almost immediately, a terrible searing agony, as if he were being unstitched, cell by cell, and each cell a small mouth screaming the outrage of its mortality.

At that instant he knew the pain of Daniel in the furnace, of Joan at the stake, even Christ on the cross, of all the saints and the martyrs ever devoured by wild beasts, or torn apart on the wrack, or pierced by hot pincers. As the blade descended, cutting through the muscle and fat of his body, laying open the soft internal organs for the maggots of corruption that heralded new life, he understood the pain he felt was not only his pain but the pain of every living being that had ever existed upon the earth, from amoeba to man, and that was the lesson, the horror, and the salvation all rolled into one.

For to experience that pain was the only way to short-circuit the instinct of survival so deeply woven into the fiber of our being. Only then could we be entrusted with the superhuman strength enabling us to escape once and for all the fear and pain that constituted all existence. Only then could we feel the love necessary to destroy the bonds of instinct and grasp that which makes us godlike.

Only then could we become strong enough to strangle ourselves.

Itzak looked up one last time into the face of the Angel of Death, into the empty eye sockets stretching back to the time before life, before earth, before God himself. He looked into that stern, stiff, uncompromising face and no longer saw the pain or the horror or the uncertainty of death but the most incredible vision of all.

He felt the warmth travel up his spinal column as his life rushed up to embrace the end.

"Jakob," he whispered.

His brain exploded like a hydrogen bomb.

And for one split second Itzak Groetsch was the light in the dark.

About the Author

Michael Cecilione lives on the Jersey Shore with his wife, Christine. He is the author of one previous novel, *Soul Snatchers*, and is currently working on his third.

414